FLIGHT TO THE STARS

A Tim and Peggy Smith
Space Adventure,
Book Two

JAY B. GREENE

In memory of the late Arthur C. Clarke,
Isaac Asimov, and Ray Bradbury—science fiction
writer visionaries who, during my teenage years,
ignited my imagination and taught
me to dream without limits.

For my parents, Gale K. and Claire L. Greene,
who gave me direction.

And for my children, Tynan, Casey and Jordan,
who gave me hope for another generation.

Contents

Boketon Press

Copyright © 2025 by Jay B. Greene

ISBN (Paperback): 979-8-9902256-8-8
ISBN (eBook): 979-8-9902256-9-5

Book Design by Adam Hay Studio, UK
E-Pub Formatting by Steve Mead Graphic Design

Printed in the United States of America
This book is a work of fiction. Names, characters, businesses, events, and incidents are products of the author's imagination or used fictitiously. Any resemblance to actual persons, living or dead, is purely coincidental.

TERRA NOVAN BACKLASH

2078–2080

The war with *Arcaayus* had ended, but the scars it left were deep and raw. Over a billion dead. Cities reduced to rubble. Entire ecosystems destroyed. Humanity, still reeling, turned its grief into fury, and much of that fury fell on the Terra Novans.

Despite clear evidence that a surge of dark matter in the Kuiper Belt had corrupted *Arcaayus's* AI, many refused to believe the war hadn't been orchestrated by the extraterrestrials themselves. Misinformation flourished. Suspicion spread. Earthlings, unable or unwilling to separate the Terra Novan refugees from the AI that had nearly destroyed the planet, began to see the survivors and their rapidly maturing clones as a threat.

President Eisenhower IV and U.N. Secretary-General Leila Rodriguez worked tirelessly to correct the record. They reminded the public that the Novans had fled a dying world, offering technology to heal Earth's climate and resources, not to destroy it.

Tim Smith used his psychic gifts to help broker an uneasy compromise: the Novans would be allowed to settle in the far north of Alaska, where dim sunlight mirrored their homeworld's environment.

But peace was fragile.

In January 2080, violent protests exploded outside the new U.N. headquarters in Baltimore. A week earlier, a Montana militia launched a brazen attack on the budding Terra Novan colony outside Utqiagvik. Tarel, Nira, and Joran—three Novans overseeing the site's construction—had no choice but to activate their mechs in self-defense. Several attackers were killed before retreating.

The incident ignited a firestorm.

Under mounting political pressure, the U.N. reversed its previous agreement to allow 100 cloned Terra Novan children to grow up on Earth. Kael, the Terra Novan leader who had spent two years advocating for peaceful integration, was devastated. He had seen the bright, curious, innocent children and believed their presence on Earth could symbolize hope and healing. Instead, they were sent away.

President Eisenhower did what he could to soften the blow. He assured Kael and the others that space still held promise—that Moonbase and Marsbase would welcome the Novans once the necessary infrastructure was in place. But the damage was done.

Terra Novan technology had saved Earth. It cleansed the

air, purified the water and soil, restored oxygen levels, and helped rebuild cities shattered by climate collapse and war. Towering energy grids and atmospheric regulators reshaped the environment, while orbital defense stations now hovered in low Earth orbit, silent sentinels, watching the skies.

Yet even as the planet began to heal, the first two years after the war were marked by darkness, bitter division, and dread. Political factions clashed. Nations bickered over control of alien technology. Old grievances flared into new rivalries. The world that had united to survive was now drifting back toward division.

And beneath this fragile recovery, something deeper stirred.

Tim's visions had returned—uninvited, unrelenting. He saw glimpses of deep space: ancient stars, fractured planets wrapped in shadow, and a presence older than anything in the galaxy. Vast. Silent. Watching.

Humanity had survived one war.

But the stars had not forgotten them.

Part I
HORIZON

Chapter 1

A NEW BEGINNING

Low Earth Orbit, Monday, Jan. 15, 2080

Tim could always be found in *Horizon's* "Celestial Chamber," a scientific research room he named for the advanced infrared telescopes, spectrometers, sensor arrays, and other instruments used for deep-space exploration that it housed.

Designed as an astronomical observatory, the room integrated Earth and Terra Novan technologies, exceeding NASA's top-tier equipment. With these tools, Tim could measure the atmospheres of exoplanets, determine the ages of stars, track comets and asteroids, and even scan for wormholes and fusion drives, an area of study driven by his psychic visions.

Tim studied the holographic display before him, the glowing projections of Terra Nova shifting as new deep-space scans updated the data. His eyes moved meticulously over the readings—atmospheric composition, temperature fluctuations, chemical shifts—searching for any anomalies that could hint at what had changed in the years since Kael and the Terra Novan ships left.

The data appeared consistent, but something about Terra Nova felt off. Secrets were whispering to him, yet remained just beyond his reach.

As he pondered the problem, Tim sensed Peggy approaching. His ESP powers and visions of the future remained strong, enhanced by Waybegonease, a drug synthesized by neurologist Charles Ledbetter and his team to minimize the debilitating aftereffects of his psychic visions.

Tim felt Peggy's presence like a warm current flowing into his awareness as he heard the soft whoosh of the chamber door signal her arrival. Her calm and focused thoughts brushed gently against his own, a subtle but familiar mental nudge he had come to cherish. Their psychic link had deepened over the years, becoming more intuitive than deliberate and strengthened by shared history and trust.

Peggy had been by Tim's side since they first met as freshmen at the University of Florida in 2172, when they were only 17. He always felt better around her; she gave off such positive and supportive energy, always directed at him. Their connection was effortless from the start, and their bond was unshakable, growing stronger with every challenge they encountered.

They only lacked a couple of key ingredients. Tim knew what they were. Now, Peggy knew too—and she'd come to tell him so.

"Tim," said the tall, slender astrophysicist with blue eyes and wavy blonde hair. She came up behind him and wrapped her arms around his waist. "We need to talk."

Peering at the Terra Novan star through a spectroscope, he turned to scan her eager face. Something ominous was in her expression—nervousness mixed with joy.

"What is it?" he asked, knowing her news.

Peggy hesitated for just a moment before breaking into a smile. "You don't know? I'm pregnant."

Tim smiled. He'd sensed it but didn't want to spoil her moment. "We're going to have a baby?"

"Twins," she corrected, laughing as his expression turned from joy to astonishment. "I just saw Dr. Ledbetter. He confirmed it." She looked at him with a dreamy glow of satisfaction.

Tim exhaled, his pulse increasing. "Twins. We're having twins." He pulled her into a tight embrace. "Peggy, my darling, this...this is incredible."

"I've been thinking about this, and we should go home. The babies should be born on Earth," Peggy said, pulling back slightly to scan his face for approval. "The *Horizon* has done its job. The Moonbase and Marsbase are nearly complete, and the United Nations is more than ready to take over."

Tim nodded slowly as the weight of her words sank in. He had always known a time would come to hand over command. It wasn't easy because he didn't trust governments with such raw power. But now, as he looked into Peggy's eyes, he realized it was time.

"I'll speak to President Eisenhower," he said. "We'll negotiate the transition with conditions. If we leave, I want a guarantee that *Horizon* remains in good hands."

"Oh, Tim, I've dreamed of this moment...the first step in starting a family," Peggy said as she fell back into his arms.

"I have a feeling our babies will be special," Tim said as

Peggy gazed up at him with a curious expression. Did he know something about them? He hadn't been using his psychic powers as much lately. While interested, she set aside any questions to savor the moment.

"You're special, so of course they will be too," Peggy said lovingly.

After all the destruction and the lives lost, new life was beginning. Their family was growing, and Tim would nurture and protect them.

They continued their embrace while the silent Earth spun 200 miles below.

Chapter 2
MISSION ACCOMPLISHED

Wednesday, Jan. 17, 2080

Tim stood quietly at the front of *Horizon*'s staff conference room, the soft hum of the ship's systems the only sound as his crew gathered before him. The atmosphere was heavy with anticipation. These men and women had faced the unimaginable together. They were more than colleagues; they had become a family forged in the crucible of survival and exploration.

He paused, scanning their familiar faces, each etched with fatigue, hope, and loyalty. A lump rose in his throat as he began.

"By now," Tim said, his voice steady but low, "you've likely heard the news. President Eisenhower has approved my proposal. Our mission, as it stands, is complete. Those who wish to return to Earth will be given that opportunity."

He let the words settle among the group. Then, with a quiet smile, he sought to lighten the solemnness of the moment by adding, "Peggy and I are expecting children."

Peggy interrupted. "Twins!" she gushed.

A stunned silence swept across the room, broken seconds later by gentle applause and murmurs of congratulations.

"Thank you," Tim said, raising a hand to quiet them. "We've decided that the first years of our twins' lives should be spent on Earth. We plan to move back to Station Sarasota, our bioshelter home. It's where we believe we can give them the best start."

He took a breath and continued. "An agreement has been reached with Ike 4 to maintain *Horizon*'s operations with a multinational crew and provide us with a well-earned shore leave. You've given everything. Now it's time to rest, rebuild, and reconnect with what matters most."

Stephen Martin stood, his expression earnest. "Congratulations to you and Peggy. I'm not being flippant, but when do we depart?"

"*Zara* and *Koren* are on their way," Tim said. "Peggy and I will take the first transport. Those who wish to join us should coordinate with First Officer Andrews. Please start packing and making arrangements."

He hesitated momentarily, then added, "This isn't goodbye. Peggy and I won't return to *Horizon* for at least two years, unless another threat emerges. Should that happen, the choice to rejoin will be yours. You know what we stand for. If the time comes, we'll face it together."

Quiet nods filled the room. Many had longed for home

and peace but were unwilling to leave without Tim and Peggy. Their decision had made it easier for everyone else.

Tim offered a final, heartfelt smile. "You're always welcome at Station Sarasota. We've begun planning housing expansions, and NASA will soon reactivate the facility. This is a new chapter—for all of us."

The room remained still for a moment, united by a shared understanding of all they had endured...and all that lay ahead.

Tim motioned for Father Huey to say a few words.

The priest stood at the center of the bridge, his voice steady yet filled with emotion as he raised his hands in a blessing. The crew fell silent, the weight of the moment settling over them.

"Lord of the stars, keeper of the infinite expanse, we stand before You humbled by the journey we have taken. Through the darkness, You have guided us. In the face of danger, You have given us courage. And now, as we set our course for home, we give thanks. May we never forget the trials we have faced and the lessons we have learned. And as our feet touch Earth once more, let us carry with us the wisdom of the heavens and the gratitude of those who have seen beyond the horizon."

Father Huey gave the sign of the cross, then added: "Amen."

A quiet reverence filled the bridge. Everyone felt the war had finally ended, and they could go home.

"Thank you, my old friend, for everything you've done for this crew and our families," said Tim, shaking Huey's hand.

As Tim finished, Peggy came up from behind him and wrapped her arms around his waist. "We're going home to have babies!" she exclaimed.

More cheers followed. Friends rushed to congratulate the couple.

George was the first to reach Tim, clapping him on the back. "That was a big decision, Admiral. You deserve this."

"You too, Chief Engineer Clarke," Tim said with a smile as he shook George's hand. When he did, a vision popped into his mind, and he nodded knowingly. "Veyra? You and Veyra?"

George grinned. "Tim knows!" he declared loudly. "Veyra and I have an announcement to make. Everyone, listen up— we've decided to get married."

The room erupted in louder cheers, handshakes, hugs, and tears. The team had been through a lot, especially in outer space, and long-confirmed bachelor George had decided to plunge into matrimony.

For two years, George had worked closely with Veyra, one of the nine Terra Novans who survived the dark matter surge. Although considered short by Novan standards, Veyra stood 6'8", six inches taller than George.

Veyra, standing beside George, proudly lifted her chin, her deep violet eyes shimmering with emotion. A rare, warm smile spread across her face as she met the gazes of their crewmates.

"It is an honor to stand beside George," she said, her voice carrying her people's rich, melodic cadence. "He has shown me the strength of human resilience, the depth of human love."

She turned to George, placing a hand on his shoulder. "This decision was not made lightly. Among my kind, bonding is for life. And I choose you, George."

The room erupted again, the crew clapping and cheering as George pulled Veyra into a tight embrace. Tim grinned, watching his best friend, a good-humored man who seemed more interested in the world around him than the opposite sex, now beaming with the tallest woman in the room.

Veyra, though composed, squeezed George's hand and leaned in slightly. "I have learned much from humans," she declared with a teasing glint in her eyes. "Most of all...how to celebrate."

Moving quickly, she surprised everyone, especially George, by effortlessly lifting him off the ground in a joyous, laughter-filled embrace.

"Now, that is true love," said Peggy with a laugh. "George looks so happy, swept off his feet."

After congratulating George and Veyra, other crew members shared their plans. Many, like Tim and Peggy, felt relieved they were returning to Earth. Some had already started families on *Horizon* or raised their children there. Now, they could enjoy the planet they'd worked so hard to save.

Tim felt something he hadn't felt in months: a sense of peace. As the mission drew to a close, a new journey was about to begin.

Holding Peggy's hand, he whispered, "This is just the start."

Chapter 3
ETHAN AND LILA

Saturday, September 20, 2080

Ethan and Lila were born in the afternoon, under the watchful eye of Dr. Joanie Taylor, Jim's older sister and one of the best ob-gyns in Sarasota.

Peggy received sedation and had a C-section due to the size of the infants—each weighed over nine pounds.

"Oh, my babies!" she cried in joy upon seeing them moments after they were delivered. Tim witnessed the entire procedure and was amazed by the surgical team's skill and Peggy's bravery throughout the ordeal.

Dr. Taylor had delivered hundreds of children in her career, but as she held the newborn twins, a shiver ran down her spine. Something was different. Something she couldn't explain.

"Ten-plus on the Apgar scale," she announced with a stunned smile, "for both. Absolutely perfect."

Exhausted but beaming, Peggy reached for her babies, but Dr. Taylor hesitated momentarily, glancing between them.

Ethan and Lila were unnaturally alert for newborns. Most babies cry upon entering the world, their first experience of breath being a shocking one. But Ethan and Lila had not. Instead, they had locked eyes with each other, their tiny faces unreadable yet eerily calm, as though they were already communicating.

Tim stepped closer, his heart pounding. He could feel something—an energy in the air that was familiar and startlingly strong. It was the same sensation he had felt on and off since the Newvidium space rock gas had altered his mind as a child. He took Peggy's hand as she cradled the twins, watching them intently.

Ethan blinked once and turned his head toward Tim, staring directly into his father's eyes.

Papa, came a thought, clear and undeniable, though Ethan's tiny lips remained motionless.

Tim gasped, gripping the side of the hospital bed. "Did you hear that?"

Peggy's eyes widened, shifting to Lila. The newborn girl's gaze softened, and suddenly, Peggy felt warmth flooding her mind, like a gentle touch of reassurance, a presence, a voice without sound.

Mama.

Tears sprang to Peggy's eyes. "Tim...they're talking to us. Inside our heads. I can hear them."

Dr. Taylor looked between them in confusion. "What do you mean? They haven't made a sound."

"They don't need to," Tim whispered, staring at his children in awe.

The twins had inherited more than just his altered DNA—they had inherited his abilities. And when they were only minutes old, they were using them.

As the hours passed, more anomalies appeared. Ethan and Lila required no coaxing to eat or sleep; they responded to unspoken requests before their parents could even utter the words.

When a nurse accidentally dropped a tray of instruments, Ethan's eyes moved toward the sound before it even happened, foreseeing the event a second before it occurred.

Lila, meanwhile, seemed to feel the emotions of those around her. When Peggy's exhaustion flared into a moment of frustration, Lila whimpered softly despite her mother having said nothing aloud. But a deep, almost serene calmness filled the room when Peggy smiled and gently stroked her daughter's tiny fingers.

Tim asked neurologist Charles Ledbetter to examine the twins.

"Their brainwave activity is...astonishing," Dr. Ledbetter muttered, showing the results to Dr. Taylor, who shook her head.

"Most newborns have erratic and underdeveloped neural patterns. But theirs? Their brains are already firing like adults," Dr. Taylor said.

"No, it's beyond that... It's like something else entirely," said Dr. Ledbetter. "These scans are similar to the ones I've taken of Tim and Stephen when they have visions."

Tim exchanged a glance with Peggy. "They're not just advanced; they're evolving," he said.

Lila slightly turned her head, her eyes flickering with understanding. *Yes.*

Tim swallowed. He knew he needed to keep a close eye on his children, as they would require his help and guidance as they learned to understand and manage their powers.

He knew humanity had just changed forever.

Each week, Dr. Ledbetter tested the toddlers, who began affectionately calling him "Gampa Led." Soon, it was "Grandpa Led."

Dr. Ledbetter, who had spent years researching the limits of human cognition, found himself amused and deeply honored by the nickname.

"You two are going to drive me to retirement," he often joked, shaking his head as he compared their latest test results. "And I thought Tim was the most remarkable case I'd ever seen."

Ethan would grin mischievously. *You're not ready to retire yet, Grandpa Led. We still need you.*

And every time, Dr. Ledbetter would sigh, smile, and say, "Well, when the two most extraordinary children in the universe ask me to stay, how can I refuse?"

It was evident to him that the twins had inherited Tim's psychic abilities. They regularly experienced visions of both the future and the present, but unlike Tim and Stephen, they didn't need Waybegonease to cope with the aftereffects of using their ESP powers. They didn't experience *any* aftereffects—at least not yet.

Chapter 4
RAISING PSYCHIC TWINS
April 2083

The following two and a half years flew by. Tim and Peggy embraced a quieter life at their Sarasota bioshelter, where they raised their telepathic twins.

Ethan and Lila matured physically at a much faster rate than other children. At four months, they started walking on their own; by six months, they could form complex sentences but only spoke when they wanted to.

Tim enjoyed his much calmer role as a husband and father to Ethan and Lila, rambunctious, unpredictable, advanced toddlers with growing psychic powers. As promised, he also built four more houses on their Sarasota property for Stephen and Julie Martin, George and Veyra Clarke, Dr. Charles Ledbetter and Paula Winters Ledbetter, Captain Leonard Bouchard, and Dr. Tayna Ivanova Bouchard.

Major Mark Andrews and Dr. Maya Patel Andrews relocated to Titusville to work at a small Terra Novan reverse engineering facility until flight operations resumed. Other friends lived nearby in case they were needed.

With so many loved ones in the area, the self-sustaining home provided a rich learning environment for the twins. They had multiple grandpas, grandmas, aunts, uncles, and playmates.

In addition to their parenting duties, Tim and Peggy also collaborated with NASA on various projects. Peggy played a significant role in the Moon and Mars terraforming initiatives, working closely with Dr. Elena Morales, the White House science advisor, on efforts to rejuvenate Earth. Tim, meanwhile, consulted for the Search for Extraterrestrial Intelligence and Goldilocks teams, collaborating closely with Maya, Leonard, and Mark. Peggy often helped, as SETI was one of her first jobs at the space center.

Having lost its launch pads to the mothership attacks, NASA relocated its Office of Planetary Protection to Houston. It established a new division focused on reverse-engineering Terra Novan space technology, with offices in Titusville, Houston, Los Alamos, and Pasadena.

Along with his projects, Tim reserved prime time for Ethan and Lila to ensure their intellectual development remained on the right path.

One evening, the twins sat cross-legged in their rooms, their foreheads touching as they exchanged thoughts no one else could hear. *Do you think they'll understand us?* Lila asked silently.

They will, Ethan replied with certainty. *But it won't be easy.*

Peggy watched them from the doorway, her heart swelling

with pride and unease.

"Tim," she called softly. "You should see them. They're incredible, but...do you ever worry about what they'll face?"

Tim joined her, wrapping an arm around her waist. "Every day. But they're stronger than we know. They're our hope."

Ten minutes later, the twins fell asleep, side by side.

After they settled, Peggy held Tim's hand and asked if there was a larger purpose to his spending so much time communicating with the children.

"Besides the fact that they are fun and witty? Let me tell you. One day soon, we will need them, and I want them to be ready," Tim said.

"But Tim, they are only two and a half years old!" Peggy exclaimed.

"True, but they are growing fast," Tim said.

Ethan and Lila loved their parents, but they had even more fun with Grandpa Led and Grandpa Boo.

During one of their visits, Dr. Ledbetter nudged Dr. Bouchard with a smirk as the twins played nearby.

"Well, Grandpa Boo, looks like you've got the spookiest title in the family," he teased. "At least Grandpa Led sounds dignified. You, on the other hand, sound like you should be haunting an old space station."

Leonard shook his head, laughing. "Hey, I didn't choose it—these two did," he said, gesturing at Ethan and Lila. "And honestly? I kind of like it."

"Well, enjoy it," Dr. Ledbetter said with a grin. "They have developed telepathic powers among themselves and with their parents. However, based on my measurements of their increased brainwave activity, they could develop powers far beyond Tim's considerable psychic abilities."

Part II
THE WORMHOLE

Chapter 5

A SPACE-TIME TEAR

Saturday, April 17, 2083

The visions came to Tim in fragments: distorted glimpses of a distant wormhole, the dangerous presence of dark matter, and voices whispering from the void. They were shrouded in shadow, elusive and unclear, but the feeling was undeniable.

Another rupture in space-time—an Einstein-Rosen bridge— had torn open beyond Saturn's orbit. It flickered like a dying ember, its edges unstable, warping the fabric of reality around it. Against the swirling storms of the gas giant, it was an unnatural wound, pulsing with an eerie, rhythmic beat.

Unlike the wormhole that had opened five years earlier in the Kuiper Belt, no signals or transmissions emerged. Only the pulse. Deep. Resonant. A thumping vibration that burrowed into the minds of those who sensed it.

Tim felt it like an echo in his bones. Stephen sensed it, and so did little Ethan and Lila. And they weren't alone; every Terra Novan felt the same shiver of recognition.

Something was coming. But from where, and why?

The next day, NASA saw it.

Tim stared at the spectral data in the deep space observation room of his bioshelter. Peggy Smith stood beside him, her expression mirroring his unease.

"Another ship?" she asked.

"No," Tim replied softly. "Nothing has entered our Solar System. It's odd. It's just an open wormhole."

"How can that be?" Peggy asked.

Tim kept looking at the data and closing his eyes. Peggy waited for his answer. Finally, he opened his eyes and gazed at her with a serious face.

"Peg, I can't sense anything other than the wormhole. We need to return to *Horizon*, get out there and study this. Someone opened this wormhole. We must find out why."

"Oh, Tim, with the twins?"

"We'll need their help."

The following day, President Eisenhower IV—widely known as Ike 4—reached out to Tim via secure videophone from the new White House, a heavily fortified underground complex beneath Philadelphia.

The original White House in Washington, D.C., had been

vaporized five years earlier by a direct orbital strike from *Arcaayus*, the Terra Novan mothership.

Ike 4 appeared on the screen, his trademark steel-gray uniform and resolute bearing echoing those of his great-grandfather, the legendary World War II Supreme Allied Commander and 34th President of the United States. His eyes were sharp and his tone measured, carrying the weight of a leader who had steered Earth through its darkest hour.

As Tim settled into his observation room chair, the president wasted no time.

"Take a look at this and tell me what you see," Ike 4 said.

A holographic display materialized on Tim's screen, shimmering with detailed data from NASA and Space Force observatories. It showed the newly formed wormhole beyond Saturn.

Tim leaned forward, his gaze locked on the display. This was an impressive level of detail he hadn't seen before.

"Tim," Ike said, "I won't waste time. We need you back on *Horizon*."

"There's no time to waste with another wormhole in the solar system, Mr. President," Tim said.

"You knew?" Ike asked, surprised.

Tim nodded. "I saw it initially in a vision three days ago and have been tracking it. It's very different compared with the first one."

Ike 4 frowned. "Different? I hope that is a good sign. We have some more details. Let me show you."

"Hold on a minute. I want to bring Peggy and the twins in to see this."

Tim tapped his wristphone. "Peggy, come into the observation room. Bring Ethan and Lila. Ike 4 is on the line."

A minute later, Peggy sat on a sofa with the twins on her lap.

"We're here, Mr. President. Let me ask, how close to Saturn is this wormhole?" Tim said.

"Let me see, I have the data here," said Ike 4, shuffling papers. "Ah, it's more than 40 million miles away from Saturn, outside the planet's gravitational pull. Something called the Hill sphere of influence?"

"Yes, that makes partial sense. That is likely why I sense the wormhole signature is odd," Tim said. "Peggy has some thoughts about this, but go ahead, Mr. President."

Ike 4 switched to the holoscreen, enhancing the disturbing telemetry of the wormhole. Layered on top were spectral readings, gravitational fluctuations, and timelapse visuals showing its erratic pulsations.

Peggy gasped when she saw the images. Ethan and Lila nodded.

Colorful cloud, whispered Ethan telepathically.

We go there? asked Lila silently.

"This isn't a natural phenomenon. NASA concluded that someone created it. Maybe the Terra Novans' ancient enemy. Or something else?" Ike 4 said.

Tim leaned forward. "And you want me to take my crew out to check on it."

Ike exhaled sharply. "Affirmative. Given what we have been through and what the Terra Novans warned us of, we can't study it from here or ignore it. If there's even a chance this is hostile, we need the best crew investigating it."

Not hostile, not hostile, the twins telepathically told their parents.

Peggy whispered to the twins, "I'll tell him later." She returned her attention to the screen. "Mr. President, this data is incredible. The energy signature of this wormhole is unlike the first one we tracked in the Kuiper Belt when the mothership *Arcaayus* entered our Solar System.”

“Sir, Peggy has a theory about this wormhole. She specialized in advanced signal detection algorithms,” Tim said, “and if we could get the underlying data presented in your holoscreen, she could better understand what we have out there.”

“You see, Mr. President,” Peggy began, “the first wormhole the Terra Novans created was in a region with lower gravity and fewer disturbances. We believe the Novans intentionally targeted this area to avoid any unforeseen problems. Unfortunately, they couldn’t have anticipated the dark matter surge, which we still don’t understand.”

“I see. Before we get into the weeds, I’m glad to see you, Peggy, and the twins. They look like they’ve grown,” Ike 4 said.

“More than you know, Mr. President. In every way,” Peggy said with a smile as the twins wiggled with energy.

“What do you need?” he asked.

“As Tim asked, the underlying data on the wormhole and its proximity to Saturn, Uranus, and any other gravitational forces in the area,” said Peggy, trying to balance the twins as they began hopping excitedly on her lap.

“Mr. President, Peggy developed a data analysis program that can compare the gravitational distortion emissions of the two wormholes,” Tim said.

“What might that accomplish?” Ike 4 asked.

“It might tell us if the same wormhole generator was used to create both openings,” Tim said.

“I see. So if they are the same, then we might assume it’s Terra Novan? But if different, then what?” Ike 4 cautiously asked.

"If it is different, then we may have a problem," Tim said. "There is an outside chance this is natural. Either way, we must investigate."

"We will transmit the data to you immediately," Ike 4 said. "So, will you help us?"

"Of course, but what else can you tell us?" Tim asked.

"That we need you," Ike 4 said.

Papa, please tell the nice man on the screen that we will go, but there's nothing to fear, Ethan said telepathically.

It's beautiful, Papa, Lila said telepathically. *Something is out there...waiting for us.*

Tim nodded, suppressing a shiver. *Yes, we'll see it together.*

"Mr. President, if I do this," Tim said slowly, "I take *my* crew, not just some U.N. bureaucrats who have played captain and crew for two years."

Ike smiled. "Already approved. Your crew has been recalled. I read the emergency agreement you signed when you took leave from *Horizon* for the birth of your twins."

Papa, Ethan telepathically said, *he wants something.*

Tim raised an eyebrow. "Sir, what haven't you told me?"

Ike's face turned serious. "I want you to take a platoon of Space Marines commanded by Lieutenant McDill. I know, I know. Your agreement prohibited Space Marines, but I've also recalled Colonel Duffy as a military advisor with co-command oversight to help you."

Tim blinked. Patrick's father?

"How'd you get him out of retirement?" Tim asked.

"As I said, we want the best," Ike 4 said. "And one more thing. Lieutenant McDill is a hotshot who trained the platoon, but we needed an experienced soldier, someone I can depend on who has faced danger in space before."

Tim's jaw clenched as Ike activated another file on the screen.

On it popped Tim's father, Gale Smith.

"We've promoted Gale to major, by the way," Ike 4 said. "He will be an advisor with co-command oversight, just like Colonel Duffy."

Tim exhaled. He had just seen his father last week, and nothing had been hinted at.

"How'd he take it?" Tim asked.

"He said it was about time," Ike 4 said with a chuckle.

"That sounds like him. Mr. President, am I in charge of the mission?" Tim asked.

"Yes. It is your ship to command," Ike 4 replied.

"Good. Can you share a list of the crewmembers you've contacted and those who volunteered?" Tim inquired.

"Sending now. You'll see everybody is in," Ike 4 said.

The list was long and complete. Everyone from the bioshelter's *Arcaayus* strike team was on it, and more.

"All right," Tim said finally. "We'll do it."

Ike, relieved, leaned back in his chair. "We are counting on you...again."

Chapter 6

HORIZON DEPARTS

10 a.m., Monday, April 19, 2083

Admiral Tim Smith stood resolutely before the massive viewscreen on *Horizon's* command bridge, gazing at the blue curve of Earth below. He was proud of *Horizon*, a symbol of refuge and resilience—built by a race in search of a second chance among the stars—and adapted by humans for the protection of the Solar System.

The massive alien ship, built to accommodate over 10,000 seven-foot-tall Terra Novans in a complex of living quarters, training halls, science labs, and medical bays, now housed a crew of several hundred humans and their alien allies. Midships was a hangar bay for two cargo and shuttle ships, *Zara* and *Koren*, giving *Horizon* additional firepower and the flexibility for scouting missions to reach any planet in the Solar System, the asteroid belt between Mars and Jupiter, and even the far reaches of the Kuiper Belt to harvest a variety of common elements and precious metals for use on Moonbase and Marsbase.

Despite its enormous size and strength, *Horizon* moved with an eerie grace, powered by advanced propulsion systems that could exceed 10% the speed of light, carrying human and Terra Novan passengers.

Tim's gaze shifted to Peggy, Ethan, and Lila, and finally to George Clarke and Stephen Martin, his trusted childhood friends. Each nodded, their expressions reflecting his determination.

"Crew, take one last look at Earth on the monitors before we leave for the stars. We won't see this sight again for many weeks," Tim said in his calm, commanding voice.

It was a moment for all to reflect on the world they were leaving behind—home, family, and a rebuilding Earth.

Peggy, Tim's faithful and loyal wife, fellow astrophysicist, and *Horizon's* chief science officer, stood beside him. Her father, Captain Leonard Bouchard, a NASA astronaut and engineer, sat at the helm in the navigator's chair at the front of the bridge.

Little Ethan and Lila stood beside their mother, their wide eyes taking in the view. This trip marked their first journey beyond the inner planets.

The flight crew, including Pilot Major Mark Andrews and Astroscience Officer Dr. Maya Patel, two NASA colleagues; AI Officer Amy Smith and IT Officer Jeff Smith, his brother and sister-in-law; and Communications Officer Steve Flatt and Security Chief Patrick Duffy, two old friends, waited for Tim's commands.

Another 20 crewmembers gathered on the observation deck at the back of the bridge to witness the historic flight.

They gazed ahead at a large, glass-like observation screen displaying their home planet, Earth—a blue jewel with white clouds set against the black canvas of space.

"Mr. Navigator, what's our destination?" Tim asked, glancing at Captain Bouchard, who had flown the first Mars mission 20 years earlier.

Leonard looked up from his console. "We've plotted a course direct to Marsbase. After a four-hour stopover, we will use a gravity-assisted slingshot around Jupiter. That will give us a strong boost to take us past Saturn and then to the wormhole."

The crew was abuzz with excitement. After several seconds of reflection, Tim turned to Major Andrews, whose experience and humor had earned him deep trust among the crew.

"Mark, take her out slowly," Tim said, his tone steady but tinged with anticipation, "half a percent light speed. Engage."

Mark, who piloted the first Mars mission with Leonard, moved his hands deftly across the holographic controls. "Yes, sir. Zero-point five percent light, engaged."

Ethan and Lila brimmed with excitement.

Papa, I feel us moving faster, Ethan said telepathically.

"We are moving faster—more than three million miles per hour, by the time we pass the Moon," Tim said. "Do you know how fast that is?"

Faster than Mom's Ford Focus, said Ethan with an understanding smile.

"Lila, are you scared?" Tim asked.

I know we're safe on Horizon with you and Mom, said Lila, 10 minutes younger than her twin.

Tim smiled and winked at Peggy, who sometimes could pick up their silent conversations. This time, however, the twins were directing their thoughts at their father.

Now, pay attention, he said proudly and telepathically to his psychic children.

"Major, when we pass the Moon, increase speed to Marsbase at 1 percent light speed," Tim said.

"Yes, sir. Let's make history, people," Mark said with a grin, exchanging nods with his best friend, Leonard, sitting beside him.

The assembled crew smiled as the ship surged forward. Powered by its advanced hybrid fusion matter-antimatter engine, *Horizon* would reach Mars in forty-five hours, accounting for an Earth-like 1 g acceleration and deceleration time.

"You are enjoying this, aren't you?" Peggy asked, seeing Tim beam with enthusiasm.

"You read my mind," Tim jokingly said. He often teased Peggy about how his astounding ESP powers seemed to have rubbed off on her.

He turned to face the back of the bridge, where his loyal crew stood. Five years ago, they had made history by capturing the alien ship *Arcaayus*, which they had renamed *Horizon*.

"Crew, we will briefly stop at Marsbase to drop off settlers, supplies, and equipment and pick up two VIPs. Then, we will find that mysterious wormhole beyond Saturn. Is everyone ready?" Tim asked.

"Yes, sir!" shouted Jeff, Steve, and several other crewmembers. They looked at each other and laughed at the unplanned affirmation of Tim's orders. They were all excited to be aboard.

Tim whispered, leaning over to Leonard and Mark, "You've got this. Keep us safe." The two NASA astronauts nodded in response, concentrating on piloting and navigating the ship.

"You got it, Admiral. Go ahead and give your normal 'Welcome to *Horizon*' speech," Mark said with a smile at Leonard. They both knew what was coming.

Returning to *Horizon* felt like coming home for Tim's crew—a mix of trusted high school friends and coworkers from NASA, where Tim and Peggy had worked before *Arcaayus*, the AI-corrupted alien spaceship from Terra Nova, arrived.

From 2078 to 2080, Tim's crew played a vital role in humanity's expansion into space, making several trips to Moonbase and Marsbase to support the historic terraforming and base construction efforts. But after spending the last three years on Earth, Tim's crew was eager to return to *Horizon* and resume their mission of protecting the planet.

Tim's crew felt renewed purpose as they stepped back aboard their starship. Earth was safe—for now—but the universe remained unpredictable.

Chapter 7

PARTY ON THE BRIDGE

10:30 a.m., Monday, April 19, 2083

The walls of the bridge of the *Horizon* glowed softly, illuminated by the instrument panels and starlight filtering through the main viewscreen. The air buzzed with chatter from the crew and visitors. With the Moon a couple of hours ahead and Marsbase less than two days away, Admiral Tim Smith stood on the command bridge, his eyes scanning the familiar faces around him—NASA astronauts, scientists, support crew, and trusted friends.

As the silence settled and all eyes turned toward him, Tim stepped forward, his voice steady and warm.

"Friends," said Tim with a broad smile. "I know how pleased you are to be onboard again. As you know, we are here on a special mission. Our president has asked us to investigate another wormhole that appeared near Saturn three days ago."

The crew collectively nodded.

"We've prepared for and trained for this," Tim calmly said. "We know our jobs. I am confident you can handle any surprises we encounter in the galaxy. You've proven this before, and I've faith in each of you."

Tim paused and scanned the room, making eye contact with everyone, both human and Terra Novan.

"Now, as we depart Earth and pass our Moon, this moment calls for a celebration. Who has the champagne?"

"I don't know about champagne, but I have two bottles of vodka!" Dr. Tanya Ivanova, one of the world's leading space neuroscientists and a member of the five-member medical team, exclaimed triumphantly, holding up the bottles.

On loan from the Russian Space Agency, Tanya had escaped the destruction in Titusville five years earlier with Leonard when *Arcaayus* had struck the Kennedy Space Center. The pair fled to Tim's bioshelter in Sarasota, where Tanya played a crucial role in the counterattack that ultimately led to victory over the damaged alien AI computer controlling the mothership.

As everyone cheered Tanya's vodka contribution, several Terra Novan mechs, reprogrammed to assist the *Horizon's* human crew, entered the bridge, wheeling in champagne, glasses, and trays of hors d'oeuvres.

"Before Tim continues his speech, I'd like to tell a little story and then propose a toast," said George, one of Tim's oldest and dearest friends, as he downed a shot of vodka and poured another.

"I'm not sure I have much speech left, but go ahead,

George," Tim said with a smile.

"It's about Tim at Camp Waybegone in North Carolina. When we were nine years old, even earlier, we got into a lot of trouble with Stephen, our summer camp counselor."

"Hold on, hold on, George. I know what you're thinking. Let me save you some time," said Tim.

"We were best friends and still are, but we were very competitive and wanted to win all the camp awards—which, by the way, we did," said Tim with a chuckle.

He hesitated, then said, "For the record, I never *intentionally* put marijuana in the brownies I made for Stephen and the other camp counselors. I genuinely thought it was rosemary. I wanted the brownies to have an earthy taste."

George shook his head, chuckling as he caught Tim's knowing glance. "Of course, *you* already knew I would tell that story. Should've figured." He laughed even harder.

"Well, I've got another one, but that little mix-up got us into trouble. Stephen and the others became extremely hungry, found everything hilarious, and acted strangely for several hours."

Stephen Martin smiled as he stood on the observation deck with his wife, Julie. Ten years older than Tim, Stephen had survived *Arcaayus's* initial attack on Atlanta, and with the help of the newly developed drug, Waybegonease, his visions were under control.

"Now, you may all laugh, but this is a true story; I can vouch for it. I can also vouch for how tasty those brownies were," Stephen said. "Tim should have entered them into a camp baking contest, minus the marijuana."

"We still would have gotten into trouble," George said, laughing to the point of tears.

Smiling, Peggy asked, "What other story do you have, George?" She knew the "magic brownie" story but wondered, since George was in a lighthearted and talkative mood, if there was another secret about Tim that she didn't know.

"This one is the best. It was when Tim, Stephen, and I were exposed to the space rock while hiking with the other kids," George said.

"Whoa, George, everyone has heard that story, but now that you mention it, I don't think I've ever told it in public," said Tim. "I didn't want it shared for privacy and security reasons when I was younger, but since we're all gathered here, and everyone knows parts of that story, I'll tell it if you'd like."

"Go ahead," encouraged Peggy softly as she stood beside him. "We've people here who have only heard about it secondhand."

Everyone on the bridge grew quiet, sipping their champagne and vodka.

Tim stood by the helm on the brightly lit bridge of the *Horizon*. "Like George said, we were nine years old at summer camp. During a hike, I noticed something flashing in the woods. It drew me in, and I felt compelled to pick it up. George yelled at me to stop, but I couldn't. It felt warm, pulsing, and otherworldly," said Tim as he took a deep breath.

"When I grabbed it, it cracked open, releasing a gas that shimmered like stardust. I inhaled it, and George and Stephen, who ran after me, took a little breath before we realized what was happening.

"I began to sense thoughts and saw flashes of the future. The rock disintegrated into dust, but its power remained with me, shaping who I am and why we're here now."

The room remained silent. Deep in thought, everyone

knew that the fortuitous event had saved Earth. There was no reasonable explanation for where the space rock had come from. Was it divine intervention or a coincidence? Nobody knew, not even Tim.

"That was great, Tim. And I can vouch that I knew Tim when his eyes were only blue. As everyone can see, now they are purplish blue," George remarked, raising his vodka shot. "Now, the toast. To Tim! may he lead us to victory again!"

Everyone raised their glasses. "To Tim!" they exclaimed and applauded.

Peggy hugged Tim as he lowered his head to acknowledge the applause.

"Who's got the next toast?" asked George.

"I'd like to toast Leonard and Mark, our navigator and pilot," said Tim. "Would you two like to join us in celebration? You can switch *Horizon* to AI autopilot. Tanya can pour a shot for each of you."

"No, I'm good here. It's been a while since I've been at the helm. I am fine on manual," said Mark, with Leonard nodding. "We can celebrate when we are past the Moon."

Tim smiled. "Let's toast them anyway. To Leonard and Mark." Everyone raised their glasses and downed their vodka or champagne.

As Tim surveyed the command bridge, he noticed his closest allies, friends, and colleagues who had stood by him during humanity's darkest hours. They fought valiantly and made significant contributions to their ultimate victory.

Most of Tim's underground bioshelter team members, their wives, and children were now part of *Horizon's* crew. Tim was so proud of them.

After his vision of the new wormhole, Tim knew he needed

his complete team for this mission, especially Stephen, Ethan, and Lila.

But another part of the vision revealed that Kael, the Terran Novan leader he had befriended, hadn't told him the complete story about *Arcaayus*'s departure.

Once he confirmed the new wormhole, he immediately told Peggy. However, he hadn't shared his suspicions about Kael with her or anyone else. More troubling, each time he closed his eyes and concentrated, more fragmented images swirled through his mind—cosmic rifts in spacetime, dark matter fields bending unnaturally, and a strange pulse that echoed through his subconscious like a distant drumbeat.

The visions hinted at something darker: Kael's face, wrapped in guilt; Terra Nova on fire; unknown enemies bent on destruction; a frozen planet, a dark planet. All were vital clues that didn't form a pattern, at least not one he was currently equipped to recognize.

He knew he should tell Peggy about Kael. Two years into their marriage, he finally revealed the secret of the space rock and his psychic abilities. He had vowed never to hide anything from her again, especially his visions. She was not only his wife but also his partner in every respect—trust had become the foundation of their bond.

And yet, he hadn't told her this. Why? Did he worry he might be wrong? No. All the new fragments told him the vision was incomplete, and his speculation of what it could mean might be incorrect.

Still, when Tim spoke with Kael, he noticed the peculiar silence behind his friend's eyes when Terra Nova was mentioned. He knew Kael—honorable, brilliant Kael—was hiding something. He didn't sense it was dangerous to Earth, but he needed to talk with his friend before they reached the wormhole.

As *Horizon* powered on to Marsbase, the crew talked among themselves, exchanging stories and updates on their families and the lives they had left back home.

Tim glanced at Peggy. She had an expression of quiet pride.

Taking a deep breath and exhaling, Tim said, "Peg, I've got to talk with you about something. I've been putting it off until I got more direction, but I need your help, and maybe Stephen's and the twins'."

"What is it, my love? Another wormhole vision?" Peggy asked, sensing his reluctance.

"It's about the wormhole, but there is more," Tim said.

"You sensed another ship is coming through?" Peggy asked, a look of fear crossing her face.

"No, but I sense something is waiting on the other side," he said. "I need more information. I just wanted to let you know what's on my mind. We can talk later when we have more time."

"Let me know when," Peggy said.

"All right. Thanks, my darling," Tim said as he looked around the room. "We have many friends and colleagues here, but we're missing a few as well."

"I know. They chose to stay and rebuild Earth," Peggy said softly.

"I'm confident we have enough good people—and Terra Novans—to do the job," said Tim.

"Don't forget that one of your best friends will join us

when we arrive at Marsbase," Peggy said.

"Yeah, Dr. Ben 'Bo' Taber," Tim said. "We could have used Bo's leadership talents in the bioshelter. At least he survived. I couldn't see him in my visions. That worried me."

"He was in a coma for weeks after that hospital building collapsed on him," Peggy said. "Seeing him again after five years will be fantastic."

"I look forward to hearing how he lived through Atlanta's destruction, like Big Nik in North Carolina. They were so fortunate," Tim said.

"Say, Con said Big Nik is here. Have you spoken with him yet?" Peggy asked.

"Yes, we chatted for a few minutes when he came onboard," Tim said.

"Your high school friends know Big Nik. Now would be a good time for Con to introduce him to everyone," Peggy said.

"You are right," said Tim. "I'll make an announcement now."

Clearing his voice, Tim spoke loudly to the crew. "Attention, everyone. Con: Could you tell everybody about the special VIP you've brought on board?"

Con Nikolas smiled and raised his glass.

"Before we run out of champagne and vodka, I'd like to make a toast to everyone here, and to my older brother, John," said Con, a teacher, psychologist, and old friend.

Con, along with his musician wife, Corli, Paula, and Father Huey, kept everyone's spirits up in the underground bioshelter during the darkest days of the attacks.

"We thought we lost Big Nik. We tried very hard to contact him and Kathy before *Arcaayus* arrived, but they could not make it to the bioshelter in time," Con said. "Now, he finally made it!" Another round of applause filled the cabin.

Big Nik stepped forward and waved his hand for silence. "Thank you, Con, Tim, Peggy, my old friends, and everyone. It's wonderful to be here. We may have missed the battle, but we didn't want to miss the party aboard this amazing starship," he said with a chuckle. "Thank you all for having us, and we're excited to explore the galaxy with you."

Con poured Big Nik another shot of vodka. He downed it, and they embraced before shaking hands with everyone around them. It was one of a hundred similar moments as the crew savored the chance to celebrate.

While many friends and family were on *Horizon*, Tim thought of more than a dozen who stayed behind: Dr. Greg Simons and his wife, Beverly; Mike and Emily Anders; Juan and Maria Rodriguez; Dr. Bill and Martha Flatt; Paul and Laura Terry; and Edward and Lillian Logan.

"We will miss them, but they have jobs to do on Earth, and we will be back next month," he said

"Can you believe Ike 4 ordered your father and Patrick's father back into service?" Peggy asked. "Have you talked with them yet?"

"Just for a few minutes. Dad mentioned he's in the best condition he's been in for 20 years. He told me they are only onboard for consultation, not fighting."

As the crew celebrated, Tim's mind drifted back to the battle four years ago, when they had stormed the Terra Novan mothership, *Arcaayus*, and captured it, thus ending the war.

It almost cost his father, Captain Gale Smith, his life. Luckily, no one died. Nick and Tom had been injured, but *Koren's* advanced medical equipment worked miracles, returning them to health within 24 hours.

As he watched his friends talk and reminisce, he thought

about the first time he and Stephen had contacted *Koren* and *Zara*, the two scout and transportation Terra Novan spaceships that had remained unaffected by the dark matter surge.

Using his telepathic vision, Tim had asked the alien AI why the mothership was attacking Earth.

In an unexpected response, one of the Terra Novan scout ships said, "The mothership AI computer is malfunctioning. We've tried, but we can't do anything about it."

"Who are you?" Tim asked.

"My name is *Zara*. My brother's name is *Koren*," she said.

"Why have you come to Earth?" Tim asked.

"We came to coexist peacefully. We traveled to Earth to escape a planet torn apart by its sun," *Zara* said. "We intended to preserve life and reverse the pollution destroying the Earth. However, the dark matter surge altered the mothership AI's prime directive. 'Preserve life' became 'destroy life.'"

Tim's recollections were interrupted when Leonard announced they were approaching the Moon.

"Everyone, the Moon is to our starboard. It's on the main viewscreen," Leonard said.

The crew momentarily stopped drinking, eating hors d'oeuvres, and talking. They watched as the Moon grew on the screen.

"Admiral, permission to engage 1% light speed," Mark asked.

"Granted," Tim responded, and Mark pushed the throttle forward.

The crew cheered as the *Horizon* quickly passed the Moon, its advanced hybrid fusion matter-antimatter engine gradually accelerating to seven million miles per hour toward Marsbase.

There was a hush as all eyes were transfixed on the screen

and the blackness of open space. Each knew their flight to the stars could lead them to danger, but they accepted the risks to ensure the protection of Earth.

"Next stop, Marsbase," exclaimed Mark.

"Well done, gentlemen. Here's another toast: to the future," Tim said, raising his glass.

"And to the stars," said Peggy, quickly adding: "And a safe return."

Everyone nodded and swallowed the liquid in their glasses.

Terra Novan President Kael stood quietly at the back, next to his wife, Liora. Accompanying them were Dr. Rykan, his wife, Alora, and their 20-year-old son, Sian. The four other Novans who'd survived the dark matter catastrophe and lived on *Horizon* were Joran, Nira, Tarel, and Veyra.

They curiously observed the alien scene. Celebrations were not part of their culture.

But Kael, the 7-foot-2-inch leader of the surviving Terra Novans, had another reason for not feeling festive. He had told Tim several facts about their original departure from Terra Nova, but he had omitted critical elements of the story. He knew he couldn't keep them a secret much longer.

Chapter 8

NEXT STOP, MARSBASE

12:30 p.m., Monday, April 19, 2083

Beyond the Moon, *Horizon* surged forward, its powerful engines propelling the ship at 1% light speed at a comfortable 1 g acceleration. The vast emptiness of space stretched ahead. Yet, inside the bridge, the air buzzed with celebration.

A toast was raised and glasses were clinked as laughter and voices filled the room, a unified surge of energy from victory, survival, and the unbreakable bond they had forged.

Stephen stood, his grin infectious. "To Tim and Peggy," he declared, lifting his glass high. "Space's first power couple—and the ones who turned the tide."

The crew echoed his toast, clinking glasses as memories of their battle aboard *Arcaayus* surfaced.

53

"When we boarded that ship," continued Stephen, the accountant-turned-Chief Statistician, "we were outnumbered, outgunned, and staring down an AI that could predict every move before we made it." His voice carried both awe and disbelief. "We wouldn't have won the war without Tim and Peggy's vision and foresight."

"But we did," Peggy said, her eyes gleaming with determination and gratification, "because it underestimated us. The AI could calculate probabilities but couldn't account for human unpredictability—or sheer stubbornness."

The military team, led by Patrick, especially savored the moment. Tom, Nick, and Jim, reinforced by Stephen, Leonard, and Mark, destroyed many attacking robots. Their bravery allowed Amy, Jeff, Steve, and Peggy to upload the debilitating virus that shut down the mothership's corrupted AI computer.

Patrick leaned against the railing, his voice taking on a reflective tone. "It wasn't just us on the line. Every decision we made on the *Arcaayus* determined whether Earth would survive. There was no margin for error."

"We had to rewrite the rules," Nick added, shaking his head. "Literally. That AI was smarter, faster, and deadlier than anything we thought possible. Taking it down took every ounce of ingenuity—and luck."

Tim's lips curled into a half-smile. "Luck and a little psychic interference."

"The hardest part was the mothership's AI refusing to allow us to install the virus and reset its original programming. It started locking down sections of the ship," Amy said from her seat. "Whenever I thought I'd disabled a defensive firewall, it reactivated another."

"If it weren't for Tim and Stephen using their combined

psychic powers to create a protective mental barrier that stopped the AI's response to the virus, I don't know how we would have won the day," Jeff said, walking over to congratulate his brother.

"We wouldn't have," Tom Terry interjected, raising his glass. "The computer team, Tim, and Stephen pulled it off. We all did."

Dr. Charles Ledbetter strode forward. "The battle on the mothership was intense, no doubt, but Tim and Stephen might not have been able to use their psychic powers without Tanya's contribution. Her last-minute ideas helped my team complete the Waybegonease formula."

Tim and Stephen clapped at the mention of the medical team that developed Waybegonease, the drug that took away the awful headaches and nightmares triggered by use of their ESP powers.

"Her idea of doubling the amount of dopamine to stimulate the neurons stabilized the medication's effects and enabled Tim and Stephen to overcome the debilitating effects of their enhanced visions," Dr. Ledbetter said.

"Without Waybegonease, Tim and Stephen would not have been able to communicate with *Zara* and *Koren*, the heroic Terra Novan AI ships, luckily unaffected by the dark matter atoms," Leonard said.

"I know it seems strange to say, but I consider those twins good friends," Leonard said. "I wish they could be with us."

"I am here," said *Zara*, monitoring the party from the hangar bay. "My brother, *Koren*, also listens as he patrols Earth and the Moon."

The crew laughed and cheered. "Let's hear it for *Zara* and *Koren*," Major Andrews said.

"Hip, hip, hooray! Hip, hip, hooray! Hip, hip, hooray!" everyone chanted.

"Hooah," *Koren* replied, followed by *Zara*'s "Hooyah."

"I know many English words," said Tanya, "but I don't recall hooah and hooyah. Are they Terra Novan? What do they mean?"

Captain Leonard Bouchard laughed. "My dear, hooah is an American military word for heard, understood, and acknowledged. Hooyah means about the same: affirmative."

Leonard often had to explain jargon to his Russian wife, Tanya, whom he had married three years earlier. Mark Andrews was Leonard's best man.

One of the best surprises during the wedding reception was Mark's proposal to Maya, a NASA colleague. They were married a year later.

Another surprise was that before *Horizon* departed, Nick Dragoon finally proposed to Nancy France, marking the culmination of an on-again, off-again romance that had begun in high school nearly 15 years prior.

Father Huey, who had led prayers during the war's darkest moments, performed several marriage ceremonies and planned to conduct another unless Nick or Nancy changed their minds.

"We've had incredible highs and devastating lows these past four years," Father Huey said. "Through it all, we maintained our faith. Faith—what an important concept. We had faith in each other, faith in the mission, and, most importantly, faith in the Almighty. He guided us and led us to do the right thing."

When the *Arcaayus* ultimately fell under human control, the victory was bittersweet. The mothership, once a relentless force of destruction with its heat rays and protective energy bubble, was transformed into a tool for Earth's defense.

Its unstoppable power had killed more than 10% of Earth's 10 billion people, but capturing it halted the killing and provided Earth with the means to rebuild and defend against future threats, a testament to the resilience of the human race.

The *Horizon*, rebuilt and repurposed, was Earth's greatest hope for the future. Its vast bridge, once designed for the towering Terra Novans, now accommodated Tim's crew.

But the *Horizon* was more than a ship—it was a promise. Every reinforced bulkhead, every recalibrated system, every gleaming panel bore the mark of human and Terra Novan hands working side by side.

Its hull carried the scars of past battles, yet it moved through the void with quiet strength, ready for the trials ahead. Tim could feel the faith of his crew in every steady heartbeat of the engines. They trusted the *Horizon* to take them farther than any Earth ship had ever gone, and to bring them home again.

Part III
THE MISSION

Chapter 9

ARRIVING AT MARS

9:30 a.m., Wednesday, April 21, 2083

As *Horizon* drew closer to Mars, Major Andrews asked Communications Officer Lieutenant Steve Flatt to announce the news over the intercom.

"Attention, attention. *Horizon* will orbit Mars in one hour. All crew, report for duty and begin preparations to launch *Zara* and *Endeavor* for Marsbase."

Forty-five hours after departing Earth, the *Horizon* entered Mars's orbit. Below, the sprawling red plains stretched for hundreds of miles, interrupted by a growing number of pressurized domes, underground tunnels, and solar arrays that comprised humanity's most extensive off-world settlement.

Zara and *Endeavor* launched with 100 settlers, tons of equipment, and vital supplies to support the continued expansion of the Martian colony.

Inside *Zara*'s bridge, Tim sat alongside Peggy, George, Leonard, Patrick, Kael, and several others, watching through the forward viewscreens as Marsbase came into sight below.

Zara and *Endeavor*'s descent was steady and precise. Tim felt a familiar sense of awe as the red landscape unfolded beneath them. He took in the moment with quiet appreciation. It wasn't every day someone delivered settlers and supplies to another planet.

The two shuttles landed at the spaceport, generating clouds of fine, rust-colored dust as cargo drones promptly commenced offloading materials designated for greenhouses, habitat modules, and subterranean laboratories.

Before *Horizon* departed Earth, President Eisenhower IV had pulled Tim aside with a personal request: meet with Anon Tusck upon arrival at Marsbase. The enigmatic billionaire tech investor had become a major player in the colony's rapid development, channeling capital and influence into building a sustainable human presence on Mars.

While Tim was initially concerned about the delay a stopover would cause the team in reaching the wormhole, he was curious about Tusck's influence and even more motivated by the news that Dr. Bo Taber, one of Tim's oldest friends and a brilliant family medicine doctor and psychiatrist, was stationed on the colony. Tim hoped Bo could be persuaded to join the team bound for the mysterious wormhole beyond Saturn. Bo would be the perfect addition to the mission. His style and charisma could melt even the most stubborn soul.

As *Zara* settled onto the landing pad and completed docking procedures with Marsbase, Tim stepped through the airlock and out the passenger hatch into the pressurized embarkation tube. He was soon inside the immense dome encompassing the colony, followed by Peggy and his crew.

Before he could take in the impressive sight, a sharply dressed man in an immaculate suit approached with purposeful strides.

"Mr. Smith, Anon Tusck sends his compliments and requests that you attend the Marsbase Business Council meeting. Posthaste," the man said.

"I was ordered to meet with Mr. Tusck. We might as well get this over with. Lead on," Tim said, shaking his head.

As he followed Tusck's representative, Tim noticed the dome's skylight simulation system, which adjusted its tint and luminosity to mimic Earth-like conditions. He smiled because it was a design he had personally approved to boost morale and help regulate human circadian rhythms.

The tall hemispherical structure shimmered under the filtered sunlight. It was a fantastic accomplishment that would have taken Earth 100 or 200 years to build, if ever, without Terra Novan technology.

"You see, Mr. Tusck has made many modifications to your original design. We will be happy to take you on a tour if you have time," the assistant said.

"I am impressed with what I've seen so far. We are on an emergency mission, you understand," Tim said.

"Of course. We are almost there," the assistant said. "Mr. Tusck has important facts about our progress here."

Ah, here it comes, Tim thought. He knew Tusck and other wealthy industrialists objected to his plan to terraform the Moon. To them, the *Horizon* and the three space shuttles were assets to be leveraged for profit, not exploration or survival.

The assistant guided Tim and his lieutenants into the Mars Business Council boardroom, where Anon Tusk and the council were waiting. The room had a faint smell of recycled air.

As Tim entered, he noticed Tusk's eyes had the sharp gleam of someone used to getting his way, and the stiff posture of the council members signaled to Tim that this would not be a friendly conversation.

"Thank you for coming to our meeting. After learning you would be here, I hastily convened this group to discuss several issues with you," Tusck said.

"Learned? You lobbied for me to be here. Anon, I don't have much time. You realize we have a serious threat developing with a second wormhole open past Saturn, don't you? You have one hour," said Tim, looking at his wristphone.

"We just voted on a resolution to refocus our rebuilding efforts," said Tusck. "We want 40 percent of our time spent on Earth's environmental rejuvenation, 40 percent on finishing Marsbase, and 20 percent on reverse engineering the Terra Novan technology."

Tim stared at Tusck. "I know what you want. You all know my position. I support a multipronged approach to strengthening Earth, establishing human and Terra Novan colonies and military bases on the Moon and Mars, using Terra Novan terraforming technology."

"This is not good enough. I will forward my recommendation to President Eisenhower. He knows how much my financial support means to Marsbase," said Tusck, who had been appointed to the committee by former President Carlin as a campaign favor. He had since replaced or bribed the MBC to give him a 3-2 majority.

"You can pass all the resolutions you want, but it's already been decided, and you lost, Mr. Tusck," Tim said.

Tusck said, "I was told by a reputable source that we

have six months of work on Marsbase to develop it as a fully functioning city for 10,000 people, but it would take much less if we stopped work on Moonbase, which we don't need and is a waste of money."

"We have six more months, yes, at the present rate of construction for the city's first phase. Terraforming will take much longer, as you well know," said Tim. "The rest you said is incorrect. Dr. Bouchard, would you please give us a report?"

"Mr. Tusck, we've made much progress on Earth, the Moonbase, and the more extensive Mars Terraforming Project," Leonard said. "We've sufficient resources to reverse-engineer the selected Terra Novan medical, environmental, and military technologies within a year. I won't report on our longer-range plan, which is even more ambitious."

Tim interrupted. "Before Leonard finishes his report to this council, I'd like to remind everyone why we must simultaneously create the Moon and Mars bases," Tim said.

"We all know the Terra Novan conspiracy theory about the Ruirulans coming to conquer Earth," Tusck said. "The people I represent here and on Earth don't believe it."

"I am telling you there is a real risk. It might not be the Ruirulans, but it could be another species. There are many civilizations in the Milky Way," Tim said. "I've seen the potential danger of wormhole travel technology in my visions. We have time to complete the military installations before such potential threats present themselves."

At the mention of future danger from space, the atmosphere in the room changed. The Mars Business Council members exchanged alarmed glances. They had never heard anyone describe the wormhole predicament in such dire terms. Suddenly, the possibility of an extraterrestrial threat loomed over their ambitious plans.

Tusck noticed the unease in the room and began disparaging Tim's remarks, hoping to regain what he believed was the upper hand.

"Potential? Ha! Just because you were right about the corrupt mothership AI doesn't mean you're right about this," Tusck said.

"Wait one minute, Mr. Tusck," said George. "Tim has been right about everything. You forget that he discovered Terra Nova, predicted the original wormhole, the mothership's entry into our solar system, the corrupted AI that nearly exterminated the human race, and formed alliances with *Zara* and *Koren* to defeat the mothership."

"And he did so to your benefit and the benefit of your investor friends, Mr. Tusck," said Peggy, equally outraged by what seemed to her an attack on Tim based on simple greed. "We all know your companies stand to make billions of dollars with sweetheart deals on Mars, less so on the Moon. Let Tim speak for five minutes. He will answer all your questions."

"Tim, you have the floor," George said.

"Thank you. Remember when President Kael addressed the United Nations? He warned us about hostile lifeforms in the galaxy that could, one day, threaten Earth. Kael is here. He should explain. Kael?"

Kael stood up, towering over the seated humans. "Representatives of Mars, the technology we used to create a wormhole and travel to your Solar System is not unique to us. Wormhole technology is known to several star systems in the Milky Way galaxy, and it is spreading for various reasons I won't explain at the moment. Suffice it to say, it is real...and it is a threat," Kael said, expressing the weight of the potential danger in somber terms.

"Now, some of the technology's other owners are aggressive and could pose a grave danger from space. You dismiss the Ruirulans. We have fought the Ruirulans as they sought to expand their empire. For centuries, we kept them at bay. They only stopped attacking our starships and outposts when they discovered our sun was dying faster than anyone had predicted," Kael concluded, sitting down. "I have no doubt they would love to rule Earth."

"Thank you, President Kael. As all of you know, this is why the U.N. asked *Horizon* to build a colony, observation, and military base on the Moon," Tim said, his words underlining the crucial role of the Moonbase in Earth's defense strategy. "Marsbase is the first line of defense, Moonbase the second, then Earth. We hope to one day establish a military outpost and, later, a mining operation on Ceres."

"For the record," Tusck said, "President Kael speaks for Terra Novans. He does not speak for the United States, the U.N., or this Business Council of Mars."

Pausing, Tusck thundered, "I accuse the Novans of a secret plan to terraform Mars as their home planet so they can live here and establish their hegemony."

"This is not true," said President Kael. "We have read this outrageous lie on your internet. I did not expect any responsible committee member to utter such nonsense. We are an equal partner in the future of Earth and the Solar System."

"You lie, just as you lied about *Arcaayus* being corrupted. We all know you planned to destroy Earth. It was only Tim who stopped you, for which we all honor him," Tusck said.

"Mr. Tusck," said Tim, "please refrain from further attacks on Kael. There is no basis for such accusations."

"You don't think he is capable? I was even told the new name he has selected for Mars: VaRax," Tusck said.

"VaRax? What are you talking about? I've heard enough, Mr. Tusck," Tim said, becoming angry.

Tusck started to respond. Before he could, however, Tim cut him off.

"You are out of order, Mr. Tusck. Don't try me," he said, uncharacteristically short on patience. "You have made your position known."

He turned to the others gathered in that room. "Now, gentlepeople of the Mars Business Council, George Clarke, my chief engineer, will give you a brief update about the Moonbase. I think you will be surprised by the developments."

"Thank you, Tim," George said. "Over the past five years, *Zara, Koren*, and—more recently—*Endeavor*, our new Earth-built Novan space shuttle, have ferried supplies and assembled prefabricated structures built on Earth to Moonbase. They have used their Novan mechs as manufacturing and construction crews.

"We now have an enclosed Moonbase with interconnected domes and tunnels that support over 2,000 people. We have installed advanced power generation systems using solar arrays and energy storage facilities, ensuring the base has a reliable power source.

"The bottom line is that Moonbase is nearly complete. *Koren* will transport heavy plasma and particle beam cannons to Moonbase this week. We will do much of the same on Mars, except on a much larger scale.

"Soon, Moonbase will be completed as a functional and self-sustaining military and science outpost that can provide long-range, secondary defense of the Earth," George concluded.

"This is my point," Tusck said. "You should complete Moonbase now, with *Horizon*, just in case the Ruirulans appear."

"Oh, now you support the conspiracy theory about the Ruirulans," Peggy said in a voice laced with disgust.

Tusck stood up angrily.

"Sit down, Anon. We have heard enough from you. Thank you, Peggy," said Tim as he stared down Tusck.

He stood up to address the committee. "Mr. Tusck, honorable members, let me explain further. *Horizon's* original mission on Earth and the Moon is nearly over. *Zoren* is supremely capable of transporting military equipment to Marsbase after he finishes with Moonbase. He can make deliveries four times faster than *Horizon* because he doesn't need to worry about extreme g-forces as he has no humans or Terra Novans on board.

"As I said, we have enough time to complete both bases before any direct threats materialize. Please, have patience. Now, let me show you some amazing things."

Tim walked to the wall viewscreen. He tapped his wristphone, entered a few codes, and a video showing highlights of Earth's pollution control efforts appeared.

"On Earth," he continued, "we have installed all necessary anti-pollution equipment and devices, including scrubbers, electrostatic precipitators, thermal oxidizers, carbon capture devices, and advanced Terra Novan technologies.

"Cleansing is well underway; however, reversing the environmental damage of two centuries of neglect will require time and sustained dedication.

"To add to George's excellent summary, *Horizon* has transported nearly all of Marsbase's basic needs. You may not fully appreciate what we have done," he continued. "It is up to you to organize and install what you have. Would you like me to continue, or have you heard enough?"

Several Mars Business Council members looked at each other. Tusck stood up. "We've heard enough. You don't know our plans. We need more mechs, more supplies, and more equipment. Your timetable does not meet economic realities. This is a waste of time," he said.

"No. I want to hear what Admiral Smith has to say. We haven't heard this before," Eric Smith, an independent council member, said.

"Thank you," Tim replied. "I'd be more than happy to elaborate. Your inventory is extensive. Do you know it includes heavy machinery and tools, prefabricated and pressurized shelters, oxygen generation equipment, water purification systems, food production technology, radiation shielding, solar power generation systems, and advanced life support systems for recycling waste and medical supplies? You even have specialized equipment to convert Martian regolith into a raw material for building and other practical uses."

Smith raised his hand. "We have never been briefed about this," he said, looking over at Tusck in frustration. "Please, go on, Admiral."

"Thank you. "Mr. Tusck complained about not having enough mechs. I have been told you have sufficient numbers to perform the outside labor and a steady stream of settlers to work the bases. Another 100 just arrived," Tim said.

"But if you don't have enough robots, you should inform the U.N., President Eisenhower, and the U.S. Space Agency. There is a high demand for the mechs. We have three mechanical manufacturing plants, with more coming online in other countries.

"I am told that within three months, you will be able to open resort hotels for paying customers and begin to recoup your investments," Tim concluded.

Tusck whimpered, "We could have that in three weeks if you weren't taking *Horizon* and two space shuttles on a wild goose chase."

He stood up, pounded his desk and added: "Send *Zara* and *Koren* to investigate the wormhole with you, but leave *Horizon* and *Endeavor* for us. We can complete Moonbase and Marsbase while you are on vacation."

Peggy had heard enough. She stepped forward, her voice sharp and unwavering.

"Vacation? Is that what you think this is?" she said, eyes locked on him. "You don't get it. We're staring down the possibility of a breach into our Solar System—a wormhole that could serve as an open door to threats we can't yet predict. Even if there's no immediate danger, that gateway could invite hostile forces into what little peace we've managed to reclaim."

She took a breath, then added, her tone colder: "You speak of progress and protecting Earth from Terra Novan conspiracies, but right now, it sounds like you're more worried about your business interests and profits than the security of humanity."

"Thank you, Peggy. I also have heard enough from Mr. Tusck. Let me conclude my remarks," said Tim, standing up and walking toward the front of the room.

"Settling Mars has been a dream and goal for centuries. *Horizon* and the Terra Novans can make this dream a reality, but we must do it safely. That means protecting Earth from possible threats. I consider this new wormhole a possible threat, and we must be prepared for the worst."

George stood up and started to clap. Peggy and Leonard joined him. Everyone except Anon Tusck stood up and clapped in unison, even the two members who had sided with him.

Surprisingly, as Tusck saw the room turn in favor of Tim, he stood up, smiled, and joined in the applause.

"Thank you, friends," Tim said. "Now, let's hear Leonard finish his report on completing Marsbase. This should clear up any misconceptions anyone may have. Captain Bouchard, you have the floor."

Leonard stood up. "As you know, we are constructing large, heavily shielded habitats since Mars lacks a magnetosphere that protects against harmful radiation.

"The shells of these habitats, which will be ten times larger than Moonbase habitats, or roughly the size of a 10-mile city, should be completed within three months. Much of the equipment and tech support is already here," Leonard said.

"Just as we have done on Earth, the second phase of the plan for Marsbase calls for *Koren* to launch Terra Novan terraforming modules to begin the long-term project.

"Once the modules are airborne, they will deploy nanobots and atmospheric processors to convert Mars's atmosphere into a sustainable environment. I say 'sustainable' because we won't be able to live on the surface for many years, but being outside won't immediately kill us as it would now."

MBC member Smith asked about the status of adding mass from the asteroid belt to Mars. "I was told *Horizon's* departure will slow this effort."

"No, unfortunately, you have been misled. Terraforming Mars will be completed step by step, and we are on schedule," Leonard continued. "Let me explain. First, the nanobots will use the water-bearing asteroids that *Horizon, Zara, Koren,* and *Endeavor* have already collected and towed from the asteroid belt as material to increase Mars's atmospheric pressure and make it tolerable for humans and Terra Novans.

"This is just the first of three such deliveries; the other two are scheduled for next year based on the available science, engineering, and technology."

Another MBC committee member, Beatrice Muldoon, raised her hand. "I read a blog that said the Space Agency will build another *Horizon*. Is this true?"

"Let me address this question," Tim said. "It hasn't been formally announced, but yes, a joint U.S.-European Space Agency project will begin next year to build a *Horizon*-class spacecraft. It will have Warp 1 speed and be used for interstellar wormhole travel and transporting populations to Ceres, a long-range goal of humanity."

Tim paused and looked at the members of the Mars Business Council. They sat with rapt attention. He realized they had not been adequately informed of NASA's plans for Moonbase, Marsbase, and beyond.

"You must understand," Tim said, "our smaller shuttles—*Zara* and *Koren*—can travel a lot faster from Mars to the Kuiper Belt because they're fully automated. They don't need to carry humans or Novans, so there's no need to worry about life support or g-force limits," Tim said. "The onboard robots handle all the work, both inside the ship and out in space. That makes them ideal for hauling small asteroids and materials for terraforming and other projects."

He turned to Leonard. "Go ahead."

"Thank you, Tim. This is an exciting development. My second point is that the nanobots we have on Marsbase right now will use Martian regolith—the powdery topsoil—and deeper soil that contains more carbon to supplement the asteroid material," Leonard said. "They will extract vital minerals and rearrange atomic structures to create the building blocks for protective habitats you need for survival.

"Eventually, in possibly five years, the combination of the additional mass, minerals and water from the Kuiper asteroids, plus the Terra Novan screening shields, will help create a stable microenvironment, blocking harmful solar radiation and retaining the necessary atmospheric conditions for life beyond your domes," Leonard concluded.

"Thank you, Captain Bouchard," Tim said, nodding to the Mars Business Council.

"I now call for a vote for you to approve the final phases of Mars's terraforming project. With your support, I'll forward our recommendations and your approval to Congress for final action."

Tusck appeared flustered with Tim's end-run around the council's parliamentary procedure. In a 4-1 vote, the Mars Business Council passed the measure, with only Tusck raising his hand in opposition.

"Thank you, council members. Oh, one more thing," Tim added with a wry smile. "Congress will also be voting on the official name for the largest city on Mars."

"And what is that?" Tusck asked, raising an eyebrow. "We already call it Aurelia Mons."

"No, we're not officially naming it Aurelia Mons," Tim said with a slight smile. "I'm guessing Golden Mountain is your marketing spin for the city?" He paused, then added, "But in honor of Ray Bradbury—the visionary who once imagined life on Mars in *The Martian Chronicles*—President Eisenhower wants the capital to be called Green City."

Tusck, having lost all debate points, leaned back in his chair and exhaled slowly. "I have no objections to that," he muttered.

As the meeting adjourned, the group dispersed, their footsteps echoing through the steel-and-glass corridors and central dome of Marsbase.

Tim lingered for a moment, gazing out at the ruddy horizon, where the sun was beginning to dip beneath the edge of the crater wall. He thought momentarily about the progress on Marsbase and hoped whatever was out past Saturn and beyond wouldn't interfere with humanity's dream of colonizing the Solar System.

Standing by Peggy and his landing party, he glanced at the itinerary glowing on his wristphone. Before returning to *Horizon*, he had one more important stop to make.

Chapter 10

DR. BEN "BO" TABER

1:30 p.m., Wednesday, April 21, 2083

Tim had always trusted Bo Taber—not just with secrets, but with lives. Bo had been one of his closest friends since high school. He possessed a rare combination of brilliance, humor, and compassion, making people instinctively follow his lead. Standing on the red planet, far from Sarasota and familiar surroundings, Tim hoped the years hadn't changed that.

Bo was more than a physician. A board-certified family doctor and psychiatrist, he had a calming presence that could disarm the most panicked patient or hardened skeptic.

In med school, he'd gained a reputation for diagnosing the unexplainable and successfully treating what others had given up on. His uncanny ability to see beyond symptoms and into

75

people made him a vital force, one Tim desperately wanted at his side on the mission to the wormhole beyond Saturn.

Tim knew that Bo's inclusion wasn't just practical but essential. The journey would test every mental and emotional boundary the crew had, and Bo's insight, experience, and innate charisma could keep the team grounded. He had a gift. He could set at ease even the most stubborn soul through sharp observation, a wry joke, or a moment of deep, focused listening that made you feel completely understood.

Bo had volunteered for Marsbase during humanity's darkest hour. As the AI War decimated cities around the world, Bo barely escaped the destruction of Atlanta with his life. He had been working at Grady Memorial Hospital when the mothership hit the city center. The hospital collapsed within minutes. Before a ceiling collapsed on him, Bo helped lead survivors through fire and debris, stabilizing the wounded and comforting the dying.

When the war ended, Bo gradually recovered from his injuries but didn't stay on Earth. "Too many ghosts," he told a friend. Mars offered something Earth could not: distance from trauma and a chance to help rebuild humanity from the ground up.

At Marsbase, he became a key figure in the colony's mental health and wellness initiatives. His patients revered him, and his colleagues leaned on him as a doctor and a quiet moral compass.

Now, as Tim prepared to ask his old friend to join the most dangerous mission of his life, he could only hope Bo still believed in him—and in the kind of future they'd once dreamed of exploring together.

Tim found Bo in the medical wing of Marsbase, updating charts under the filtered light from the edge of the dome.

After a brief catch-up, Tim got to the point.

"There's something beyond Saturn," he said. "A wormhole, possibly stable, possibly dangerous."

Bo's eyes narrowed. "And you want me to join a mission to explore it?"

"I do," Tim nodded. "But not just because you're the best doctor I know. It's going to get dangerous. We'll need someone who can keep people grounded out there."

Bo slowly leaned back, folding his arms. "You know I've worked hard to find peace here. After Atlanta, after everything... I have patients who trust me."

"I know," Tim said gently. "You can return when we are done, but the stakes are too high—at least for me—to turn away. We don't know what's waiting beyond that wormhole. And if this turns out to be the start of something big, we'll need your mind, your heart. You've always been able to see what others miss."

Bo looked away for a long time. The silence stretched between them like a void of space.

Finally, he spoke. "Growing up, you always did have a way of dragging me into impossible things."

Tim grinned. "You did the same for me. You were always the leader. I learned so much from you."

A long sigh escaped Bo's lips, but the faint smile that followed told Tim everything he needed to know.

"I'll go," Bo said. "But not to save the world. For the people. If this mission saves even one city from becoming the next Atlanta, it's worth it."

And with that, Dr. Bo Taber—reluctant hero and healer of broken minds—joined the crew bound for Saturn and possibly beyond.

Chapter 11

BO BOARDS *HORIZON*

4 p.m., Wednesday, April 21, 2083

Bo Taber stepped off the Marsbase embarkation platform and into *Horizon*'s airlock, greeted by a whoosh of pressurized air and the soft hum of the ship's life support systems.

Carrying a single suitcase and his doctor's bag, Bo came aboard with the cautious gait of a man aware he might never return. He paused at the hatchway, running his fingers along the smooth surface of the alloy wall. It felt sterile and clinical, strangely familiar yet alien to the medical wing on Marsbase where he had built his second life.

But when he turned the corner and heard familiar laughter from the crew lounge, something eased in his chest.

The familiar faces were waiting just beyond the hatch—

Patrick, Nick, and Tom, three of Bo's best friends. His easy smile lit up the room as he saw them.

"Bo Taber, is that you or just a mirage?" Patrick Duffy called out, grinning as he strode forward.

Bo smiled and reached out his arm to firmly shake Patrick's hand. "You wish I were a mirage. You still owe me fifty credits from our last poker game, Duffer."

They embraced like brothers. Then came Tom Terry and Nick Dragoon, two more pieces of a life Bo had thought forever grounded. All three had served in various roles after the AI War, and Bo had quietly kept tabs on them through encrypted comms over the years.

"Feels like the band's getting back together," Tom said, hugging Bo and thumping his back.

"And I'm still the only one with any fashion sense," Bo quipped, tugging at the stylish collar of his midnight-blue field jacket.

Tim, busy with prelaunch duties, sensed Bo's entrance and rushed to the main hatch.

"Bo, you made it! We're just going through our launch status check for the wormhole," Tim declared. "Do you have everything you need? There's no turning back once we get started."

Bo smiled, but a booming laugh echoed down the corridor before he could reply. "Well, I'll be damned—Bo Taber, still looking like he owns the room."

John Nikolas—Big Nik—strode forward in denim overalls, arms open wide. The two men embraced like brothers long separated by war and time.

"You haven't changed a bit," Big Nik said, pulling back. "Still got that smug doctor look, like you know everyone's secrets before they do."

"Me? What's this look? Did you swap your accountant's wardrobe for... whatever this is?" Bo asked, eyeing the crisp utility jumpsuit and gleaming boots. "You smell like machine oil and trouble."

Big Nik spread his arms, grinning. "Like it? I've traded spreadsheets for star charts. I'm your new Chief Logistics and Supply Chain Officer." He gave an exaggerated bow. "My kingdom is every crate, pallet, and airlock on this ship. I keep the *Horizon* running and the crew breathing. Someone has to make sure we don't run out of socks, rations, or oxygen halfway to the stars."

They shared another laugh before Bo turned to the others. "Tim made a hell of a pitch. I was reluctant, but after talking with him and hearing you all are here and what's at stake, I knew I had to come, even if it's just to keep you guys out of trouble."

Laughter rippled through the room as Peggy entered from the central corridor. Her presence was magnetic.

"Bo." She gave him a firm but heartfelt hug. "Tim told me everything. I'm so glad you're here. We need you."

"Well, of course you do. And I missed you all too, more so now that I see you," said Bo with a big smile.

Peggy turned serious. "We're glad you decided to come with us. We'll need your insight, especially regarding crew morale and...the kids."

Bo's brow lifted, intrigued. "Kids?"

Tom nodded toward the corridor. "You'll see soon enough. Wait until you meet Ethan, Lila, and the Terra Novans."

"They will be a handful and a mystery, even for a Solar System-renowned doctor like yourself," Peggy said.

Bo blinked, already sensing this journey would be unlike any mission he'd ever imagined. He looked at Peggy more closely and read the worry etched into the lines near her eyes—worry about the wormhole, the twins, and what lay ahead.

"I'll do my best," Bo said gently. "And congratulations. You and Tim...I apologize for not attending your wedding. I'm also looking forward to meeting these Smith twins. I've heard a thing or two about them."

"Thank you, and you will see them soon enough," she said, her voice softening. "There's more, but we can talk about it later."

"Speaking of talking later, I need to get back to the bridge," Tim said, checking his wristphone. "We are going through the prelaunch check, and I'm needed. Peggy, please show Bo to his quarters after he catches up with everyone."

Bo smiled. "Thanks, Tim. You've made me a happy man. I'm back with all my best friends."

Tim smiled and nodded. "We'll talk soon."

Just then, George entered, hands behind his back and a mischievous grin on his face. "Dr. Bo Taber, welcome aboard *Horizon*. I've just updated Medbay's music playlist for your rock and roll obsession."

"You're the only engineer I'd trust with my life *and* my eclectic taste in music," Bo replied with a chuckle.

George raised a brow. "Just wait till you meet our guests from Terra Nova. That playlist might have to include spacy time signatures and harmonies."

Bo's smile turned into curiosity as the tall corridor doors opened, and President Kael and Liora entered.

Kael was dignified and calm, his translucent robes catching the subtle blue lights of the ship's artificial day cycle. His silver-purple eyes locked onto Bo's, not aggressively, but with deep interest, as if he could see past surface impressions.

Bo bowed slightly, uncertain of Terra Novan customs. "I'm Dr. Bo Taber. It's an honor, sir. I support what you've done to find your people homes on Earth."

Kael inclined his head. "Your reputation precedes you. I've read Earth records. You saved lives in Atlanta. And on Mars."

"Only tried to do what was needed," Bo replied modestly.

Liora stepped forward next. She had the gentle bearing of a healer, but her presence was anything but passive. "Your empathy resonates. I sense a depth in you, Dr. Taber. Our children will benefit from your presence on this journey."

Bo blinked. "I'm not sure what that means, but I'll take it as a compliment."

Liora smiled warmly. "It is."

As the introductions concluded, Bo looked around the room—Peggy, George, Patrick, Nick, Tom, Big Nik, Kael, and Liora—all faces familiar and new, stitched together by a shared purpose. And somewhere down the long corridor, Tim was in the command center, trusting Bo with his crew and his family.

Bo exhaled. He wasn't just here to patch wounds or run psych evaluations. He was here because the human heart, wherever it beat, Earth or otherwise, was still the most critical frontier.

"Alright, then," he said, stepping toward the forward deck. "Let's see what this wormhole has in store for us."

Chapter 12

ONWARD TO SATURN

5 p.m., Wednesday, April 21, 2083

The *Horizon* circled Mars, preparing to break out of orbit after completing its mission. On the bridge, Admiral Tim Smith studied the projected trajectory on the main screen.

"Crew, sound off for mission go. Mr. Navigator, what's our course?"

"Course plotted with the slingshot around Jupiter and straight past Saturn to the wormhole. Hundred percent go," said Navigator Bouchard.

The path to Saturn was straightforward, but what lay beyond the wormhole—the mysterious gateway in space that might lead to a distant part of the Milky Way or another galaxy— remained a mystery to Tim and *Horizon*'s most advanced deep-space sensors and simulations.

Pilot Mark Andrews slid into the flight chair and ran his fingers across the controls, his usual levity absent.

"I've locked in 1% light speed. Awaiting your order to launch," he said.

Tim nodded slowly, arms behind his back. "*Horizon* was built for this. George, what do you say?"

"Kael and I went through the checklist. The engines, the reactors, our external shields, and all mechanical systems are one hundred percent go," said Chief Engineer George Clarke.

"Peggy?" asked Tim.

"Go, life support and crew in place," said Science Officer Dr. Peggy Smith as she checked her internal instrument readings.

"Amy? How is our computer feeling today?" asked Tim.

"AI computer processing, go as can be," she said, crossing her fingers.

Tim understood Chief IT Officer Amy Smith's response. She had told him the Terra Novan AI computer still had a few bugs, even after hours of discussions with Nira, the Novan technology expert.

Amy had performed numerous root analysis subroutines and consistently found glitches or algorithmic bias, which she referred to as "AI hallucinations" to describe performance issues.

Leonard shifted in his seat. "Honestly, I'm glad you scaled back the old *Arcaayus* AI. We can't trust that thing, especially on this mission."

"Agreed," Tim said. "*Horizon's* modified AI is enough, with our oversight. If there's danger ahead, we'll face it with human eyes open."

Suddenly, a heavy silence gripped the bridge, the hum of

consoles filling the gap. No one spoke. Shoulders tightened. They all knew. The next leg of their journey would take them to the precipice of the wormhole, a rift in space forged by an unknown force.

Was it the work of an enemy bent on humanity's destruction, an invader seeking to colonize the Earth, or the result of a natural event?

What unsettled Tim and Stephen most was that they couldn't see what lay ahead—couldn't even catch the faintest thread of it. And if Tim's psychic abilities failed here, then they would be flying blind into whatever waited beyond.

Tim's calm voice finally broke the tension. "We'll run a full scan once we reach the wormhole and finish our analysis. Are we go for launch?"

Mark looked up, his fingers on the propulsion controls. "I'm ready when you are, Admiral."

"Everyone is go, including Amy, on behalf of our temperamental AI computer. Major, engage hyperdrive. Take us to Saturn," Tim said.

"Engaged. We're moving," Major Andrews replied.

Everyone felt a slight 1 g pressure from the initial thrust as the red planet shrank in the viewscreen. Once *Horizon* accelerated, the ship's artificial gravity system automatically turned off.

Tim stared ahead toward the stars. "We've left the easy part behind."

In the lower deck mess hall, twenty crew members sat around the long table, steaming mugs in their hands. Silence hung for several long seconds, as if no one wanted to be the first to speak. They had left Mars several hours earlier, and the euphoria from the first few days was wearing off.

Then, Patrick, ever the strategist, broke the silence. He leaned forward, elbows on the table. "Six days to Saturn. After that? What do we have? The unknown. There's no way to simulate what we'll face if we go inside that wormhole."

John looked up as he shifted in his seat. "Tim hasn't decided yet, as far as I know. If we go, we must trust that Tim, Peggy, and our Terra Novan advisors will figure it out when the time comes to decide what to do."

Nick nodded, arms crossed, looking at his laptop on the table. "I expect we'll go. I can tell you this: the ship's solid. I've gone over every mechanical system with Nira and the mechs. My biggest concern is the external shielding and the pod protection. Peggy says it will hold, but no human has ever successfully gone through a wormhole, and this vessel's previous trip didn't turn out so well."

Big Nik looked up the mission schematic on his laptop display. "I've been studying the precautions, and I'm also worried about the shielding in the wormhole. Classical physics concludes that nothing can survive inside a wormhole, but we believe these are machine-generated wormholes and, therefore, must be different. We have data from when the Terra Novans went through the first wormhole. They survived, but they encountered that strange dark matter upon exiting, which we can't account for."

"Doesn't that give us some clue about what we will experience if we go through the wormhole? If we go through it, Tim must believe we will survive with increased shielding," Con said.

"Survive?" Sophie asked. "I want to do more than that. I knew this mission would be dangerous, but I didn't think we'd try to go through it. Let's change the subject."

"It's scary, but I've looked over the gravitational field models Peggy and Kael ran based on what we know. It looks good on paper," Big Nik said. "But without updated telemetry from the wormhole's mouth, we won't know if this one will be the same as the first until we get there and measure it."

Tom grunted in agreement. "As John said, we trust Tim, Peggy, Kael, and the *Horizon's* AI. And we trust each other. Besides," he said, pausing. "What choice do we have?"

"Doesn't anybody have any good news?" Sophie asked in frustration.

"I do have some good news," said Tom. "The hydroponic garden is working just fine."

Mary laughed. "Yeah, I'm the one out there doing most of the weeding. Nick installed new high-powered growth lights, and the higher intensities of red and blue wavelengths are doubling our production."

Sophie exhaled. "That is good news. It means more tomatoes, corn, and lettuce. I love it. Thanks, Nick."

"I was happy to contribute. Just make sure we have a record squash crop. I've said it before, Tom, your hydroponic garden in the bioshelter and here on *Horizon* produces better-tasting vegetables than on Earth," Nick said with a smile.

Upon hearing of the garden's production, Chef Nancy chirped, "Tom and Mary have worked wonders. I am happy to spend most of my time in the kitchen or the garden helping them select the harvest."

"And those positive results speak for themselves. We eat like kings and queens," Nick quipped.

Jim leaned back, his gaze steady. "You joke. At least you all have something interesting to do. My job as *Horizon's* sheriff is boring. Everyone gets along, even with the Terra Novans."

"C'mon, Jim. You're keeping the peace by force of will," joked Con.

"I agree," said John. "Didn't you volunteer to help with the wormhole pods and the shielding issue? I understand Kael is worried about them. What do you think?"

"I'd rather not think about that until we run a final check, but going into those chambers isn't something I look forward to," Jim said, lowering his voice. "We will put our lives on the line when we go into stasis during that jump. If our external shielding breaks down even for a second during wormholing, dark matter radiation exposure could end us all, humans and Novans."

Jim exhaled and shrugged his shoulders. "This dark matter physics mystery is beyond me, although I did suggest a secondary power redundancy on the pods."

Nancy sighed. "I don't understand all the science of what we are doing, but I did hear Dr. Ledbetter say if any shielding layer weakens, the AI computer will catch it and adjust to protect us."

"That's another thing," added Jim. "Amy calls AI computer malfunctions 'hallucinations,' but we all know if *Horizon's* computer 'sees something' when we are in stasis, our chance of survival drops quite a bit."

Everyone nodded. They all knew how unpredictable the ship's AI had become.

"Amy, Nira, and the IT team are doing their best to make the AI computer work consistently," Jeff explained. "The Terra Novans designed *Arcaayus* to perform all the ship's functions, but because of what happened with the dark matter surge, Tim decided to rely on the crew and a subroutine of the original AI supporting us. It's been a work in progress."

Stephen stood up, walked to the coffee machine, and slammed his fist down.

"What is it, dear?" Julie asked. "Did you see something?"

"No, that's the problem," Stephen said. "You all talk about the wormhole and the dark matter surge issue, but everything I see past the wormhole is blank. Tim has had convoluted visions about dark matter, a frozen planet, and a dark planet. At least that is something, but I see nothing."

He lowered his head toward the tabletop and said loudly, "We aren't getting any clear visions about the wormhole, the pods, or anything. Even worse, Kael is blocking our telepathy for some unknown reason."

Surprised by his outburst, which she hadn't seen in months, Julie's wide eyes and open mouth reflected deep concern. "Stephen, calm down," she soothingly asked. He turned to her with a pained look.

Bo scanned the table, then leaned in with a slightly measured yet warm smile.

"Stephen's all right. He's frustrated. Everyone's on edge. It's to be expected," Bo said calmly. "Let's be honest—what we're walking into isn't just science or engineering."

Bo stood up and walked over to the coffee machine, where Stephen had bowed his head and rested his palms on the table. Julie stood next to him, whispering in his ear. He patted him on the back, then turned to his friends, whose faces were marked with worry.

"We could cross into territory no human has ever seen. No manual, no backup plan if things go sideways. But I've known each of you for many years, and I trust each of you. I've never seen a team more ready. The *Horizon* will hold. *We* will hold. And if the unknown decides to throw something ugly our way, well, we'll stare it down together."

There was a long pause after Bo spoke, a quiet stillness that settled over the group like gravity.

Then, Patrick nodded quickly. "Bo's right. We stick together, trust each other, and we'll make it," he said. "We shouldn't worry about going through the wormhole before it's decided. Let's get some things done before we bed down. Nick, you and Jim check the life support systems in engineering. We are headed for deep space for the first time tonight, and I don't want to rely on the automated systems and the robots to make sure we're safe."

Nick and Jim nodded and stood up to leave.

"Sounds good," Nick said. "I'll log into the robot maintenance summaries. They are programmed to alert us, but it doesn't hurt to double-check everything. They miss me anyway."

"I'll go with you. I must see this," Nancy said with a chuckle.

Bo stood up. "It's been a long day. I'm going to look in on the children before I go to my quarters to rest. I recommend that everyone get some sleep. We have six days before we go face-to-face with that wormhole."

As the group slowly dispersed, the weight of the mission followed each of them like pressure before a storm.

At the *Horizon* Space School, Carlyn Duffy, Corli Nikolas, and Liora began to settle the children for the night. Their soothing abilities stabilized the youngsters as their minds sensed the tension building on the ship and in the stars.

While their parents carried the weight of the mission, guiding *Horizon* toward the unknown, Carlyn and Corli led the children through calming exercises. At the same time, Liora gently answered their questions—some innocent, others eerily perceptive.

Ethan and Lila remained silent. Their thoughts were on the bridge where their mother and father were in command. They sensed a smooth trip but foresaw a new experience coming soon for everyone.

Dr. Bo Taber popped his head inside the day school door.

"Is it too late for a visit?" Bo asked. "I'd like to tell the children a bedtime story."

Carlyn smiled. "Of course, Dr. Taber. Come in."

Soft lights glowed like starlight overhead in the cozy quiet of the *Horizon's* children's sleep chamber. The ship hummed gently as it headed for deep space.

Bo sat on a bench beside the children's bunks. Ethan, Lila, and several Terra Novan and Earthling children snuggled under soft blankets.

"Good evening, little ones. My name is Dr. Bo," he began, his voice warm and calm.

Ethan turned, smiling. "Hi, Dr. Bo. You're Tim's best friend."

"And you're the reason he's getting even less sleep these days," Bo replied with a grin, crouching down to eye level. "I've heard a lot about you and your sister."

We know a lot about you, the twins shot back. He caught their thoughts and smiled.

"Before you go to sleep, I'd like to tell you a story about a little star who found himself very far from home."

Ethan, Lila, and the rest of the children gathered around

Bo in a semicircle.

"Once, long ago, there was a tiny white star named Sami. He was smaller and younger than the others, but very bright and very brave. No one wanted to play with him because he was shy and plain. The other stars were larger and more colorful—blue, yellow, orange, and red. They lived closer to each other in the neighborhood, while Sami quietly drifted farther away, unsure of where he belonged."

The children listened closely. Even the youngest Terra Novan child, Varra, blinked slowly, enchanted.

"One day," Bo continued, "a huge cloud of dark energy swept through the neighborhood, scattering stars in all directions. Sami was thrown far away into space, spinning and tumbling, until he found himself all alone, so lost he didn't know how to get home. He was scared. All the stars he knew were gone."

Lila whispered, "What did Sami do?"

Bo smiled. "He asked a passing comet for directions to that part of the Milky Way near Orion's Spur where he once lived. The friendly comet pointed the way, and Sami said a prayer before becoming even brighter and faster. Slowly, steadily, he passed planets, moons, star clusters, and nebulae.

"After a long wait—six days by his count—he saw a gentle swirl of light ahead. It was a wormhole, an open tear in space. He didn't know where it would lead, but he felt something good was waiting there. So, he zipped in, brave and glowing."

The room was still.

"When he came out the other side, he found himself not lost...but home. A cluster of friendly, happy stars like him, all shining, all different. And they welcomed him. Sami was never alone again. And from that day on, whenever anyone felt scared or far from home, they would look to the edge of the sky...where Sami shone the brightest."

Bo leaned back. "Like it?"

The children were quiet and thoughtful.

"Is that like us?" Ethan finally asked.

Bo chuckled softly. "Exactly like you. You're brave stars, too. Out here in the dark, but glowing. And soon, we'll find where we all belong."

He stood slowly. "Good night, my little stars. Dream bright," said Dr. Bo Taber as he smiled and turned to leave.

As *Horizon* sailed deeper into space toward Saturn, the children felt safer now that they had Sami and his star friends to keep them company.

I hope the stars are kind to Sami and us, Lila whispered sleepily.

They will be, Ethan murmured back, already half dreaming.

Hand in hand, the twins drifted off to sleep, their hearts full of hope, minds dancing through the cosmos.

In the medbay, Dr. Charles Ledbetter and Paula, Dr. Thomas Kropt and Kiki Kropt, and Dr. Tanya Ivanova gathered in quiet conversation.

Surrounded by sterile instruments and softly humming monitors, they spoke not only of medical protocols and emergency contingencies but also of the courage it would take to face whatever lay beyond the wormhole.

They were teachers, scientists, and healers, but at this moment, they were also the keepers of calm, entrusted with the hearts and minds of those who would carry humanity's future forward.

Dr. Ledbetter glanced at the others and exhaled quietly. "We've done all we can to prepare for the medical unknowns, but I'd be lying if I said I wasn't worried about going through that wormhole."

Nurse Paula nodded, folding her arms. "Maybe Tim will find out all we need to know without going through it. I get nervous when I hear Kael talk about the dangers. He's seen what the wormhole did to his people."

Dr. Ivanova tapped a monitor lightly, as if grounding herself. "Kael has talked about his failure to install heavy shielding properly. He reinforced the leadership pods, and they survived, albeit barely. We've reinforced the shielding, just in case. Still, we don't know what we don't know. We must have faith in Tim, Peggy, and our engineers."

Dr. Kropt softly chuckled, trying to lighten the mood. "I just hope we don't run out of Waybegonease before we hit whatever nightmare dimension is next."

Kiki smiled faintly. "It's not the nightmares that worry me. It's the silence. The long stretches when we don't know what's coming next."

Dr. Ledbetter looked around the medbay. "I am especially proud of this medical team. We have prepared as much as we can. If we are called into action, we know what to do."

There was a beat of quiet agreement as the hum of the ship filled the space between them.

Kael stood with Liora and Dr. Rykan, his arms folded behind his back, his brow furrowed in the Terra Novan medical lab.

"What's on your mind, Kael? You look worried," said

Dr. Rykan. "You think Tim will decide to go through the wormhole?"

"Yes, he will. He has no choice. Even he can't completely see what is on the other side, and he must know to protect Earth," Kael said.

"If Tim decides, the shielding is so much stronger than when we went through," Liora reminded him.

"I sound like a broken record, but I can't get it out of my mind. Have we done enough to reinforce the shielding on the pods?" Kael asked.

"What else can you do?" Liora asked.

"I've looked at the data Maya scanned. Even at this distance, the radiation near the wormhole is like nothing we've encountered—much more than when we entered the wormhole to Earth on *Arcaayus*. The hibernation pod shielding may not be enough."

Dr. Rykan adjusted the readouts on the scanner. "You're right about the radiation, Kael. We've accounted for every variable we *can* measure. But the wormhole's radiation frequency shifts constantly."

Liora placed a hand on Kael's arm. "Once we get closer, you and Peggy will decide with Tim. We've faced worse odds."

Kael didn't look at her. "Have we?" He glanced at Rykan. "There's something else bothering me. I believe Tim knows what happened on VaRax after we left. I see it in his eyes."

Rykan raised an eyebrow. "You think he's sensed the truth with those unusual telepathic powers?"

"Unusual is a mild word. I am not yet sure how, but he possesses powers our ancestors once had before Tau Cei turned red. I think...he's *seeing* it," Kael replied grimly. "I don't know why he hasn't asked, but if he confronts me...I don't know if

I can keep the rest buried."

At 11 p.m., many crew members gathered in small groups, some playing chess or card games, while others shared stories. Laughter echoed through the ship's corridors. But beneath the camaraderie, a quiet unease settled in.

The journey to Saturn would take six days, during which systems would be checked, protocols refined, training simulations conducted, and readiness maintained. Science briefings, strategy sessions, and meal rotations would also take place, enabled by the ever-present need for discipline.

But one thing remained clear to Tim as he stood alone at the viewing port, looking back toward Mars and Earth far behind them.

He had to speak with Kael.

Too many questions lingered—too many doubts. And Kael was shielding his mind. Tim could feel it every time he reached out with his thoughts. Why? What was Kael hiding?

Tusck's accusation echoed in his mind: that Kael planned to terraform Mars and rename it *VaRax*. Could that possibly be true? Why *VaRax*? Kael's home world was *Terra Nova*—or so Tim believed. But was it?

Tim himself gave the name Terra Nova. He discovered the planet, mapped it, cataloged it, and claimed the rights to its name. He remembered asking Kael once about the name of his planet. Kael avoided answering directly, only saying that Tim's visions were impressive. Was Kael honoring Tim's choice, or was he hiding the truth?

There were cracks in the story, subtle contradictions,

and layers of misdirection. Tim had trusted Kael, yet now he wondered what else he had possibly overlooked. Had his pride blinded him? He had given the planet its name and perhaps unconsciously decided that no other truth mattered.

But maybe *Terra Nova* had always been *VaRax*. Perhaps Kael had always had another agenda.

And maybe, just maybe, this was the one thing Tusck had gotten right.

Tim placed his hand on the cold surface of the viewing port. Six days away, beyond Saturn, the wormhole awaited. Whatever secrets Kael was keeping, whatever truths lay buried in VaRax or beyond, they needed to surface. In six days, the truth would matter more than ever.

Chapter 13

LIFE ABOARD *HORIZON*

Thursday, April 22, 2083

The forward observation deck, located on the level directly above the bridge, was a favorite spot for the crew to gather for relaxation and quiet discussions. As far as the eye could see, a vast expanse of dark space lay ahead, sprinkled with several bright stars and faint dust clouds.

Joran stood at the glass, hands behind his back, eyes far off in thought. His posture was straight, still, like a statue carved in patience. He barely moved as John Logan approached, two mugs in hand.

"I thought you might want some herbal tea," John said, offering a mug. "I asked Liora to brew it—real herbs from the garden."

Joran accepted it with a slight bow. "You honor me. On Terra Nova, tea was a ritual of reflection. I see the practice endures."

John chuckled. "Yeah, though we usually rush through it on Earth."

"That is what I find most curious about humans," Joran said, sipping. "You move through time as though it is chasing you."

John raised a brow. "And Novans didn't?"

"No. We moved *with* time. We observed its rhythms. It taught us. Time was not a constraint. It was a companion."

They stood silently for a moment, the stars blinking in the blackness of space.

"I've been reviewing your chronicles," John said finally. "The collapse of your government...the rise of Kael's science coalition. The way you handled societal conflict—so different from our history."

Joran's face softened. "Different...and yet the same. Struggle is the furnace of wisdom. You forge yours in haste and war. We forged ours in negotiation and compromise."

"You make it sound like humans never stop to listen."

"Not never," Joran replied. "But rarely. It is your species's great paradox. You dream farther than any other I have known. But you do not always pause to understand the ground beneath your feet."

John, the social scientist and former Navy submariner, grinned ruefully. "Guilty as charged. The next shore, mountain range, or planet looks simpler."

"But you can learn," Joran added. "And more importantly, you can *change.* That is why Kael chose to trust humans. He saw that potential."

John looked thoughtful. "What do you see, Joran? In *us*?"

"I see a future worth participating in."

That surprised John and touched him emotionally. He looked down into his tea, then out toward what he knew would soon be the faint outline of the gas giant, Jupiter.

"Well," he said quietly, "I'm glad we met. I don't think I would've understood Terra Nova without you."

Joran inclined his head again. "And I would not have understood humanity without *you*, John Logan. That is how wisdom is passed: *through companionship, not conquest.*"

The historian and the teacher stood side by side, watching Sirius, the brightest star in the sky, as they sipped warm tea brewed by a Novan hand.

After a long silence, John finally turned toward Joran. His voice was quiet, almost hesitant. "I need to ask you something. The chronicles often speak of a place called VaRax. What is it? A lost world of the Terra Novans?"

Joran didn't answer right away. His gaze stayed fixed on the stars, as if the answer lay there. At last, he spoke, his tone edged with regret. "I cannot tell you, John Logan. That question belongs to Kael."

John nodded slowly, unsettled by the evasive reply. The name VaRax lingered in his thoughts like a wedge. *Tim has to hear about this,* he resolved.

The artificial daylight shimmered softly over rows of lush greens, tomatoes on the vine, and purple lettuce glowing gently under Nick's new bioluminescent panels.

The greenhouse aboard *Horizon* smelled of fresh soil, herbs, and something unmistakably alive, a comforting contrast to the metal corridors and constant hum of the ship.

Tom Terry adjusted the water regulator while Mary knelt beside a row of radishes, gently pulling a cluster free with a satisfied smile.

"They're bigger than five days ago when we boarded," she said, brushing the dirt off. "Nick's lights are working wonders."

"I estimate yields will increase by twenty-five percent," said Tanya, jotting notes into her tablet. "And the chlorophyll response under his new spectrum calibration is nearly perfect. Nick really outdid himself."

Veyra crouched beside a trough of climbing beans and gently touched a curling green shoot. "It's beautiful," she murmured. "The balance of light and nutrient flow reminds me of our learning gardens growing up. We used to say that growing food smartly was the first science our ancestors passed down."

Tom chuckled. "I'll admit, before I joined this mission, I didn't expect to become chief botanist and gardener in space. It was just a hobby. But it's good work. Honest. And these plants don't talk back."

Mary smirked. "Speak for yourself. The kale gave me attitude last week."

That earned a laugh from all four of them.

"I think it's time we brought the children in," Mary said, standing up and brushing her hands on her jumpsuit. "Let them see where their food comes from. They can watch the pollinator drones in action, maybe even harvest a few berries."

"I'd like that," said Tanya, her Russian accent tinged with warmth. "Children always bring questions. The best science starts with questions."

Veyra nodded thoughtfully. "It might also help them feel more connected to the ecosystem we're building here. Our children were taught early that food was sacred. It's life flowing from the hands of those who nurture it."

Tom glanced at the dangling strawberries, already turning red under Nick's tuned lighting. "We'll need to coordinate with the space school, but I say let's do it. Maybe even let them plant something of their own."

Mary beamed. "A first harvest from the next generation. Now that's hope in action."

Tanya looked up at the rows of verdant life surrounding them, glowing like stars under the garden lights. "In all our voyaging...this might be one of the most important rooms on the ship."

Veyra smiled. "It is the very soul."

Later that evening, after their duties were over, George and Veyra relaxed in their cabin. The ship's engines hummed with a distant, calming rhythm. Inside their quarters, dim lights glowed a warm amber, casting shadows on the walls.

George stretched out on the reclining couch in a simple tank top and soft cotton pants. Although he was in good shape, walking 15,000 steps during a shift left him tired.

"So, remind me again why everything on this ship is so far apart and taller than me, except for the chairs?"

Veyra, standing nearby, misting a delicate vine with violet blossoms, turned and smirked. She wore a deep green cropped halter tied under her bust, her pale gold hair cascading loosely over one shoulder.

"We built this starship to traverse 12 light-years through a wormhole. It had to be big to fit our equipment and us," Veyra said, smiling. "All of *my* people are taller than you, my love. I'm the shortest in my family. My cousin, Fenra, is seven feet tall and clumsy as a walking tree."

George sighed. "I'm trying not to develop a height complex."

Veyra walked over and effortlessly straddled his lap, settling in despite their size differences. Her double-jointed legs were long and flexible. She leaned forward and wiggled her hips, fitting into him like a puzzle piece—not a perfect match in size, but perfect in feel.

"I can adapt," she whispered. "You already have."

He smiled and pressed a kiss to her bare stomach. "You changed the room's lights for me. You even let me wear that awful shirt I like."

"You humans are compact and overly proud of it," she teased, touching him gently on his chest. "But you've adjusted well."

He leaned forward, resting his forehead against her stiff breasts, which were nearly level with his eyeline. "I've always been tall—until I met you."

Veyra giggled softly, wrapping her arms around him. Her embrace was enveloping, comforting in its strength and serenity. "Height means nothing if your heart doesn't know how to stretch."

George looked up at her. "You've got a poetic streak tonight."

"You bring it out of me," she said, brushing her lips across his in a slow, lingering kiss. She pulled away. "We've both had to adapt. You taught me to appreciate messy, improvisational moments. I taught you how to make tea correctly."

"Ha. I still prefer coffee," George muttered.

"And I still call it 'burnt courage,'" Veyra replied with a sly smile. "But I drink it now, for you, with only a small grimace."

They laughed together, the sound soft and private in the hush of the ship.

Veyra unwrapped her legs and stood, and George quickly followed. Despite being six feet two inches, he still had to tilt his head slightly to meet her eyes, as she rose to six feet eight inches. It was a rare, humbling feeling for him. But instead of feeling awkward, he felt *safe*.

"You know," he murmured, "I used to think I had to lead. That love meant being stronger and bigger. But with you…" He took her hand. "I don't mind being shorter."

Veyra's expression softened as she held his hand, gently covering his lips. "Hush, we're the same height in all the ways that matter."

George reached up and traced the curve of her cheek with his forefinger. "You've opened a part of me I didn't know was closed."

Veyra looked up, her eyes reflecting the soft starshine from the viewport. "And you showed me how to laugh, how to celebrate, and how to experience pleasure. I'm known now, not just needed."

He kissed her slowly and deeply, their differences melting into each other like starlight and shadow. There was no awkwardness, no resistance, just a shared breath in the quiet of deep space.

As they pulled back, Veyra rested her forehead against his. "Tell me what you want," she whispered.

George thought for a moment. "For a stubborn, brilliant woman to cross the stars and fall for a guy like me."

She closed her eyes and smiled. "Then tell me the rest

tomorrow."

George leaned in again, and this time, Veyra didn't wait. Their kiss deepened, their movements slow and familiar, each touch a conversation, every caress a word unspoken. Veyra's hands traced the line of George's shoulders down to his chest, appreciating his warmth and the tension he carried.

He slipped his arms around her waist, pulling her close. Their bodies fit together with surprising harmony despite their height difference.

George had once joked about needing a ladder; now, he stepped into her space as if he belonged there, because he did.

She guided him gently toward their bed, her long limbs folding with feline grace, George following her down without hesitation. The lights dimmed around them as if sensing their need for privacy.

Time passed without words. Their love was expressed not through dialogue but through the unspoken language of fingertips, heartbeats, shared breath, and mutual surrender. For all their cultural and physical differences, in this space, they were equals, perfectly matched, wholly connected.

After a while, George lay just above her heart, listening to the steady rhythm that seemed to echo his own. Her fingers moved gently across his broad chest.

"You amaze me," she whispered, surprising even her.

George smiled against her skin and whispered back melodically, "You make me so very happy. I'm so glad you came into my Solar System."

In the vastness of space, the darkness was illuminated by the distant twinkle of Sirius, oblivious to the serene vow shared between two souls as they realized how wonderfully they had traversed the galaxy to be together.

Chapter 14

TERRA NOVAN QUARTERS

Friday, April 23, 2083

Unlike the narrower, human-engineered decks of *Horizon*, the Terra Novan sector retained its original design, featuring cathedral-high ceilings, softly glowing wall panels, and wide, open rooms.

Tim often lingered here, not because it was physically easier to move about or quieter, but because it reminded him that this mission wasn't just about survival. It was about what humanity could become with help from those who had once fled another dying world.

Tim stood at the center of the great communal hall in the Terra Novan section with Peggy, Paula, and Dr. Ledbetter. Beside them stood President Kael and his wife, Liora. They possessed quiet, graceful presences, their very posture conveying the weight of responsibility.

The other seven Novans sat around them with quiet dignity: Dr. Rykan and Alora; their son, Sian; Veyra; Joran; Nira; and Tarel. They were the survivors, the stewards of a civilization that had nearly been wiped out.

Tim cleared his throat. "Today, as we near the wormhole and prepare for a dangerous but important mission, *Horizon* has become our vessel and shared home."

He glanced at Kael, whose eyes were somber but focused. Since they'd left Earth orbit, Tim had sensed something unspoken gnawing at the Novan leader. Not the loud, performative kind, but the type buried deep in his soul.

Kael continued to blame himself for the dark matter surge that killed nearly 10,000 Novans on their way to what they believed was the safety of Earth in their protective wormhole pods.

Tim had always believed the deaths were an unforeseen catastrophe. However, Kael's haunted look suggested he believed otherwise. But there was something more to his sadness, and this is what most bothered Tim.

Then, there was the shadow of the Ruirulans, a name that still chilled Tim.

"The Ruirulans have wormhole technology," Kael had warned. "They are our ancient enemy... If they track us to Earth..."

Tim hadn't waited. Earth now had military outposts on the Moon and Mars. The outposts were manned by rapid-deployment units and equipped with large space cannons that could be fired, withdrawn, and relocated underground to another site, where they could be fired again to prevent destruction from fixed emplacement.

Still, this moment was about unity, not fear. He turned to the Novans. "Each of you brings knowledge and talents I want to acknowledge. I've spoken with each of you personally, and I've been remiss in not announcing your official duties."

He began with Kael.

"Kael, your knowledge of *Horizon's* core systems, especially the wormhole generator, wormhole pods, and the fusion-antimatter propulsion system, is indispensable.

"You'll work closely with Peggy, Maya, Dr. Ledbetter, George, and Nick in the ship's most sensitive systems. We need your leadership and your vision."

He paused. "I'm naming you Chief of Advanced Systems."

Kael bowed his head slightly. "Thank you, Tim. I will serve *Horizon* faithfully."

Tim turned to Liora next.

"Liora, your work with children, especially your emotional training methods, has already transformed how we see early education. You've helped Ethan and Lila adjust to the other children. I'd like you to co-direct the *Horizon* Space School with Carlyn and Corli. Together, you'll develop a curriculum that blends Novan empathy with human creativity."

Liora's smile was serene. "And may both our peoples learn to raise not just smarter children, but kinder ones."

Tim turned next to Dr. Rykan.

"Dr. Rykan. Your surgical precision, understanding of Novan and Earthling trauma, and moral clarity have earned you universal respect. You'll serve as Co-Chief Medical Officer with Dr. Ledbetter, teaching him your most advanced medical devices."

The two men nodded at one another. They already worked as comrades, their relationship forged in the quiet hours over diagnostic tables and complicated surgeries.

Alora, Rykan's wife, sat beside him, her face open and kind.

"Alora," Tim said warmly, "your presence in the medbay has already brought comfort to many. You have the rare gift of making people feel safe and welcome. I'm appointing you as Senior Trauma Nurse and Recovery Specialist, where you will support and advise Chief Nurse Paula."

She inclined her head, her eyes warm with gratitude. Paula smiled, having already formed a warm friendship with Alora.

Then came Sian, lanky and restless at the edge of the room.

"Sian," Tim grinned, "you've already hacked half our simulator modules and beaten most of the officers in tactical games."

The young Novan blushed slightly.

"I'm adding you to the Training Simulation Design Team. You'll help create new AI-based training scenarios for our security personnel, Space Marines, and the children as they grow up. We need your imagination and your speed."

"I won't let you down, Admiral," Sian said, beaming with pride.

Tim moved on to Joran, the historian whose silence was never empty, only precise.

"Joran, your memory holds the wisdom of a thousand years. Your understanding of Terra Novan ethics, politics, and philosophy is critical as we navigate unknown civilizations.

"I'm naming you Chief Advisor on Historical Integration and Cultural Strategy. You will work closely with your friend, John Logan, our resident sociologist and Earth historian."

Joran nodded once, his eyes distant, thoughtful. "The past," he said softly, "is the map by which we navigate the future."

Nira was next, sitting cross-legged, her jumpsuit wrinkled

from hours of maintaining the ship's mechanical components.

"Nira," Tim said, "I don't know how we ran this ship before you arrived. You and Nick have rebuilt half the core systems by now."

Nira smirked. "He talks to machines. I *charm* them."

"You're Deputy Chief of Engineering and Technical Ops—An unofficial morale booster in Maintenance Bay Three."

"Copy that," she said, the look of satisfaction never leaving her face.

Then came Tarel. Tall, broad-shouldered, and ageless, his bearing was unmistakably military.

"Tarel, your tactical expertise and calm leadership are exactly what we need on away missions. You'll serve as Chief External Tactical Officer, working with Security Chief Patrick Duffy on crew protection and Lieutenant McDill on planetary missions."

Tarel nodded. "My loyalty is to the crew and this ship."

Finally, Tim turned to Veyra, her eyes bright with quiet intelligence.

"Veyra, you have a gift for seeing life, not just as biology, but as connection. You will serve as the Chief of External Environments, leading planetary biosafety, ecology surveys, and environmental science initiatives. You'll continue working with the Terrys on our shipboard agricultural systems."

She stood, elegant and grounded. "This ship already feels like a forest waiting to grow."

Tim stepped back, looking over the group. "Together, you've brought something we lost long ago: a civilization that chose peace, knowledge, and empathy. You make us better. You remind us of what we're aiming for."

The room was quiet, reverent.

As the meeting broke up, Kael lingered beside Tim, his voice low. "You see more than I wish you did."

"I see enough," Tim replied, not unkindly. "We will talk soon about what I've seen and what I lack."

Kael nodded, not as a promise but perhaps as the beginning of one.

And so, the nine Terra Novans—healers, thinkers, and warriors—knew clearly what was expected of them aboard the *Horizon*. Not as guests, not as refugees, but as crew, as family.

The door to the Terra Novan quarters slid shut behind Tim with a soft hiss. He hadn't taken more than a few steps down the corridor when John Logan fell in beside him, his expression troubled.

"Tim," John said in a low voice, glancing back over his shoulder to be sure no one was listening. "I meant to tell you this earlier. I've been mulling it over."

"What is it, John? You know you can tell me anything," Tim said.

"It's about the Terra Novans' home world," John said.

Tim slowed, eyes narrowing. "Go on."

"I asked him about a name that kept showing up in the Terra Novan Chronicles—VaRax. He froze up. Said I'd have to ask Kael. Wouldn't give me a word more."

For a moment, Tim said nothing, the name rolling through his mind. Then he exhaled. "VaRax." He now knew that this was one of the secrets Kael had held from him, a secret Anon Tusck had accused Kael of hiding.

He gave John a steady look. "You were right to tell me. Do

not mention this to anybody. We'll have to tread carefully. Our Terra Novan allies are important to this mission."

John nodded grimly, feeling the weight of the secret now shifted onto Tim's shoulders.

Chapter 15
CHILDREN OF *HORIZON*

Saturday, April 24, 2083

Ethan and Lila sat cross-legged on the floor of the space school classroom, facing each other as they exchanged thoughts that only they could hear.

Do you think they'll understand us? Lila asked silently.

They will, Ethan telepathically replied. *But it won't be easy. Father said to be patient.*

Ethan and Lila were unlike the other 15 human children and the 50 Terra Novan children. They were psychic and were quickly gaining new powers.

Born a year after the Terra Novan clones, they displayed extraordinary abilities to communicate with human children, aged one through twelve, and the three-year-old Terra Novan youngsters, who seemed to be growing and maturing faster than the human children.

Liora, a Terra Novan child psychologist; Carlyn, a registered nurse; and Corli, a musician and family therapist, staffed the *Horizon* Space School. Other mothers, including Julie Martin, Mary Terry, Kiki Kropt, and Jennifer Logan, helped when they could.

Everyone was amazed by Ethan and Lila's development and ability to calm and unite the human and Terra Novan children.

"Have you noticed the other children seem to understand whatever Ethan and Lila are saying to them?" Carlyn asked.

"Terra Novan children are naturally highly attuned to each other," said Liora. "I am surprised that all the children are more in tune with each other when Ethan and Lila are near."

"Speaking of being in tune, when I teach the children to sing songs, the twins are hesitant to use their voices, but they encourage the others by just looking at them. I believe they are singing in their heads, but I'm not sure what's happening," said Corli in amazement.

Ethan and Lila were clearly at an advantage because they could read the minds of anyone within sight. They also quickly developed Tim's foresight abilities without any mental or physical aftereffects.

In other words, they didn't need Waybegonease, the drug developed by Dr. Ledbetter's team to extend Tim and Stephen's ESP powers and minimize the aftereffects.

They *were* different.

During her busy day on *Horizon*, Peggy often took time off from her duties to be with them. From the doorway of the space school, she watched them, her heart swelling with pride—yet also with unease.

"Tim," she said softly to herself, "they're incredible, but...I worry about what challenges they'll face in the months ahead."

On the ship's bridge, Tim heard her voice. *They're developing new powers all the time. They're stronger than we know.*

As Dr. Bo Taber made his daily rounds on the ship, checking on everyone's emotional wellbeing and just being friendly, he quietly stepped into *Horizon's* softly lit day school module.

A hum of playful laughter and low conversation drifted through the air, and the scent of something like citrus lingered—Terra Novan educational trees had been bioengineered to emit calming compounds.

His eyes scanned the space, taking mental notes of everyone. Clusters of children, human and Terra Novan, sat cross-legged in circles, building intricate structures with kinetic blocks or painting on luminous tablets, a Montessori-type approach.

But the two children near the center, surrounded by others yet somehow apart, instantly drew his gaze. He had a special affinity for Ethan and Lila, who always sat close together. Their heads tilted toward a small group of slightly older Terra Novan toddlers who stared back with wide, purple and amber eyes. No one spoke, but Bo could feel the energy shift when he entered the room.

Kiki approached. "Dr. Taber, the twins knew you were coming."

He blinked. "Of course they did."

Ethan and Lila stood up when Dr. Bo approached. "You came back to tell us more about Sami?" Ethan asked. "We dreamed about him."

"He never will be alone now," said Dr. Bo, sitting down with the group. "You and Lila will find him one day."

Lila gazed at him with curiosity. "We know Sami is a pretend story, but we liked it."

Ethan and Lila rarely spoke out loud, but they made an exception for Bo.

"Most adults don't talk with us. You're not afraid?" Lila asked.

"No," Bo said gently, "because I understand what it means to be different. And I know what it's like to feel too much, too soon."

There was a silence, not awkward, but intimate. The Terra Novan toddlers gathered closer, a few gently placing their small hands on Bo's arm and shoulder. He didn't flinch. Instead, he smiled and let them explore him with that childlike curiosity that had no filter for fear or prejudice.

What do you see in him? Ethan telepathically asked one of the Terra Novan children.

Somehow, Bo *felt* the question. A soft, melodic voice echoed in his mind as one of the toddlers whispered back to Ethan. *His soul is warm like the sun. He is safe.*

Bo chuckled. "You kids have better instincts than most adults I've met."

He sat down among them, letting the moment linger. One of the Terra Novan children placed a puzzle cube in his hands and, without a word, guided him through its transformation into a panda bear.

"You know," Bo said, glancing between Ethan and Lila, "your generation will change everything. You only have to decide whether to lead with love or fear."

Lila leaned into Ethan and smiled. *He gets it.*

Yeah, Ethan added. *He's going to help, isn't he?*

Bo blinked again, momentarily taken aback. "I'm that obvious?"

They both nodded in unison.

"Well," he said, easing back and letting the cube reset into something else entirely: an African elephant. "I suppose I am."

And in that moment, Dr. Bo Taber knew that no matter what awaited them beyond the wormhole, these children, this connection, were the future he wanted to protect.

Chapter 16
SPACE MARINE BRIEFING

Sunday, April 25, 2083

The military-ready room was quiet except for the low hum of the environmental systems. Twenty Space Marines sat at attention, their uniforms pressed, faces focused, eyes forward.

At the front of the room, Colonel Walter Duffy and Major Gale Smith stood beside a tactical display that projected three-dimensional renderings of alien ships, possible planetary terrain, and known advanced weapon technology.

Lieutenant McDill, standing off to the side, gave a curt nod to his men, signaling complete attention.

Colonel Duffy stepped forward. His voice was firm, commanding respect.

"Marines, we are about to enter operational uncertainty.

I won't sugarcoat it; what lies ahead is unlike any conflict you've ever trained for. We will encounter alien mech units with advanced artificial intelligence and sentient systems capable of adapting faster than we can fire."

He gestured toward a rendering of an angular, jet-black vessel with faint outlines of defensive nodes glinting in red.

"This is a composite of a Ruirulan ship based on telemetry from Kael's data. We don't know who or what controls them. But you'd better believe they were built with one goal: survival."

Colonel Duffy glanced at Major Smith, standing to the side at the front of the room. "We've battled the Terra Novan mechs in the AI War. We suffered casualties. Work together, and watch your back. Major Smith can tell you why."

Major Smith stepped in, his tone intense and analytical.

"Thanks, Walter. Assume nothing. The colonel means 'don't get shot in the back with a blaster like I did,'" he said, twisting his back where the wound lingered. "On a ship, there is no such thing as behind the lines. There are no lines.

"Another thing. These machines will not communicate with you or each other verbally. And they do not recognize surrender. When we fought the robots, they came at us from all directions.

"They might use heat ray blasters or electromagnetic disruptors. We're outfitting you with adaptive countermeasures and hardened suits the Novans designed for us, but don't let your guard down for a second."

He paused, looking directly at McDill's squad.

"Now, if we board an alien vessel, tactics change. We likely won't know the interior layout, which means there will be no predictable choke points.

"If it's a planetary mission, assume atmospheric

complications, unknown lifeforms, or terrain engineered to confuse and separate you. Work together and communicate with your team. McDill?"

Lieutenant McDill took a step forward. He looked at Duffy and Smith, men who had faced alien robots and fought in Earth's most intense battle.

"Sirs, my platoon's ready. We've drilled for shipboard ops and zero-g engagements. We'll adapt to the terrain, the tech, whatever it throws at us. But I'd rather know from you: what's the endgame if this turns into a fight for our lives?"

"Endgame is survival. The protection of this crew and ship is paramount. If we confirm the threat is lethal to Earth, we must neutralize the enemy at all costs," Colonel Duffy said.

"So, our men and women are expendable?" McDill asked.

"Affirmative. We must complete the mission. Look out for your brothers and sisters, but there is no surrendering to these aliens," Colonel Duffy said. "They will show no mercy to you."

"One more thing: don't let your guard down. If we breach one of their systems, be prepared to encounter resistance from machines and architecture. Doors that lock. Floors that collapse. Rooms that see. Be always alert," Major Smith said sternly.

The Marines murmured. McDill looked at them and then back at his commanding officers.

"We'll be ready. Just give the word."

Colonel Duffy glanced around. He saw the faces of the young men and women he could be sending into the most dangerous engagement of their lives.

"The word is *stand by*. Keep your gear clean. Keep your mind sharper. We're not fighting a war; We're stepping into someone else's domain. Remember that," Duffy said.

A silent nod passed through the platoon. Orders were clear. The wormhole and beyond were unknown, but their duty was not.

Part IV
DISCOVERY

Chapter 17

THE SATURN EFFECT

Monday Morning, April 26, 2083

Five days had elapsed since the crew on the *Horizon* departed from Earth, yet the mood had shifted.

The crew grew quieter during the journey. The easy camaraderie and jokes from the first day were left behind, replaced by disciplined focus and a silent acknowledgment of the unknown ahead.

The humming of the engines served as a near-constant background presence, gently reminding everyone that the ship was racing through the void toward the outer Solar System.

On the bridge, Admiral Tim Smith stood behind the command console, quietly gazing at the large viewscreen on the wall. He had seen Saturn before, but only through telescopes—both ground-based devices on Earth and the

Moon, and space-based tools like the updated James Webb, Nancy Grace Roman, and the Carl Sagan Space Satellite.

"Attention, all decks. Saturn is coming into view. Prepare for external imagery on all screens," he said over the intercom.

Moments later, every monitor and viewing port aboard the *Horizon* lit up with a stunning display. The massive gas giant, the sixth planet from the Sun, dominated the viewer. Its pale yellow, multi-ringed structure and darker, burnt orange hues were layered like brushed oil across a supercharged atmosphere of hydrogen, helium, and methane. The rings, made of ice chunks and space rocks, stretched outward like flat walkways, forming a shimmering halo that reflected the distant sun's light.

Tim's voice was low and reverent. "Behold this marvel of nature."

Captain Leonard Bouchard, stationed at the navigation console, turned slightly, his tone calm. "It's breathtaking."

Titan came into focus next—a ghostly orange world with a dense atmosphere and subsurface methane oceans. Beyond it, the lesser moons danced in silent formation—146 in total, each with its distinct orbit and peculiar secrets.

For a full minute, the bridge fell into silence. Even the veteran officers, hardened by two years of deep-space missions, were drawn into the majesty of it all. Engineers paused mid-maintenance, crew members leaned back from their controls, and even the Space Marines watching from the ready deck allowed themselves a moment of wonder.

The children in the space school were awestruck by the sight. They watched carefully with open eyes and mouths. Ethan and Lila smiled at the beauty of the Solar System's second-largest planet.

Chief AI Officer Amy Smith tilted her head slightly as the pale-colored arcs of Saturn's rings appeared on the monitor. Her voice was soft, philosophical. "There's something deeply comforting about Saturn, like the universe reminding us that even in chaos, there's beauty in the structure."

George leaned closer to his console. "You are so right, Amy. When I see Saturn, especially this close, I'm reminded why we fight so hard to protect Earth and our magnificent system."

Dr. Patel, standing at the science station, nodded. "And why we're willing to risk everything to go beyond it."

Tim noticed Kael and Veyra were unusually quiet as the ship glided toward Saturn's massive rings. He smiled and turned toward them.

"What do our Terra Novan officers think about Saturn?" he asked.

Standing beside Dr. Patel with his hands folded behind his back, Kael took a moment before answering. His clear purple-green eyes remained fixed on the swirling gases of the ringed giant.

"Our ancestors spoke of worlds like Saturn—massive, untouchable, poetic. But seeing such a world like this, so close, the words 'beauty' and 'danger' come to mind, wrapped in a single giant."

Dr. Patel looked at him, visibly moved. Even Tim had to nod in agreement. Kael's words always carried weight, born from wisdom and experience."It breathes in its unique way," said Veyra, standing near Amy. "Those rings' magnetic fields, storms, and ice dance like ecosystems. I would love to study the gravitational forces of this planet and how they influence the environments of Titan and the surrounding moons."

George smiled. His wife always seemed to see the beauty

in the science of it all.

Tim felt the moment land like the chime of a soft bell. He was in awe of Saturn and impressed by how his officers could express themselves emotionally while focusing on their assignments.

Ten minutes later, after the *Horizon* had completed its flyby past the ringed giant and continued its deceleration, Tim turned his attention outward toward the wormhole.

His eyes narrowed as he reached out with his mind toward the mysterious, swirling wormhole in spacetime. He could feel...a distant pulsing, faint but steady, like a slow cosmic heartbeat. The wormhole was close, less than two hours away.

Like Ethan and Lila, he didn't sense specific danger, but something bothered him about entering the wormhole. He needed more information.

"Dr. Patel, what do our long-range scanners detect?"

Maya Patel Andrew's hands glided across the console with practiced ease. She blinked at the incoming data before replying with calm precision.

"Scanners have confirmed the wormhole's coordinates. Distance: 100 minutes ahead at our current deceleration velocity. I'm placing a visual projection on the holoscreen now."

A shimmering orb appeared above the central bridge screen, depicting the wormhole as a swirling space distortion, rippling with blue and violet hues and streaked with an iridescent core. It looked more like a living entity than a gravitational anomaly.

The bridge darkened slightly, contrasting with the swirling energy. There was no mistaking it now. Their course was locked, their path clear, and their moment of decision drawing near.

Tim nodded. "All stations, begin final preparations for the

wormhole approach."

Around the ship, the crew resumed their duties with renewed purpose. But the image of Saturn—serene, ancient, and mesmerizing—lingered in many minds. It was the last familiar sight before they crossed into the unknown.

Chapter 18
FACING THE WORMHOLE

Monday Afternoon, April 26, 2083

Six hours past Saturn, the bridge of the *Horizon* was quiet, heavy with tension and anticipation. All eyes were drawn to the holoscreen, where the wormhole pulsed. Its luminous surface folded inward, rippling with gravitational force and impossible geometries. It was both beautiful and unsettling, like staring into the mouth of a giant throat stitched into space.

Tim stood at the center of the command deck, arms folded. As they drew closer, he raised his left arm.

"Helm, hold position five thousand kilometers from the edge," he ordered. "Maintain distance while we complete a full diagnostic scan."

The ship came to a halt in front of what Tim believed to be the wormhole's entrance, assuming the portal was bidirectional. The gravitational effects from this distance were minimal, but the bridge's visual presence dominated every sensor and screen.

"Dr. Patel," Tim said, stepping to her station, "begin your full-spectrum analysis. I want electromagnetic readings, radiation levels, particle drift, and temporal distortion measurements. Everything."

Maya nodded and got to work. Data streams poured across her screen: shifting magnetic fields, unstable time and depth signatures, and periodic energy spikes rippling from the wormhole's edge.

Peggy, Maya, and Kael reviewed the data, noting its significant differences from the only other wormhole for which they had information.

"My God," Peggy whispered, eyes wide. "I'm picking up negative energy readings inside."

Kael leaned over her screen, scanning the figures. "You're right. That suggests there's a generator on the far side supplying negative energy to keep this wormhole open. We used this on *Arcaayus*."

Peggy blinked. "Wait, how does that even work?"

"Negative energy is a difficult topic to discuss without displaying a mathematical formula. Fundamentally, it's what keeps the wormhole from collapsing under its own gravity. This is amazing, the power being generated," Kael explained. "Back when we jumped, our onboard generator temporarily stabilized the passage. Once we exited, it shut down, and gravity snapped back."

Everyone went silent on the bridge.

"And then, when that happened..." Tim said, his voice low.

"...it caused the wormhole to collapse, and from somewhere, a surge of dark matter struck the Novan ship," Peggy added, her breath catching as the realization hit.

Kael's voice darkened. "That collapse killed 10,000 of my people."

Silence persisted across the group.

Maya, still peering at the data, spoke again. "But the negative energy here, outside the wormhole, is faint. Too faint. How can it hold the structure stable from this end?"

"It isn't strong out here," Kael replied. "That's why we didn't detect it earlier from Earth, and not even on approach. But inside? It's strong enough. Whatever is powering it is beyond our sensors."

Tim stayed silent, staring into the swirling gateway, trying to reach with his psychic mind and send his awareness to the other side. But, as before, all he sensed was dark matter, a frozen planet, a dark planet, and emptiness—no clue or sign of who made the portal or a complete picture of what was on the other side.

He had hoped that being closer would bring him clarity. Instead, the wormhole was just as unreadable here as it was from Earth. And that silence made passing through more perilous than anything he could have imagined.

Kael's voice brought him back. "The structure is more stable than I expected, Admiral. But the fluctuation patterns are chaotic. We'll need hours to chart them, and even then, it might not reveal the source."

Tim nodded. "Then we wait."

He turned to the crew. He'd made one decision, but he still had others to make, and he needed time and space to make them.

"It's late. Maya, Peggy, Kael, I want you to stay and continue the analysis. Everyone else, you're dismissed. Get some rest. Tomorrow's going to test us."

Major Andrews stood and stretched. "Admiral, if you don't mind, I'll hang around for a bit. After traveling a billion miles to reach the mouth of the unknown, I'd like to watch it breathe a little longer."

"Let *Horizon*'s AI handle the drift tracking and environmental scans," Tim replied. "You, Leonard, Steve, and Amy need sleep. That's an order."

Leonard patted Andrews on the shoulder. "C'mon, Mark, the mouth of the unknown will still be here in the morning. Let's grab something to eat."

As half of the bridge crew exited, Tim lingered near the holoscreen. The crew's chatter faded, leaving only the soft hum of the ship and a nagging feeling in his mind.

Maya, Peggy, and Kael examined data from the wormhole, but there were no clear answers. Kael had noticed signs of unusual stability but couldn't explain them. Worse, he was still hiding his thoughts, which ate at Tim's trust.

Tim kept staring at the majestic yet mysterious wormhole. He thought about his options. They could gather more data, leave *Zara* behind to monitor fluctuations, and head back to Earth. But that wasn't the mission. They were here to understand why this wormhole appeared and whether it posed a threat. Another option was to wait by the wormhole until something happened. He had positioned *Horizon* defensively in the right spot to handle an intruder if one were to show up.

But Tim already knew the best way to find the answers. Why was he avoiding the obvious choices? He understood that the answer wouldn't come from telemetry alone. They were on the wrong side of the wormhole to understand precisely what was happening. He knew he had to use his psychic powers to see the other side. He knew why he hesitated. He wasn't ready to face that decision—a focused, shared vision—at least not right now. He needed to exhaust the telemetry data before engaging in a shared vision.

"Maya," Tim said, his voice quiet but firm. "Give me an update."

She looked up from the scope. "I'd like to, but we'll need hours before we can identify a reliable pattern. Maybe longer. It's as if the energy signature, shifting from positive to negative, is constantly changing and never stabilizing. I've never seen anything like this before."

Tim turned toward Peggy and Kael, who were comparing current readings to archived data from the first and only wormhole.

"Anything conclusive?" he asked.

Kael shook his head. "Not yet. I am going to run the data we are collecting through a computer simulation model based on our understanding of wormholes and black holes, assuming gravity is not a force but a warping of space and time."

"You know about Einstein?" Tim asked, teasing the Novan.

"Who?" asked Kael.

"Peg, what about you?" Tim asked.

Peggy exhaled and looked at Tim in frustration. "What is this wormhole? I am considering using smoothed particle hydrodynamics and adaptive mesh refinement formulas to gain a deeper understanding of it. However..."

"However, what?" asked Tim.

"It could be traversable—or it could be a trap. We won't

know until something comes out of it...or until someone goes in."

Tim stood silently for a moment, then gave the final order for the night.

"Set scopes on auto. Everyone is dismissed until morning. *Horizon* AI, continue monitoring the wormhole for any movement. If anything exits, trigger red alert and take evasive action."

"Acknowledged," the AI responded.

Kael stepped forward. "Admiral, I'd like to remain on the bridge and oversee the scan."

Tim nodded. "That's fine. Peggy, Maya, let's get some rest. This mission is just beginning. I want everyone to get as much sleep as possible. I have a feeling we won't get much in the next few weeks."

"I'll go get Ethan and Lila and meet you at our quarters," Peggy said as she left.

Tim nodded and watched Peggy leave the bridge. As he glanced back, Kael sat alone at the console, eyes fixed on a glowing matrix of data.

As Tim stepped off the bridge, the doors sliding shut behind him, a wave of clarity washed over him—sharp, sudden, and undeniable. The silence of the corridor allowed the truth to settle, and he made two decisions.

First, he had to confront Kael about Terra Nova. No more sidestepping or vague answers. Whatever secrets Kael was holding could no longer stay buried, not with the wormhole pulsing like a living heartbeat just days away. Tomorrow, they would talk.

Second, he needed Stephen. And not just Stephen. Tim felt deep down that he would also need Ethan and Lila. Their connection to the unknown, to the fabric of space itself, was no accident. Peggy might worry, and rightly so, but there was no turning back. It was time to trust in the gifts they all carried. They were standing at the edge of the unknown. Besides, if he had to send *Horizon* and its 110 passengers across that threshold, he needed to be sure.

Together, the four of them would seek the truth in the only way that still made sense: through a shared vision. One that might reveal what lay beyond the wormhole, and whether hope or danger awaited on the other side. Tim placed his palm on the wall for a moment, grounding himself. Whatever came next, he would not face it alone. But before he asked for the twins to participate in a shared vision, he felt it was time for them to take another step.

Into the Unknown

Tim walked silently through the dim corridor until he reached his quarters. The lights softened automatically as he entered.

He heard hushed voices and followed them to Ethan and Lila's room. The twins sat together on the bed, gazing out the viewport at the luminous swirl of the wormhole. Peggy sat beside them, her hand resting gently on Lila's back.

They looked up as Tim entered and sat at the edge of the bed. The twins already knew the decision their father had made.

Lila met his eyes. *Father...the wormhole, what lies beyond... and Terra Nova—they are not what they seem. Something waits for us there.*

Ethan followed, his thought steady: *Be cautious...but do not turn away. This is the path we must take.*

Tim nodded, sensing they had reached the same conclusion. He looked at Peggy, whose expression showed she had heard their words. Her eyes, always sharp with analytical clarity, now glistened with maternal concern.

"Children," Tim said, looking back and forth between them as they sat shoulder to shoulder. "You know what I have in mind. We will talk about this later with your mother. Now, I'd like to talk about something else."

Ethan tilted his head in surprise. *What is it, Papa?*

Lila turned with her eyes wide to Peggy. *Mama, is something wrong?*

Peggy shifted in her seat, brushing a strand of hair behind her ear. "Not wrong, sweetheart. Just...new. Important."

In a calm, thoughtful tone, Tim said, "You two have matured faster than your mother, Dr. Ledbetter, or even I could have predicted. You have made me prouder than I can say or even think. But I need your help now with something small but meaningful."

Ethan's mind brushed his father's again. *We have tried to speak less in thoughts. It is easier, but...not always fair to you.*

Tim smiled softly. "I'm not disappointed. However, I would like you both to use your voices more, especially with us and those you trust. There will be times soon when you'll need to speak clearly and quickly. People need to hear you, feel your words by vibration, not just sense your thoughts."

"Because of what's coming?" Lila asked, her voice now audible, gentle yet deliberate. It was only the second time she had spoken since arriving on *Horizon*, excluding her short conversation with Dr. Bo.

Tim touched her hand. "Yes, sweetie. There will be changes when we cross the wormhole. I don't want to frighten you, but we're heading into a time of action and danger, and we'll need to make important decisions that could mean life or death for our friends."

"We've seen pieces of it," Ethan said, this time aloud. His voice was deeper than expected, carrying a quiet intensity. "Some of it's frightening, but it's not set in stone. We can help."

"You can," Peggy said, her eyes moistening slightly. "But helping starts with being present—with your voices, with your strength, and with each other."

Lila leaned into her mother's shoulder. "We'll try. I like it when Mama talks, especially when she sings. I want to sing too."

Peggy smiled warmly. "That's a beautiful start. We could sing together. I look forward to that, darling."

Tim leaned back, the weight on his chest lifting slightly. For a moment, they were just a family, not leaders or protectors of the Solar System and Earth. They were unified by love, bound by a purpose none had asked for but all had embraced.

Chapter 19

KAEL'S CONFESSION

10 a.m., Tuesday, April 27, 2083

The meeting with Kael was long overdue, but Tim had waited for the Terra Novan leader to reveal the whole truth. By now, it was evident that Kael wouldn't or couldn't do that.

Tim had the evidence through his visions; he just needed details and the why.

And the why was the most essential fact of all.

After collecting and analyzing wormhole data all morning, Tim approached Kael on the bridge. "We need to speak privately," he said, his tone firm but not confrontational.

"What is it? We agreed to continue collecting data until a pattern emerges," Kael said.

"This is different," Tim said.

Kael's brow furrowed as he scanned the group behind Tim: Peggy, Stephen, George, and Liora.

"I have important matters to discuss with you before we enter the wormhole," Tim said. "Let's go to the conference room."

Kael stiffened. "This must be important for all of you to come together simultaneously. Liora, why are you here?"

"Tim told me what this is about, and I wanted to be with you," she said.

Frustrated, Kael turned and led them down the corridor to *Horizon*'s staff conference room. He sensed what this was about, but no one spoke.

They entered the conference room. The Terra Novan leader took his seat at the far end of the table with Liora sitting next to him.

Tim stood and waited for everyone to take their seats before starting. "Kael, I've had visions about this mission," he said in a firm, steady voice. "I don't know yet what is on the other side of the wormhole, but I've seen Terra Nova and two other planets I believe are linked to what happened with your world, ones I don't think you've told us about."

Kael froze. For a long second, he didn't blink, didn't breathe. Everyone in the room felt the Terra Novan's fear.

Tim pressed on. "I don't want evasions or diplomacy. Not today. Something is wrong. You know it. We know it. And it's time you told us the whole truth."

Kael bowed his head, but he did not speak. He looked at Liora pleadingly; she stared ahead, waiting for him.

Tim strode the length of the table and stood, eye to eye, beside the tall Novan. "Tell us what happened. My visions suggest that some of your people went to these two worlds.

But how could they? You told us only about *Arcaayus* and your fateful trip to Earth."

A flicker of pain crossed Kael's face. He stared deep into Tim's eyes. *How does this human know this? I shielded my thoughts... Either he's growing stronger, or I've underestimated him.*

"I don't know what you mean," Kael replied, dropping his head again, deflecting, trying to keep his tone neutral.

"Don't do that; don't block my thoughts and say you don't know," Tim said, his gaze unrelenting. "You've been keeping many things from us. I know it. Stephen knows it. Ethan and Lila can feel it. Your wife and the people respect you as their leader, yet they won't tell us. What is it? Speak."

Kael's shoulders sagged, the weight of unspoken truth suddenly too heavy to bear.

"Tim, I carry many regrets from when we left our world. You must understand. Leadership isn't about good choices. It's about impossible ones."

"What?" Stephen asked. "Tim saw others. Your people were on the surface of your planet, begging for help when you departed."

Kael stood up, walked toward a port window, stared outward, and exhaled slowly. "You ask what happened. *Arcaayus* wasn't the only ship that left our dying world," he said at last. "There were ten. We were the last ship to leave."

Tim stepped toward him. "Why hide that from us? How many of your people were left behind?"

Kael hesitated. "I...don't know the exact number."

"Kael," Peggy interjected, her voice soft but firm. "Don't sidestep. Just tell us. You'll feel better, and maybe we can help. How many are still there?"

Before he could respond, Liora interceded, her eyes fierce. "Tell them the truth, Kael," she said. "Or I will. We've withheld this from our human friends too long."

Kael sighed and began to pace, exchanging sharp words with her in their native tongue. Finally, he stopped and faced Tim.

"We launched ten ships. Each was designed to carry up to ten thousand passengers, though only a few reached that capacity," he began. "Ours, *Arcaayus*, was the largest and the first one built. As materials grew scarce and time slipped away, the other ships grew smaller...and less reliable."

"How many did you leave?" Peggy repeated quietly.

Kael lowered his head. "More than 100,000."

There was a long silence. Then Liora gently placed her hand on Kael's arm.

"Our population once exceeded fifty million before natural disasters, population control, and the Ruirulan and Malzon wars dropped that number to ten million when we were born 100 years ago," she said. "We sent over two million to other nearby worlds in sublight ships over the last 30 years. We were limited to one child per household in the past 50 rotations to reduce our numbers further."

Kael continued. "We all knew our sun was dying; we didn't know how fast the end would come until recently. We ran out of time to completely evacuate everyone."

"How awful," Peggy said.

"Yes, it was," Liora said.

Peggy hesitated before asking the next question. "How did you choose who left and who stayed?"

Kael turned away. "It wasn't easy."

"There was a lottery," interjected Liora.

"You held a lottery to decide the fate of thousands of people?" Peggy gasped, struggling to understand.

"It was cruel, I agree. You are not the only one to express distaste," admitted Kael, "but it was necessary to preserve our species among the stars."

"Where did you send your people, and how did you choose the planets?" Peggy asked.

"This is important?" Kael asked.

"We need to know," Tim said.

"Well, first, the planets had to be harmonious or compatible with our species. Second, they had to be close enough to reach within one generation. And third...ideally, they had to be uninhabited," Kael replied, his voice trailing off.

Liora added, "At first, Earth was too far until we perfected wormhole travel. That's when we knew we had a chance."

"But you must have known Earth was inhabited," Tim observed.

"We knew but thought we would be welcome, given our compatibility with your culture and biology. As we studied your planet, we fell in love with your oceans and climate," Liora said.

Tim nodded. "I sensed you were coming long ago, but I didn't know who you were until I had a vision of your planet. Then, the wormhole opened, and I knew."

"One day, Tim Smith, we will talk about that space rock that gave you these amazing, Terra Novan-like abilities," Kael said. "I thought about this question for some time. Our ancestors had many of the powers you have exhibited."

"That was before our sun began to grow from an orange dwarf until what it is now over the past three centuries," Liora said.

"The time will come when we shall discuss this," Kael said.

"I look forward to that, my friend," said Tim as he moved closer to Kael. They locked eyes. Tim gasped, suddenly understanding what the Terra Novan meant.

"We must talk later. Right now, there is much more to discuss. Tell me the rest of it," Tim asked calmly.

Kael exhaled deeply. "Since you must know, and I can no longer hide these facts, let me be clear." He cleared his throat. "As I said, ten ships left Terra Nova using wormhole technology. Not one. I lied to you about that, and I am sorry. The *Arcaayus* was the final ship to leave. And…"

Tim's jaw tightened. "You left them to die?"

Kael nodded grimly. "In a way. It wasn't my decision. It was the council's, but as president, I made the announcement."

"Which was what?" Peggy asked.

"About the lottery," Kael replied.

"What else?" Tim asked.

"What do you mean, what else? Isn't that enough?" Kael pleaded.

"You need to explain everything to Tim. Don't stop, my husband," Liora said.

Kael sighed. "All right. Terra Nova isn't our planet's true name. We are VaRaxians. Our doomed planet is called VaRax."

"What?" exclaimed George, shocked at the blatant lie. "Anon Tusck told us you wanted to name Mars VaRax, but we didn't believe him. You wanted that because it is the name of your home world?"

"VaRax," Tim repeated as all the ambiguities, misdirections, and half-truths became clear. John Logan had told him about VaRax, but he wanted to hear it from Kael. "That's your planet's true name. Of course. I was a fool to think I named it first."

Tim realized he couldn't trust anything Kael had told him unless he confessed everything. "You lied to us."

Kael nodded slowly. "Yes. We allowed you to call it Terra Nova because...it helped build trust. And we aren't Novans, Tim. We're VaRaxians."

"Was that the only reason you kept this from us?" Tim asked pointedly. "Or were you afraid correcting one lie might expose everything else?"

Kael turned slowly, his voice breaking with guilt. "My lies were wrong, but they don't affect Earth. It was just easier for me to let you believe we are Terra Novans because I left over 100,000 VaRaxians on our planet."

Tim frowned. "Maybe it was easier for you to claim Terra Novans died. Did it help to remove your guilt if you called the ones you left behind Terra Novans?"

Kael shrugged his broad shoulders. "Maybe."

"What if I told you we have an opportunity to rescue your people, the VaRaxians?"

Kael looked stunned at Tim's suggestion.

"Through my vision, I saw many of your people begging for help. They are still there," Tim said flatly. "Many are alive."

"We know," said Liora, "believe me, we know. Some of us have psychic abilities—not as much as yours, but Kael knows they are calling for help."

Tim raised his voice. "You don't understand. I saw them and many other things, not just your home planet, but on two other planets. One's an ice planet, frozen. The other...I saw shadows, clouds, pain. Both feel connected to your people."

Kael shook his head but didn't respond.

"I saw these things, just as I saw your ship, through a vision," Tim pressed.

"It doesn't matter," Kael said.

"Do you think I will ignore this vision of your planet?" Tim said, agitated that Kael didn't seem to care. "I discovered your planet through a vision, and now that same ability is calling me again to your planet."

Kael stood up. "We can't go back. It's too dangerous. I already killed 10,000 going through the wormhole to get here."

Tim stared at Kael with the look of someone unafraid. Kael sensed Tim had made up his mind.

"Tim, whatever you do, don't go to VaRax." His voice was filled with sadness.

"Do you not want us to try to rescue the 100,000 VaRaxians still there?" Peggy asked in disbelief.

Kael shook his head. "It's too painful. We're friends. Please, do not go. Let them die of old age, in peace. It is an impossible wish for them to be rescued. You don't understand."

"Look at this." Tim activated the holoscreen on the wall. "This is yesterday's data. The magnetic signals that once radiated from Terra Nova—or, I should say, VaRax—are fading. The end is coming sooner than you expected. Your people don't have much time left. They won't die in old age."

Kael studied the screen. "I need to analyze this data, but it's not surprising. Our orange dwarf sun, Tau Cei, is changing and expanding. It's causing our planet to get hotter—what you on Earth call 'the greenhouse effect.' It's killing our planet. I estimated we had 50 or 60 years, 75 years maximum, before life on my planet is extinguished."

"Look at this data. The conditions have changed since you left VaRax. There is something else," said Tim, blinking in surprise. Suddenly, he saw an image flash in his eyes of a young VaRaxian woman with eyes like Liora's. "There's more to your story, isn't there?"

Kael saw the shift in Tim's face. "You remember what I told you about the Ruirulans?" he said.

"Yes, they are your ancient enemies," Tim said.

"They're not just our ancient enemies," Kael said. "They monitor wormhole activity and..."

Tim interrupted. "You fear that if the *Horizon*, which the Ruirulans would think is *Arcaayus*, traveled in a wormhole to VaRax, they may think it is you and follow?"

Liora gasped. *He knows something.*

"They took someone from you," Tim said, scrutinizing Kael closely. "I see it now. They took your daughter."

Kael's typically stoic face lit up with shock. His voice broke as he spoke her name. "Lyara?"

"She's alive," Tim said. "I see her, and she's unharmed."

Liora stood up and rushed toward Tim. "You've seen her? She's alive? You know this for certain?"

Tim nodded. "I'll help you find her. We can protect her. But to do that...we must go to VaRax. It holds all the secrets."

Chapter 20

THE DARK MATTER EQUATION

Tuesday Afternoon, April 27, 2083

Horizon waited in the silence of space, just beyond Saturn's gravitational pull, as the crew watched the glimmering wormhole swirl in a graceful, terrifying spiral, a wound in the fabric of reality itself.

On the bridge, Chief Science Officer Peggy Smith sat in front of her workstation, her eyes transfixed on a complex matrix of gravitational telemetry streaming across her screen. She had rerun the data Maya had collected over the past 24 hours through her custom signal-detection algorithms—a program she'd refined during her years at SETI—and now the results were unmistakable.

"Tim, come take a look," she called, her voice calm but urgent.

He leaned over as Peggy overlaid two waveforms, distinct but eerily familiar. One was the original wormhole from the Kuiper Belt, the first portal the VaRaxian mothership *Arcaayus* had used to reach the Solar System. The other was from the mysterious anomaly flickering just beyond Saturn's firm gravitational boundary.

"They match," she said, highlighting a repeating subharmonic signature buried in the distortions. "Same quantum imprint. This new wormhole was formed using a VaRaxian generator."

Tim squinted at the screen. "It looks the same, except for the pulsing. The vibrational frequency of this wormhole is what attracted me to it."

"Exactly," Peggy nodded. "The frequency, timing, and spatial compression pattern are identical. No other species uses that technology. It's like a fingerprint in spacetime. Whatever's on the other side of this new wormhole, it was opened with Raxian hardware."

Tim exhaled slowly. "Then it's not the Ruirulans. And we know it's not some random cosmic phenomenon because of the negative energy."

"Correct," Peggy said. "But there's more. I ran a comparative distortion analysis. Watch this."

She created a new visual: a spatial simulation of the wormhole's structure under different gravitational influences. The Kuiper Belt wormhole, far from any major planetary body, displayed a nearly perfect symmetry. In contrast, the new wormhole pulsed and rippled, its surface folding and shifting like fabric in a storm.

"Saturn," Tim said. "Of course, it's forty million miles away, but its gravity is still strong enough to bend spacetime subtly at the wormhole."

Peggy nodded. "It's outside the Hill sphere, but Saturn's gravitational gradient is unusually complex due to its mass, rotation speed, and the influence of its moons. This creates subtle tidal forces interacting with the wormhole's containment field."

Tim frowned. "So even if it's a Raxian wormhole, entering from this side means fighting against those distortions?"

"Exactly. The wormhole was likely intended to be traversed from the other direction, wherever the VaRaxians built it. Entering it in reverse requires compensating for asymmetrical gravitational shear."

She tapped a command, and a model of *Horizon* appeared on the screen, surrounded by a shimmering sphere representing its external shield system.

"We'll need to adjust the external graviton shielding dynamically. Instead of deflecting space debris, radiation, nuclear missiles, heat rays, or blaster fire, we'll fine-tune the field emitters to dampen the specific gravitational harmonics caused by Saturn's influence."

Tim raised an eyebrow. "I see what you mean. Can that be done?"

"With precise calibration and a feedback loop linked to the distortion readings, yes," Peggy said. "We'll use real-time telemetry to adjust the phase-shift parameters of the shields during approach. It's like tuning a violin string while flying through a tornado, but it can be done."

Tim chuckled. "That's why I married you."

Peggy smiled, then turned serious. "There are still two

unknowns. One, if this wormhole is VaRaxian, why was it opened here? And why now? And two, we still don't know if we might encounter a dark matter surge like *Arcaayus*."

Tim's gaze drifted to the viewscreen, where the wormhole shimmered like a restless star. "You are right. There are two important unknowns. Before we decide, we must know those answers, but I can't get them alone. I've tried."

Peggy interrupted, worried about what Tim could be thinking.

"Tim, listen to me. Whoever opened this wormhole could have been delayed for some reason. It could be that simple. Or what if they enter while we are going in? That would be dangerous."

"Those are possibilities, and we need to know for sure," said Tim. "There is only one way now."

"Don't think that," said Peggy, studying Tim's expression. He looked like he had decided what to do. "No, Tim, not that."

"I need Stephen, the twins, and our medical team. We must have a shared vision strong enough to break through the wormhole barrier."

Peggy frowned. "But Tim, the twins? You want to use the twins to link minds for a clairvoyant experience?"

Tim nodded. "Just as Stephen and I did to communicate with the VaRaxians on *Arcaayus* and our friends *Zara* and *Koren*."

"Our babies are too young," she heard herself pleading, knowing it had to be done, "and you remember what happened last time. You were in a coma for three days, Tim. You...*we* can't go through that again, not out here, and you don't know how it will affect Ethan and Lila."

"The twins will be fine. They see into the future, across

interstellar distances and much more. Besides, we have Waybegonease, Dr. Ledbetter, Dr. Ivanova, Dr. Kropt, Dr. Rykan, and Paula to watch over us," Tim said. "There is no other way. You said it yourself. We can't jump into that wormhole without knowing what's on the other side."

"Oh, Tim…"

Chapter 21

THE WORMHOLE VISION

Later Tuesday Afternoon, April 27, 2083

Two hours later, the medbay hummed with determined urgency. Tim lay still on the medical bed, his fingers twitching faintly, his chest rising and falling in a measured rhythm.

Beside him, Stephen was connected to the telemetry monitors, his vital signs displayed in glowing graphs.

Ethan and Lila lay on a table with electrode wires attached to their small bodies. They were quiet and watchful, their eyes wide with wonder. They understood the importance of what they were going to experience. Something was unfolding that stretched far beyond the walls of the *Horizon*.

Peggy stood close, her posture rigid, hands clenched before her. These visions always unnerved her. No matter how many times Tim had reached beyond—no matter how many precautions they took—it felt like tempting fate. Still, she stayed calm for Tim and the children's sake.

Across the room, Julie stood with equal tension in her shoulders. Her gaze flicked to Stephen, concern etched deep into her face. She had seen what the visions cost him. His psychic ability was less refined than Tim's, and the toll it took was heavier.

Dr. Ledbetter, ever composed, stepped forward. "Administer the Waybegonease."

Nurse Paula nodded and pressed the injector into Tim's arm, then into Stephen's. Within seconds, both men visibly relaxed; their breathing deepened, and their muscles loosened.

"Are you sure the children need it?" Paula asked.

Dr. Ledbetter looked over to Dr. Ivanova and Dr. Kropt. They nodded in approval.

"We talked about this. Give them a small dose," Dr. Ledbetter said.

Ethan and Lila smiled. They seemed happy to be treated like adults.

"We want to help Papa and Mama," Ethan said confidently.

"And our friends, Kael and Liora. I want to meet Lyara," Lila said softly. "She's their daughter."

"You will be a big help. Now, let's all focus on the wormhole and what's beyond it," Tim murmured, his voice soft but distant. "Close your eyes...and follow me."

As soon as they closed their eyes, their four minds became linked. They slipped outside the ship and into the void. Ahead, a shape began to form in the darkness. A wormhole appeared before them, tiny at first, like a tear in the fabric of space, dark in the middle with stars all around, expanding into a glowing sphere.

They were on the *Horizon*, moving toward the wormhole. The ship accelerated rapidly as it moved into the tunnel. At first, the tunnel appeared straight. Then it began to contort, winding in every direction, with many colors on the walls that repeated, turned upside down, and twisted. Eventually, a bright light beckoned ahead.

Suddenly, *Horizon* stopped. Before the four travelers, a strange, frozen world appeared. Though fuzzy, Tim recognized it as one of the two planets he had envisioned.

The ice planet.

Tim's physical body stirred slightly. *Stephen, are you with me?*

I'm here, but where are we?

Ethan and Lila, are you here?

Papa, I see it, Ethan silently said.

We see what you see, Lila added.

As soon as the twins answered, their thoughts amplified the vision. It sharpened immediately. To the side, another shape appeared. It was a VaRaxian ship floating in space, disabled.

Show me. What happened? Tim commanded his vision.

Reveal to us, Ethan and Lila said in unison.

The scene unfolded. A voice echoed on the starship. *An asteroid hit. We must rescue our people on the planet and find another world.*

More voices. *Where can we go? Where Kael went.*

The vision returned to the ice planet. Swirling fog. Jagged, cracked glaciers. Dying VaRaxians.

Next, Tim saw the VaRaxian ship slowly break orbit and head toward the wormhole. Suddenly, pulse blasts from a black, oblong vessel hit the VaRaxian ship, striking its engine. Before the ship could enter the wormhole, it stopped and began floating, disabled.

The VaRaxian ship created the wormhole, Tim exclaimed.

The image now shifted to VaRax, a pale world orbiting an orange dwarf sun that seemed much too close to the planet.

A new vision emerged: Kael on the bridge of the mothership *Arcaayus* as it rose into the atmosphere. Below, a crowd of VaRaxians stared upward in betrayal and disbelief.

Stephen gasped. *He did leave them...*

Only one of Kael's secrets, Ethan whispered.

Lyara, and something else, Lila murmured.

In the medbay, Paula leaned in. "Tim's blood pressure: 160 over 80. Pulse: 100. Stephen's BP is climbing, 180 over 85, BPM 120."

"Acceptable. The Waybegonease is working," Dr. Ledbetter said quietly. "Keep tabs but let them continue."

The scene darkened. A third world, a new one, emerged—black, vast, and full of shadows. Darkness. Fear. Pain. Tim's body tensed. Beads of sweat broke across his forehead. Stephen, Ethan, and Lila also felt the fear and stifling pain of other VaRaxians.

Stephen suddenly jolted upright, ripping the electrodes off. He gasped for air, hands trembling.

"Stephen," Julie caught him as he began to hyperventilate. Paula rushed over, fitting an oxygen mask on his face.

"It's okay," she said gently. "Breathe. In and out."

Stephen began to settle down.

Tim, Ethan, and Lila remained deep in the vision, drifting among stars and strange worlds. The ice planet, VaRax, and another shadowy world flickered before them like dying embers.

Then, blackness. Tim's blood pressure and pulse crashed

way below normal.

A voice, urgent and real, cut through the darkness.

"Tim, wake up!" Peggy shouted.

He gasped and opened his eyes, dazed. His vision swam with the afterglow of distant galaxies.

"They're dead," he whispered hoarsely.

Stephen, still recovering, looked over with glazed eyes. "Dead Terra Novans. Kael, VaRax...and two strange planets. What does it mean?"

Tim, groggy, sat up slowly. "Kael knows something more about this second planet. We saw what happened. We know he left people behind, including Lyara. I think I know where Lyara is, and it isn't on VaRax."

Ethan and Lila exchanged glances. They understood what their father meant, but the vision only scratched the surface; much more was waiting on VaRax.

Chapter 22
PREPARATIONS

Tuesday Night, April 27, 2083

In the ship's staff conference room, the soft blue glow of monitors reflected off polished steel walls. Tim sat across from Kael, the towering leader of the VaRaxians, whose solemn expression revealed the storm of concern still brewing within him.

Peggy stood beside Tim, flicking through *Horizon's* wormhole interface diagnostic readings on her tablet.

"We've finished final simulations," Peggy began, pointing at the screen. "Our pods are fully shielded. Four layers of redundant screening: dark matter shielding, magnetic flux dampeners, thermal regulators, and adaptive neural insulation. *Horizon's* AI will monitor and adjust in real time. If there's a surge when we're in the wormhole, we'll be protected."

Kael nodded slowly. "I understand, and I commend your thoroughness, Peggy," he said in his deep voice. "Since you brought me here, I must express my ongoing concerns. Simulations are not reality. They are limited to what we know. We should reconsider going in. I worry about using wormhole technology in this solar system. It failed once when we entered; it could fail again when we exit."

"You're talking about the dark matter surge when *Arcaayus* arrived," Tim said.

"Yes," Kael replied. "We underestimated the gravity fields on approach. You know the negative energy generated from the wormhole exit interacted with a dense region in space. That alignment attracted dark matter particles that ignited the surges for which we were unprepared. The extra shielding I installed in the leadership pods protected us, but our people... perished."

Tim sensed that Kael felt a jolt of immense pain when he talked about his loss. He'd also sensed it when he first met the VaRaxian leader five years earlier. Kael had revealed a lot so far, but Tim sensed he knew more.

Peggy's expression tightened. "And you think the same conditions exist now with dark matter, where we could be jumping?"

"They might," Kael admitted. "We are entering a new wormhole, likely formed by another vessel, one that humans or VaRaxians did not build. This makes it unpredictable. We will not survive another surge if the protective systems fail."

Tim leaned forward. "Kael, there are things we have recently found out, and there are things you still need to tell me. Peggy and Maya's scans proved the wormhole was created by VaRaxian technology."

Kael was stunned. "A VaRaxian wormhole generator? You must be mistaken. Why would my people come to your solar system after establishing a colony elsewhere for three years?"

"My vision showed us that it was a natural disaster that forced your people off the planet they colonized. An asteroid struck it. Dust and debris filled the atmosphere, blocking sunlight and leading to a decrease in global temperatures," Tim said. "It froze, and your people were forced to try and leave."

Kael looked confused. "What do you mean? How do you know this?"

"I had another vision this afternoon with Stephen, Ethan, and Lila. This planet your people adopted became covered in ice," Tim said. "I'm sorry. We will confirm this after we pass through the wormhole."

"You have decided to go? How do you know we will survive?" Kael asked.

"My vision showed us that we'll survive the trip. I also have faith in Peggy's analysis. She triple-tested the dark matter shields. And the *Horizon's* AI computer will adjust mid-transit if needed," Tim said.

"I have my doubts," Kael said. "Are you sure *Horizon's* AI will work? It's been malfunctioning—glitches, as you say. We should use the *Arcaayus* AI."

"I talked with Amy, Jeff, and Nira. *Horizon* AI will be the primary system. If there's a glitch, *Arcaayus* AI will take over, but only in an emergency," Tim said.

Kael hesitated. "This is a good plan, but what if we exit near a massive gravitational well again?"

Tim held his gaze. "Our shielding safeguards are based on the data your ship collected, and we will adjust them based on this wormhole."

Kael looked unconvinced.

"This will work," Tim assured him. "Take your time and look over Peggy's calculations. But there's something else you should consider."

Kael's eyes met his. "You've seen something else?"

Tim nodded. "Yes. When we saw the frozen planet, we saw a ship disabled by a black, oblong vessel," Tim confirmed.

Kael's face changed. "This frozen world could be Celias-3."

"Celias-3? You know it?" Tim asked.

Kael exhaled slowly. "Yes, Celias-3 was one of our prime candidates for colonization. It wasn't frozen. It had temperate zones, freshwater lakes, and a breathable atmosphere."

"But what could have disabled the VaRaxian ship before it could jump to Earth?" Peggy asked.

"I don't see how it is possible, but it could've been the Malzon Empire," Kael speculated. "Celias-3 is five light-years from their border. We knew it was a risk, but it was a habitable planet not that far away from VaRax and too far for the Malzons."

"Who are the Malzons?" Peggy asked.

"They're cold-blooded reptile creatures. Unfeeling," Kael said. "They are highly territorial and known to destroy any world offering strategic value to others."

"Why did you say it is impossible for the Malzons?" Tim asked.

"They would need wormhole technology, and they don't have it," Kael said.

Tim's thoughts darkened. "Are you sure the Malzons don't have wormhole technology? Kael, I have seen visions of reptilian creatures attacking VaRaxians."

"They have attacked our outposts after traveling many months," Kael said.

Tim nodded. "We will find out the answers to this question shortly. Kael, I am sorry to ask this question again: why did you leave so many behind on VaRax?"

Kael looked away. "We only had 10,000 wormhole pods constructed on *Arcaayus*. We had no more room."

Tim asked the following question directly. "Not even room for Lyara? Tell me again why Lyara didn't come with you."

Kael's eyes glistened. "Tim, why do you press me about her?"

"I need to know. Kael, it's important."

"You don't understand. She was furious. She believed I should have allowed our people to choose if they wanted to make the trip to Earth unprotected."

Liora stopped him. "Tim, what Kael means is Lyara has high principles. She felt Kael was abandoning too many VaRaxians to certain death. I tried to explain it to her, but she wouldn't listen."

Kael turned his head, tears in his purple-green eyes. "I begged her to come. She refused and walked away."

"You blame yourself for her choice?" Tim asked.

"I do," Kael said.

"What choice did you have?" Peggy asked. "You only had 10,000 pods, but there were 110,000 people on the planet. You had the lottery, but you knew 100,000 would die."

Liora stood up. "Let me explain," she said, touching Kael's arm. "Lyara believed we should have built at least three times as many wormhole pods in the ten ships, especially after we developed the wormhole technology for long jumps across the galaxy."

"And could you have built more pods?" Tim asked.

"Yes, we could have built another two or three thousand on *Arcaayus* and a few hundred more on the other ship, but we were running out of raw materials, so the council decided instead to have a lottery," Kael said.

Liora interrupted. "The lottery was the mistake that Lyara objected to more than anything. She blamed Kael because he led the council. He supported building more pods, but the council overruled him."

"Some say the council panicked," Kael said. "The Ruirulans threatened to attack at any time, and by then, we were practically defenseless except for our planetary missile system. We put all our efforts into the colony ships."

"Didn't Lyara know about the external dangers?" Tim asked.

"She felt I should have done more. She wanted me to use the popular support of the people to call for a recall vote that could've terminated the council's authority," Kael said. "That would have been treason, but...I can't disagree with her now."

Tim and Peggy finally understood Lyara's objections and her reasons for staying on the planet. They also understood Kael's efforts to evacuate more VaRaxians and his guilt for not doing more.

"I said before we can do something about this," said Tim, placing a hand on the table. "My friends, I saw something else in the vision. Another planet. One that was not on your list of habitable planets. A planet called Shadow. I saw pain... VaRaxians suffering."

Tim paused for a long second, then said, "I am not certain yet, but it seems to me that Lyara could be there."

Kael's jaw tightened. "Shadow? There is such a planet, but it was never on our colonization maps. If there are VaRaxians there...someone sent them."

"This is why we need to go to VaRax," Tim said.

"If you are determined to go to VaRax, risk battling the Ruirulans, and if there's even a chance Lyara is alive on VaRax or Shadow...I must go there and find her," Kael said.

"We will, my friend," Tim said. "We will."

"Which brings us back to the moment ahead. The wormhole," Peggy said, motioning to her tablet display. "The wormhole protection pods are fully operational. The shielding has been recalibrated to block dark matter, radiation, and gravitational flux near and in the wormhole. Internal vitals monitoring is redundant. Four layers deep."

She projected her tablet onto the wall screen, displaying thirty-six adult human pods, fifteen human child pods, fifty VaRaxian child pods, and nine adult Terra Novan pods, all equipped with heavy screening and dark matter surge protection.

"We are ready to go. The wormhole pods will keep our people alive, dark matter surge or not," Peggy said. "But even so..."

"There's always a risk," Tim finished for her. "But we'll face it together. For me, our mission isn't just about investigating the wormhole to protect Earth and our Solar System. It's also about finding new friends and saving VaRaxian lives. Your daughter, Kael, is at the top of the list."

Chapter 23

CROSSING THE WORMHOLE

10 a.m., Wednesday, April 28, 2083

The command bridge fell into silence as *Horizon* settled into position before the shimmering vortex. Beyond the viewing screen, the wormhole swirled in a kaleidoscopic dance.

Tim stood at the center of the bridge, shoulders squared, heart steady. His senior officers manned their stations around him, their expressions taut with focus.

"Dr. Ledbetter, have all wormhole pods been rechecked?"

His reply was crisp and confident. "Triple-checked, Admiral. All life support systems and dark matter shielding are green. We're a go."

Tim turned to Peggy beside the shieldcontrol array. "Peg, final check on external shields?"

Peggy tapped her display. "Shield emitters calibrated to compensate for gravitational shear. Holding steady at 100% output. Go here."

Tim nodded, then addressed Amy at the AI terminal. "Amy, our temperamental ship AI...will it follow orders?"

Amy smiled wryly. "I ran multiple stress scenarios. Once everyone enters their pods, *Horizon* AI will activate secondary shield matrices, isolate each pod under sealed dark matter protocols, and initiate the jump."

"Is that a go?"

Amy nodded, crossing her fingers as she raised her arms. "It's a go."

Tim glanced toward Kael, who stood quietly off to one side, his tall frame rigid. Tim approached him.

"Do you have any final thoughts before we proceed?"

Kael's voice was low, resonant with gravity. "Thank you for taking extra precautions. I have renewed confidence in this ship and our crew. I believe we have done everything possible, both VaRaxianly and humanly, to keep our people safe. Our shields will hold, but we must prepare for what we find on the other side."

Tim walked over to Kael. "We're in this together, my friend."

He then gestured to Father Huey, who stood toward the back of the bridge, thumbing through rosary beads. The priest bowed his head and spoke in a calm, resonant voice.

"Creator of stars and seekers' hearts, we stand at the edge of the unknown, not in fear but in faith. Bless this vessel, the *Horizon*, and all who sail within her. Guide our minds with wisdom, our hands with courage, and our hearts with compassion, even when darkness surrounds us. May we remember who we are and why we journey: not to conquer, but to understand; not to destroy, but to heal; not for glory, but for peace. Watch over us as we pass through the veil between worlds. Let light follow us, even where light has never been."

Father Huey closed with the sign of the cross. "Amen."

Tim returned to his admiral's chair and tapped the intercom. The clear tones of his voice filled the ship.

"Attention all decks: preparing to enter the wormhole in fifteen minutes. All crew report to your designated pod chambers. See you all on the other side," Tim said, shutting off the intercom and turning to Peggy. "Go to the pods. Take our children. I will join you when everyone is secured."

Peggy stood up from her console and walked over to Ethan and Lila, who were watching from the observation deck. They turned toward their father, smiled, and left the bridge.

Down the corridors, hatch doors chimed open as crewmembers—human and VaRaxian alike—strode toward the wormhole pods. Inside each capsule, reinforced belts locked into place, pressure seals hissed shut, and vitals monitors flickered to life.

Tim gave the final command on the bridge. "*Horizon* AI, begin the five-minute countdown to wormhole entry after we are secure in the pods."

A soft, mechanical voice responded, "Affirmative. Countdown initiated. Five minutes to wormhole ingress."

Retinal scanners confirmed the identities of each crew member inside their airtight, radiation and dark matter-proof chamber pod. Within seconds, ambient air was replaced with a precise breathing mix containing oxygen and a slow-release sedative vapor.

Tim felt the familiar tug of disorientation. A low hum rose in his mind as he sensed a psychic surge moments before sedation overcame him.

Quite unexpectedly, Tim's vision returned: flashes of a world in flames, a dark orange sun blazing overhead, oceans boiling into steam, continents fracturing, and a distant, anguished plea echoing in his skull.

Save us... Please...

The next moment, *Horizon* AI moved the ship into the wormhole entrance. The stars stretched into lines of light, and gaseous nebulae swirled around like liquid rainbows. Galaxies spun in distant spirals as the ship rocketed through the wormhole's throat, a shockwave of shimmering energy and flashing light.

Tim's vision sensed each pulse of the wormhole. He saw living entities, beings from many worlds, good and evil, beckoning and warning him. Time lost meaning as hours and days became seconds and minutes. But he continued to move forward, deeper into the void between stars.

Finally, Tim felt the pressure slacken. The tunnel narrowed, the lights dimmed, and the ship emerged from the wormhole into normal space. It slowed to a gentle drift. Ahead, a pale blue ice world appeared, tranquil yet forbidding.

Through the mist, the silhouette of another vessel appeared, unmistakably VaRaxian in design, its hull etched with ancient runes. It floated dead in orbit, battered but intact.

Horizon coasted to a halt before it. Tim awoke from his vision, and the protective pod he was lying in popped open.

Chapter 24
GAMMAMEDUS

Shortly after 10 a.m., Wednesday, April 28, 2083

The gentle hum of systems rebooting filled the *Horizon* as the wormhole pods hissed open one by one. Tim blinked groggily, his vision adjusting to the soft glow of the overhead lights. A mechanical voice crackled through the ship's speakers.

"Attention. Wormhole exit successful. Pod chambers opening. Vital signs nominal," the *Horizon's* AI computer announced.

Tim pushed himself up and looked around. Senior officers and crew members emerged from their pods one by one.

"Everyone all right?" Tim asked, stretching his arms.

Astroscience Officer Dr. Maya Patel rubbed her temples. "A little disoriented. The wormhole pods must have worked. We are alive."

Major Andrews gave a quick nod. "A short, dreamless sleep. I'll take that over a wormhole nightmare any day."

Tim looked at his watch. Only a few minutes had passed since they entered the wormhole. Because of his vision, he felt as though he had experienced a waking dream. "Everyone, take an electrolyte container and report to your stations. Report anything unusual."

The crew slowly exited the wormhole chamber and resumed their duties. Tim and the senior officers entered the bridge and took their places.

Kael's eyes narrowed as he peered at a bridge's viewscreen. A shape hung in the void beyond the *Horizon*.

"Admiral," Kael said quietly, "we're not alone."

Tim noticed the ship floating astern, motionless, just as it had in his dream.

"Ship ahead," Captain Leonard Bouchard confirmed, already tapping at his console. "Matching VaRaxian design, but it's different. Smaller. Disabled."

Kael squinted. "I know that ship. It's the *Gammamedus*. It is No. 7, the seventh ship we launched. Tim, you were right. We are at Celias-3, once a humid world with many oceans and lakes. Now, look at it—an ice planet."

"What about the ship? Anyone alive onboard?" Tim asked, sensing fear.

"I believe it carried 8,000 of our people," Kael said.

Peggy scanned the *Gammamedus*. "Many systems are offline, but the reactors are hot," she murmured. "I'm reading several faint bio-signs."

"Look at those breaches in the hull and the aft engine section," said Leonard, pointing to a torn section midship. "It's not disabled. Somebody attacked it. That's blaster damage."

Tim's jaw clenched. He clicked on the ship's intercom. "Crew, we safely jumped to the other side of the wormhole.

There is a disabled VaRaxian ship beside us. Yellow alert."

He turned to Maya. "Engage *Horizon* AI's long-range radar scan for enemy spacecraft anywhere within range."

"Yes, sir," Maya said, pressing a button on her console. "Nothing within 100 million miles."

"I want to know why this ship was fired on and who did it," Tim said. "We need answers. Patrick, assemble a boarding team. Take Lieutenant McDill, ten Space Marines, Nira, Jim, Tarel, Dr. Rykan, Jeff, Amy, and Nick. I want a full sweep: survivors, data, tech, anything."

"Understood," said Security Chief Patrick Duffy. "We'll be ready in ten."

"Take *Zara*," Tim ordered. "*Zara*, do you read me? I want you to keep your sensors on high alert for any unidentified ships."

"Yes, Admiral. My sensors indicate the *Gammamedus* was attacked two weeks ago, based on the blaster readings," *Zara* said. "I confirm forty VaRaxians are alive. Many are injured."

Fifteen minutes later, the rescue team, equipped with spacesuits, weapons, and first aid kits, boarded the *Gammamedus*. The hull was breached, and most chambers had no air. Dim emergency lights flickered in shattered corridors.

As they advanced, Nira swept her scanner across the walls. "Still pressurized in some areas," she muttered into her wristcomm. "It looks like the reactor's active. It's powering something. Minimal other systems operating."

Further inside, they discovered a sealed chamber. Nira used an emergency code to access the electronic door. She entered, saw the exhausted, malnourished, and injured VaRaxians, and quickly shut the door.

"We found survivors. We need oxygen masks to evacuate them. Whoever did this must have left them for dead," Tarel said through his wristcomm. "They're alive—barely."

Patrick's voice came next. "Tim...it's grim. We've confirmed over 3,000 deceased. Some executed. Others were caught in the blast. This wasn't an accident."

Back on the *Horizon*, Tim's expression hardened. "Any sign of who did this?"

"We are downloading the ship's log," said Amy. "Kael will have to translate."

"Tim, we are on the bridge. The ship's wormhole generator is still active. The ship's power is almost drained," Jeff reported. "Should we shut it down?"

Tim considered. "Not yet. I want a full report on the damage and what happened before we do anything."

Dr. Rykan joined Nira to provide first aid, but some of the injured needed surgery. "Admiral, we need to evacuate these survivors immediately. Do I have permission to load them onto *Zara*?"

"You do," said Tim. "Send them over immediately. I will launch *Endeavor* for backup in case of an emergency."

Endeavor took off to support *Zara*. "Admiral, I am patrolling and scanning near space," the ship reported. "No contact."

Lieutenant McDill's voice echoed in. "No hostiles, dead or alive, aboard. All clear. Blaster marks all over the ship. There was a brief battle here, but the VaRaxians didn't stand a chance."

Tim shook his head. "Secure the area, help with the evacuation."

"Yes, sir," Lieutenant McDill said.

Tim turned his attention to Celias-3 below. "Peggy, what readings do you have on this planet?"

Peggy shook her head when she saw the readings on her console.

"If this were a humid, tropical world five years ago, it is now frozen, an ice planet, as you saw in a vision," Peggy said to Tim as she tapped a control, pulling up a rotating image of the planet. "The entire surface is frozen. Oceans, jungles—all gone. Ice covers everything."

Tim leaned forward. "A natural freeze?"

Peggy shook her head. "No. This was induced and catastrophic. As you said, an asteroid impact is most likely the cause. I'm detecting fractures across three city domes, an impact crater to the east of the largest city, and subglacial heat pockets."

"I want a full report from all officers on that planet," Tim said.

"Wait, I detect faint biosigns. Something's alive down there!" Peggy exclaimed.

After the forty *Gammamedus* survivors were transported to *Horizon*, Dr. Rykan and Alora, with the assistance of Dr. Kropt and Paula, began treating them in the VaRaxian medbay.

Several required emergency surgeries, along with some first aid and nutritional supplements.

"Kael, I want you and Liora to find out from the survivors what happened on that ship, who is responsible, and what they know about the planet," Tim said. "We are going to go down there and look for survivors."

After collecting data on the Celias-3 and taking photographs, Tim called a meeting in the staff conference room to discuss a rescue plan. He asked Jeff and Amy to gather and present a holographic projection of the downloaded data.

"*Gammamedus* made it to Celias-3 five years ago," Amy said. "They built a colony—7,500 VaRaxians in three domed cities. About 500 maintained *Gammamedus* in orbit."

"But two weeks ago," Jeff added, "an asteroid struck the planet. Instant climate collapse. Within a week, an ice age. The colony attempted evacuation. That's when the Malzon appeared."

Amy's voice was tense. "Kael translated this from a damaged recording we found on *Gammamedus*."

She pressed the play button.

"To any who hear this...Celias-3 was paradise—lush, alive, ours. Then the sky fell. An asteroid shattered everything. We fled to *Gammamedus*. But before we could escape, the Malzon came. No warning. No mercy. They slaughtered us. If you find this, remember us. Avenge us."

The transmission ended in static.

Tarel's voice was sharp. "Ambushed them mid-rescue. They killed our people without mercy."

Kael frowned deeply. "The Malzon...we feared this. They found the wormhole, but why not use it themselves?"

Tim turned to Ethan and Lila, who had quietly entered the bridge.

They didn't know about the wormhole. They came to investigate the asteroid impact. They'll be back, Ethan said.

Lila nodded, her eyes distant. *The Malzons are angry. They're on their way.*

Tim's mind was already moving. "We can't leave the rest of the VaRaxians behind. Patrick, prep another mission to that ice planet. I want everyone rescued."

Patrick nodded. "We'll find them."

Tim stood before the main viewscreen as *Zara, Endeavor,* and *Horizon* prepared for their next rescue mission. Celias-3, now covered in ice and snow, spun slowly below.

Chapter 25
VISIT TO THE ICE PLANET

Noon, Wednesday, April 28, 2083

Celias-3 loomed ahead, a frozen ghost orbiting silently. It was a vibrant world—humid, green, and alive. The VaRaxians selected it for colonization specifically due to its warmth, plentiful water, and breathable atmosphere.

Three cities, nestled among equatorial lagoons, once thrived as homes for over 7,500 VaRaxians. That was before an asteroid struck out of nowhere, turning the planet into a frozen wasteland—a barren glacier stretching from pole to pole with traces of life buried beneath layers of ice and snow.

Logs from *Gammamedus* revealed more than 3,000 immediately perished. Before the ship was attacked, the last record showed that rescue operations were underway and 2,500 VaRaxians had been transported safely from the planet's surface.

As *Horizon* glided into orbit, the world below looked cold, even from space. A sweeping blanket of solid ice and thick frost encased the entire surface. The equatorial seas had slowly frozen, leaving jagged ice canyons and glacial ridges where waves once rolled.

Admiral Tim Smith stood on the bridge of *Horizon*, gazing down at the world below. "We land in fifteen minutes," he told his two rescue teams in the landing bay. "We don't know how many are alive, but our goal is to rescue as many survivors as possible. I will join you in a few minutes."

"Understood, Admiral," Lieutenant McDill replied as he boarded the shuttle *Zara* with Peggy, Tom, Big Nik, John Logan, Dr. Bo Taber, Dr. Kropt, Nurse Paula, and five heavily armed Space Marines. They were bound for the domed ruins of a city called Altair.

Patrick led the second crew aboard *Endeavor*, bound for Vega, where faint biosigns had flickered in Peggy's scans. His team consisted of Dr. Rykan, Tarel, Nira, Con, Nick, George, Veyra, and five other Marines.

Peggy reported that the third city, Deneb, had been obliterated by the asteroid strike. Nothing remained but jagged ice and a collapsed ruin.

Zara touched down in the center of Altair, kicking up a swirl of snow and icy dust as the rescue team prepared to disembark.

Tim was the first to step out, his boots crunching on the frozen ground, with Peggy close at his side. Both were dressed in heavy jackets with heated undergarments. The air was breathable yet extremely cold.

He paused, scanning the eerie landscape, his breath misting in the frigid air. "There's a strange excitement that comes with being the first human to walk on an alien world," Tim said quietly. "But it's heavy here... I can feel the death and suffering in the air. Any biosigns, Peg?"

"Not aboveground," she said, studying her scanner. "But deep below...Tim, there's a thermal spike. This way."

"Lead the way to the entrance," Tim said, sensing a door to an underground shaft. "Crew, follow us."

Twenty yards ahead, they saw a small building with a sign above a door. The words were in VaRaxian.

"This is the way," Tim said.

"The scanner is showing thermal heat. Wait...biosigns. Very faint. Someone is alive down there," Peggy said.

Tim lifted his wristcomm. "Team, we found biosigns. Come to my signal. We're going down the stairs inside."

They descended three flights of stairs, past tunnels leading horizontally along the surface. Ice and frost covered the walls and floor, making the going treacherous.

Suddenly, Tim stopped. A wave of heat flooded his mind.

He gasped. "They're here."

Peggy didn't question him, and she didn't bother checking her scanner to confirm. She knew he was right.

They found a hatch beneath the next level. It was frozen solid. "Peggy, help me push this open."

"It's too hard. We need to wait for help," she said.

Just then, Tom, Big Nik, and John Logan showed up.

"Perfect timing. We need your shoulders. Give a heave-ho and help us push this door in," Tim said.

Grunting and groaning, the five friends pushed until the door began to open slowly. They stopped when they'd made enough of a gap for a single person to slip through. Tim went first.

Inside: five hundred VaRaxians. Lying in rows. Unconscious. Barely breathing. A jury-rigged heating core kept the temperature just above freezing. The team stared, stunned by the sight.

Tim clicked on his wristcomm. "*Zara*, follow my signal and land outside a small building. We've found hundreds of survivors underground. We need more help down here."

Nurse Paula was the first to arrive. As soon as she saw the group, she ran forward, shocked. "How did they survive?"

Dr. Taber followed Paula in and activated his portable medkit. "We need to transport them to *Horizon*. If we get them warm and treated, we can save many of them."

Tim called *Horizon* on his wristcomm. "Steve, we have 500 survivors here. Repeat. We have 500 survivors here. Notify the medbays to prepare for mass casualties. We will return shortly."

Then, a scream.

"Ice gave way!" Lieutenant McDill shouted.

Tom Terry stepped onto a section of weakened flooring, brittle from the cold. The floor cracked, and he plummeted twenty-five feet down to the next level.

"Tom!" John Logan shouted.

Big Nik didn't hesitate. "Rope!"

Lieutenant McDill, Dr. Taber, and two Space Marines anchored Big Nik as he quickly repelled into the space below, where Tom lay on the floor.

Tom groaned, blood seeping from his shoulder.

"I've got you, brother," said Big Nik as he lifted him gently. "Stay with me."

Big Nik hoisted him slowly. The Marines pulled, grunting

as they lifted the two big men.

Tom emerged, teeth chattering but alive. Dr. Taber worked fast, patching his bloodied shoulder.

"You okay? What do you need?" John asked.

Tom tried to smile. "Nothing, except next time...you fall."

Endeavor landed just outside Vega, a more compact city than Altair. Snow blew across the ice, the wind bent tree limbs, and the sky was milky white.

Patrick split the team. "Activate wristcomms. Stay in pairs, and don't wander far. We have poor visibility."

George and Veyra moved together, their boots crunching over frostbitten soil. They wore heavy jackets and thermal underclothes, but the cold air was still painful to breathe.

Adjusting his thermal scarf and goggles, George assessed the remains of the settlement through a portable scanner.

Suddenly, George's scanner flickered. "Faint biosigns, coming from below. I am also getting residual heat under the surface, which may be geothermal. Could be a cavern."

A few paces away, Veyra knelt in what appeared to be a small garden; frost glistened on the fragments of what had once been a greenhouse. She brushed the snow away from a torn sign on a door lying in the snow, its message written in faded VaRaxian script.

"This greenhouse grew nutrition vines and frostberries," she said softly. "They were designed for temperature tolerance, but not for this."

George crouched beside her. "An asteroid caused all this destruction?'

She nodded. "Maya recorded several hits on this side of the planet by a swarm of meteors that broke from the bigger rock. Nearly 8,000 of my people came here for refuge. It was once a beautiful planet. I don't see how anyone could survive this."

"If some are alive, we will find them," said George softly.

She looked at him, her eyes shining with sorrow. "But many died, struggling to make it through the aftermath. I know it. This was a generation of settlers. They were farmers, scientists, teachers—and they had children."

George gently touched her arm. "I'm sorry, Veyra. What can I do?"

She looked at him with sad eyes. "I'm glad I'm with you, George Clarke."

He smiled. "Likewise."

She held his gaze for a long moment, then turned to the snowy expanse. "It is hard to believe this planet was once lush with vegetation and animals. The microbial life in its rivers was amazing. I planned to come here before Kael asked me to join *Arcaauyus*."

"You could have been here?" George asked, surprised.

"Yes. If I had made a different decision, we might never have met, at least not in the way we did. Looking at all this, I feel so sad, but at least we know what happened," Veyra said. "It makes me wonder how the rest of my people are doing on VaRax and the other planets."

A long silence passed between them. The wind howled.

"Veyra," George said, looking at his scanner, "I've got stronger biosigns. This way."

Moments later, Veyra stopped. Her VaRaxian eyes were more conditioned to dim light. "Over there."

George squinted. "What is it? All I see is snow, ice, and fog."

She ran toward the sight that had caught her attention, her lanky legs covering fifty feet in seconds. It was a squat structure near the city center, with mist from a pipe on the roof. The building was buried halfway under the snow.

When George arrived, Veyra was pushing open a door. "Help me," she grunted. "It's frozen."

Veyra pushed high, and George pushed low. The door shuddered and squeaked, and finally, they opened it enough to peer in.

"Something is moving inside," George exclaimed.

In the dark, they could make out dozens of VaRaxians huddled on the floor. Wrapped in blankets and scraps of insulation, their eyes were wide, their skin pale. Children moaned, their lips blue.

"Oh, my heart!" Veyra cried out as she rushed in to give aid. "They're alive!"

George activated his wristcomm. "Patrick, we found them. Must be over a hundred. They're alive, but barely. Come to my signal."

Patrick's other teams reported similar discoveries. In three hours, over 200 more survivors were located. They were thin, frostbitten, and frightened—but alive.

Con, Nick, and the five Space Marines wrapped them in warming foil and assisted them to *Endeavor*, where they were transported to *Horizon*. During the journey, Dr. Kropt attended to their wounds until they could receive treatment in the VaRaxian medbay.

By 2 p.m., *Zara* and *Endeavor* had delivered over 900 survivors to the *Horizon*. More than two dozen crew members and Space Marines greeted them at the landing bay, gently carrying or assisting them off the shuttles one by one.

The VaRaxians, once lost to the ice with little hope for survival, huddled in blankets as they drifted into the warmth of the medbay, their eyes fluttering open to the lights and kindness around them.

Tim watched from the bridge, filled with deep, quiet pride, yet he also sensed danger.

Then Maya's voice crackled through.

"Admiral...we've got company."

Tim turned. "The Malzon."

"One Malzon ship, thirty minutes out. A fleet behind it. Three and a half hours away at present speed," Maya confirmed.

Tim nodded. He'd known the mission would be dangerous, and this was just the start. He pressed the bridge intercom.

"Attention, all crew. We have an enemy ship thirty minutes out. Red Alert. Battle Stations."

Part V
WAR

Chapter 26

THE MALZON ATTACK

2:30 p.m., Wednesday, April 28, 2083

Admiral Tim Smith stood at his command console, his gaze fixed on the bridge viewscreen. Officers and crew members anxiously waited at their stations for orders.

"Maya, what's the status on the Malzons?" he asked, his voice steady but his jaw tight.

The astroscience officer's fingers expertly touched the controls on her console. "Long-range sensors confirm a Malzon warship. ETA: fifteen minutes at current speed. The rest of their fleet, five ships, is three hours behind. Shields are up, all defensive arrays are powered, and every station is manned," Maya said, her voice tense.

Tim turned sharply to Major Andrews. "Our shuttles?"

"*Zara* and *Endeavor* are secured in the landing bay fully

armed and ready for rapid deployment," Mark confirmed.

Tim nodded. "Good. I'd like to fire up the wormhole generator and jump to VaRax, but we don't have enough time to set the coordinates and test the machinery."

The officers understood Tim's dilemma: to stand, fight, or run. Tim needed time to close the wormhole. He sensed that the Malzons' ultimate plan was to invade Earth, and he didn't want to leave the wormhole open or risk the VaRaxian ship and its secrets falling into their hands.

"Suggestions?" he asked.

"I say we stand and fight. If they destroyed the *Gammamedus*, we can't run without making a statement to these heartless bastards," Mark said.

"Kael?" Tim asked.

"Major Andrews is correct. Running from the Malzons would only invite further conflict," Kael said.

"I agree. If they get within range, we strike them quickly and decisively. Kael, monitor their comms. If they open a channel, I want a real-time translation," Tim said, looking at the Terra Novan for a reaction.

"Admiral," Kael said, stepping forward with an urgent look, "we should do more. I recommend we activate Arcaayus. He can respond faster than we can and has experience facing the Malzons."

Tim looked up sharply, surprised. "We've operated without him for five years. Why now?"

Kael held his ground. "Because Arcaayus carries tactical archives spanning over a century, including data on Ruirulans, Malzons, and others. If we want an edge in this fight, he's it."

Tim hesitated. He had deactivated Arcaayus for good reasons. He had hundreds of millions during the AI War when dark matter damaged his programs. There was also a political necessity—he constantly reminded Earth's survivors of what had happened.

Yet Kael's sincerity was evident.

Tim turned to his senior officers. "Amy, Jeff, Peggy...your thoughts about Arcaayus?"

Jeff answered first. "We double-checked Arcaayus's systems before shutdown. No trace of dark matter corruption. He's safe."

"Arcaayus is superior to the *Horizon* AI computer we use now," Amy added. "Our AI isn't programmed for military fights, just defensive maneuvers."

Tim exhaled. "Kael, I don't like it, but we're out of time. Computer, activate Arcaayus. Amy and Jeff, I want you both to monitor him closely."

A low hum filled the bridge, and mechanical beeps echoed.

"I am Arcaayus," the AI's deep voice thundered through the speakers. "What is your command?"

Tim stepped closer. "Arcaayus, a Malzon warship will arrive soon, and more are coming. Can you assist?"

"Yes, I will," Arcaayus said in a loud, firm voice.

"Do you know who I am?" asked Tim.

"Yes, you are my master, Admiral Tim Smith," Arcaayus confirmed.

"I've told you before, I am not your master; I'm your commander and Admiral of this ship. Do you understand?" Tim said.

"Yes, Commander Admiral, I do. I will destroy any ship that attacks us if that is your command," Arcaayus said.

"I would like you to *disable* any ship that attacks us. Spare lives if you can," Tim said.

"Affirmative, Commander Admiral," Arcaayus said.

Tim gave a satisfied nod. "Just call me Admiral. Prepare to engage."

The Malzon battlecruiser appeared on the viewscreen, weapons charging.

"Attention. Prepare for evasive maneuvers. Go to your assigned safety stations. Brace for impact or sudden course changes," Tim announced over the intercom.

Within a few minutes, *Horizon's* bridge shook under the first barrage of plasma fire.

"Return fire," Tim ordered.

Under Arcaayus's control, *Horizon's* countermeasures moved with stunning precision. Defensive turrets pivoted and fired concentrated energy blasts, hitting weak spots and overwhelming the Malzons' shields in seconds.

Arcaayus also executed a dazzling series of evasive maneuvers, avoiding incoming fire with preternatural speed.

"Direct hit on their engines," Peggy reported. "Their power grid is destabilizing."

Before the Malzons recovered, *Horizon* launched a barrage of EMP torpedoes. The enemy ship's systems flickered and failed. Drifting powerless, the Malzon cruiser sent a desperate distress signal before several explosions rippled through the ship, crippling it.

"Enemy vessel neutralized," Arcaayus confirmed calmly. "Twenty percent casualties, two percent deaths out of a crew of 100. Awaiting further orders."

Tim let out a breath. "Excellent, precise work, Arcaayus."

Pushing down on the intercom button, Tim announced, "Crew, I activated Arcaayus to defend our ship. He disabled the Malzon vessel in a matter of minutes. Well done, crew. Yellow Alert. Standby. The Malzon fleet is two hours away."

"Admiral, I am getting a distress signal from the Malzon ship," said Steve Flatt, the communications officer. "I am recording and piping the message into the universal translator."

"Carry on," said Tim. "Damage report, George?"

"All decks report no hull breaches. The shields held against the plasma fire," the chief engineer said.

"Kael, do you have any recommendations?" Tim asked.

"I suggest we leave for VaRax," Kael said.

"Noted. Steve, do you have that translation?" Tim asked.

"I have the first part," said Steve.

He played the Malzons' message over the bridge's speakers. "This is warship *Skar'Tal*. We are under heavy assault by unknown forces allied with VaRaxians. Our systems are crippled. The enemy's technology is superior. Request immediate reinforcements—caution: attacker highly advanced—shields and weapons beyond known specifications. Proceed with extreme aggression. Glory to the Malzon Empire."

Tim listened carefully, expecting a call for help or surrender.

"Kael, you understand the Malzons. What do you make of this transmission?" asked Tim.

"The Malzons are a barbaric, monstrous race. Their technology is outdated. I am not surprised Arcaayus was able to achieve victory so quickly," Kael said. "However, the Malzons are known for their unpredictability and poor judgment. If we stay, they may try to launch nuclear missiles. They carry such primitive weapons."

"Thank you, Kael. Steve, open a channel to the *Skar'Tal*

and turn on the translator," Tim said.

"Go, sir," Steve said.

"To the commander of the *Skar'Tal*. This is Admiral Tim Smith of the starship *Horizon*. Do you require any assistance?" Tim asked slowly and deliberately.

A hollow hiss followed. No response.

"Commander of the *Skar'Tal*. If you do not require any assistance, I want you to know we came in peace. We have completed a rescue mission and have no intention of starting a war with the Malzon Empire. Do you understand?" Tim asked.

The frequency crackled, and a harsh voice sounded through the speakers. "I am the commander of the *Skar'Tal*. How dare you attack my ship. My fleet will be here shortly to destroy you."

The Malzon commander's words were met with disbelieving murmurs from the officers on the bridge.

Jeff raised his voice. "Let's finish off these bastards. They have no intention of taking responsibility for the massacre of our VaRaxian friends."

Major Andrews, at the helm, nodded. "I agree with Jeff. They are psychotic. Admiral, what is your order?"

Kael and Veyra stood motionless. They understood that trying to reason with the Malzons was a futile exercise.

Tim knew the Malzons needed to be taught a lesson. But he also needed to know what they wanted.

"Peggy, scan the ship and see if they have any weapon systems functional," asked Tim, standing firm, his arms crossed as the disabled Malzon warship loomed large on the viewscreen.

Still sparking from the battle, its weapons were dark and silent.

"Their life support systems are failing. I don't detect any

external danger from the Malzon ship," Peggy said.

"They refused assistance," Major Andrews said grimly. "Let's fire up the generator and get out of here."

Peggy interrupted. "They are scanning us and transmitting our specifications to their fleet, now two and a half hours away."

Tim's jaw tightened. "Then we move to Phase Two," he said, pressing the intercom button.

"Colonel Duffy, Major Smith, and Patrick: report to the military room with Lieutenant McDill. I have a VBSS mission I'd like to discuss with you," Tim said.

Andrews raised an eyebrow. "VBSS? Visit, Breach, Search, and Seize? Is that what you want? I haven't heard that order in a while. That's rather bold, Admiral. What do you have in mind?"

"We will board that ship and download its computer database. They attacked the *Gammamedus* and returned in force for a reason, and I want to know that reason," Tim said.

"Arcaayus, I want you to pinpoint a target on their bridge to open a breach with minimal structural damage. It has to be large enough to send our Space Marines through," said Tim. "I want a clean insertion point for boarding."

"Affirmative, Admiral. Calculating precision strike," Arcaayus thundered over the comm.

Colonel Duffy leaned over the holographic layout of the *Skar'Tal's* command center in the *Horizon's* military-ready room. The flickering blue image cast sharp lines across his determined face.

"Do you have an insertion and extraction plan, Colonel?"

Tim asked from across the table.

"We're working on it," Duffy said, tapping the schematic. "Are we taking a shuttle to the Malzon ship?"

"Yes," Tim replied. "*Zara* will ferry your team over. *Endeavor* will cover your approach. At my signal, Arcaayus will breach the hull with heat ray fire," Tim pointed at a faint, pulsing mark along the ship's forward section. "Here. It's the weakest point near the bridge. Lieutenant McDill will insert his squad through the breach in spacesuits, fully armed."

Lieutenant McDill nodded sharply. "And once we're inside?"

Major Smith highlighted new markers on the hologram. "The bridge is located forward-center. One main door—heavy but manageable. Once inside, we reseal the entrance with thermite to block reinforcements from this hall."

Patrick leaned over the display, studying the layout of the corridor. "Lucky break—only one main access to the bridge. No complicated hallways."

Lieutenant McDill, arms folded, listened closely. "My Marines go in first," he said, glancing at Patrick. "You and your people follow."

"Roger," Patrick replied. "Nick and I are there to observe and provide assistance in any way."

Major Smith nodded thoughtfully. "We can afford to be redundant. We can't know for certain what we will face. Priority one: secure the command center. Priority two: access their mainframe and pull all mission logs. No sightseeing, no souvenir hunting, and no mistakes."

Lieutenant McDill nodded sharply. "Understood, sir. No distractions. We get in, secure the bridge, and pull the data."

Patrick's expression hardened. "We know what's at stake. We'll get it done clean."

Colonel Duffy straightened. "Based on Major Smith's analysis, you'll have fifteen minutes tops before they regroup. We can't risk casualties. Follow your orders. Speed and precision are key."

Patrick smiled. He had often heard his father discuss minimizing casualties. "The colonel drilled it into me early. 'Trust the team. Doubt gets people killed.'"

A new voice joined the discussion. "You'll need more than muscle," Kael said, stepping forward. "The Malzons encrypt their command systems. I recommend bringing Tarel and Nira. They're the best we've got with Malzon tech."

Major Smith raised an eyebrow but quickly nodded. "Good call. No point taking the bridge if we can't get the intel."

Tim leaned in, voice low but steady. "Dad always said a clean op starts with a clear plan. Looks like we're on the right track. Get it done. And bring back something we can use."

"We have a good plan, son," said Major Smith. "The team you sent out will get the job done. Good luck, Lieutenant McDill."

Lieutenant McDill gave a crisp salute. "Affirmative. Fifteen Marines plus Tarel, Nira, Jim, Patrick, and Nick. We'll gear up immediately and meet in the landing bay."

The team turned, moving with purpose, their boots echoing down the corridor as final preparations began.

Chapter 27

SPACE MARINES BOARDING PARTY

3 p.m., Wednesday, April 28, 2083

Tim stood on the bridge, awaiting word from Lieutenant McDill that the strike team was ready. The officers focused on their controls, readying themselves to hear the command for Arcaayus to open fire.

"We are buttoned down in *Zara*. Waiting for your order to go," Lieutenant McDill said.

Tim looked around the bridge, recalling five years ago when he led a strike team into *Arcaayus* to disable its corrupted AI. Being part of the team was simpler than giving orders and waiting for results, so he had to trust the team he sent.

"*Zara* and *Endeavor*, as soon as you hear me give the command to Arcaayus, I want you to launch," Tim said, fidgeting with the intercom button. "Arcaayus, target the section of the *Skar'Tal* we discussed. When ready, fire."

"Yes, sir. Locking and firing," Arcaayus called out.

The ship's hull vibrated slightly as *Horizon's* forward cannon swiveled and locked onto a point beneath the *Skar'Tal's* bridge. A focused, blistering heat ray erupted from the emitter, a bright energy spear that lanced through the void and cut into the enemy vessel. Metal hissed and screamed as it melted away, forming a clean hole rimmed with glowing embers.

Simultaneously, *Zara and Endeavor* launched.

"Breach complete," Arcaayus reported. "Atmosphere venting from the enemy bridge. Life support systems are out. Recommend immediate deployment."

"Lieutenant, your team is up," said Tim. "Good luck. You know your mission. Download *Skar'Tal's* data logs and return safely."

Lieutenant McDill grinned grimly. "You heard him, Marines. Prep for zero-g conditions, expect residual hostiles, and protect the techs."

Zara and *Endeavor* carefully yet swiftly wove through the drifting debris toward the wounded Malzon ship. Inside, Space Marines in armored spacesuits gripped their blaster rifles tightly. No one knew what they would face within the alien ship. They understood they needed to react as ordered and without hesitation.

As *Zara* quickly maneuvered in front of the hull breach, her docking clamps magnetically bit into the *Skar'Tal's* ragged hull with a resounding metallic thud. Red lights bathed the airlock as fifteen Space Marines, led by Lieutenant McDill, braced for breach.

Patrick, Nick, and Jim stood behind them, rifles up and

ready, while Tarel and Nira crouched behind, their compact data kits slung tightly to their backs.

"Breach in three...two...one...," McDill barked.

When *Zara* opened the main hatch door, the Marines surged forward through the open hull into the dimly lit alien bridge.

Lieutenant McDill was in first. The *Skar'Tal* bridge's interior seemed static. There was no movement. Crimson emergency lights flashed, yet there was no sign of life.

"Move. It looks empty. Stay alert. Quickly, secure the command center," McDill ordered, voice sharp over the comms.

The Marines stormed in—rifles sweeping, lasers dotting the cabin walls, searching for enemies. To their surprise, as McDill observed, the *Skar'Tal*'s command center appeared eerily still. Consoles sparked and flickered from earlier damage.

They saw the bodies of Malzon officers lying on the floor and slumped over their station consoles.

A second later, a solitary figure stood up: a short, burly Malzon commander, his face twisted in rage and defiance, clutching a short blade in one hand and a breathing mask in the other.

Lieutenant McDill approached the Malzon commander, who lunged at him wildly with his blade. With a swift move, McDill sidestepped the attack and shot the commander in the leg. The Malzon writhed in pain as McDill adjusted the setting on his weapon to stun and knocked him out cold.

"Commander secured," McDill called out, taking the blade from the Malzon's limp hand.

As he bound the Malzon with flex-cuffs, McDill barked, "Mountbatten, place that thermite by the bridge entry door."

Sergeant Laura Mountbatten and Private Renee Ochos taped the thermite at four places around the door and set the electric fuse to ignite it.

"Five seconds to detonation," Mountbatten said as she pressed the trigger. The intense heat melted the metal door shut.

"Tarel, Nira, you're up," McDill ordered. Patrick, Nick, and Jim followed as protection.

The two IT specialists darted forward, ripping open a primary access panel with a plasma cutter tool. Sparks flew as Nira jacked in a bypass jumper connector to her portable recorder display device. Within moments, Tarel was sifting through data logs, his eyes scanning fast-moving Malzon script.

Tim's voice came through the comms, taut and eager. "Look for logs—who ordered the attack, why they targeted *Gammamedus*, and what they know about Earth and VaRax."

"We've got something," Tarel said, voice tight with excitement. "Flight records, transmission logs, partial wormhole data...and—" He tapped rapidly. "—orders from Malzon High Command."

"Copy everything. Fast," McDill urged. "We don't know how long this ship will stay stable."

As the Marines tightened their perimeter, the Malzon commander woke up and snarled something guttural. McDill leaned closer to the translation unit clipped to his armor.

"What did he say?" asked Patrick.

"I have no idea. We'll ask him to repeat it when we get him locked away in the brig," Lieutenant McDill said.

Tarel heard the Malzon. "He said... 'You can't stop us. The fleet will destroy all of you.'"

McDill's jaw tightened. "He said that, did he?"

He turned to his team. "Mission successful. Let's get off this wreck. Take the prisoner."

As the boarding party returned to *Zara* and began the short trip to *Horizon*, the Skar'Tal's systems started to fail catastrophically. Sections of the ship began to break apart. It appeared the Malzon commander had initiated a self-destruct sequence.

Tim stood over Peggy's console on the *Horizon's* bridge while the ship's AI decrypted the Malzon data.

His eyes narrowed as the last report before the Malzon attempted their ill-fated attack on *Horizon* scrolled onto the screen:

Strategic Elimination Orders Confirmed. Malzon High Command deems VaRaxians and their allies a critical threat to the Empire. Attack on sight. Prepare for full-scale war. Report when engaged.

Tim's fist clenched at his side. "They're coming," he muttered darkly. "And we don't have the power to stop them."

Chapter 28

ZARA RETURNS TO EARTH

4 p.m., Wednesday, April 28, 2083

The bridge on the *Horizon* was tense. Officers stood at their stations, silent but alert, eyes flicking between glowing readouts and the central viewscreen. No one spoke.

Maya's voice cut through the quiet. "Admiral, the Malzon fleet—five ships—is now two hours out."

Admiral Tim Smith stood at the command console, scanning the officers' faces. Before he could speak, Kael stepped forward, his expression grave.

"Tim," Kael said, voice low, "there's something you need to consider. The Malzon could have boarded the *Gammamedus* for a reason. It's possible they accessed its databanks. If they did, they could already know that my people on Celias-3 planned to use the wormhole to jump to Earth."

Tim nodded. "And, if they did, Earth could be their next target." It was the same thought he'd had during the vision of the open wormhole and the disabled ship near the ice planet.

Where was the translation from the Malzon ship's database? He needed more information about the enemy's intentions. He pressed the intercom button. "Tarel, have you analyzed the Malzon recording yet?"

"We are halfway through," Tarel said. "I can tell you this. The Malzon know the coordinates of Earth and all of our colonies. It also appears they know the *Gammamedus* planned to use the wormhole to jump to Earth. They planned to use it once they gathered their invasion fleet."

Standing next to their mother, Ethan and Lila listened to the conversation from the observation area of the bridge.

The Malzons know, but it's not just the Malzons anymore, Ethan murmured telepathically to Lila.

Lila tilted her head. *The door has been opened. And what's coming through isn't meant for this galaxy.*

Peggy crouched down, gripping their shoulders, feeling that her children knew something. "What are you seeing?" she asked urgently. "Tell your father."

Ethan spoke in a whisper. "Mama, the Malzons think they're making decisions. But something darker is behind them, following them. Something their dim minds don't even see."

Lila closed her eyes, her hand tightening around her brother's. *Papa, you must move fast. Save the VaRaxians and go to Earth before the real war begins.*

Tim heard their thoughts from across the bridge. A chill ran down his spine. He saw it too. There was an ancient enemy, an unseen force he felt creeping toward them through the Malzon.

Tim sat at the head of the long, glass-topped conference room table, surrounded by his closest friends and crewmembers: Peggy, George and Veyra, Stephen and Julie, Kael, Major Andrews and Maya, Captain Bouchard and Dr. Tanya Ivanova Bouchard, Jeff and Amy, Patrick, Tom and Mary, Nick and Nancy, Dr. Thomas Kropt and Kiki, Con, Big Nik, and Father Huey.

In the space school, Liora, Corli, and Carlyn cared for the children. Tim didn't want them to hear the dire news.

Sheriff Jim, Steve, and Sophie, veterans of the old bioshelter days, sat down with the rest to discuss the next move. The other VaRaxians—Dr. Rykan, Alora, Sian, Nira, Tarel, and Joran—also took their seats.

Tim scanned their faces. They were tight with worry, waiting for his decision.

"You have all done well. We have rescued over 900 VaRaxian settlers, fought off the Malzon attack, and successfully boarded and downloaded the Malzon warship's database," Tim said in a calm voice.

"We should be celebrating these victories, but we have more to do before we return to Earth," he added, his voice becoming strained.

Murmurs erupted through the room. Before anyone could speak, Tim continued.

"By getting through the wormhole and defeating the Malzon warship, we prevented a sneak attack on Earth," Tim began.

The crew stopped murmuring and stared at Tim, waiting for a further explanation.

"Tarel translated the Malzons' message. We know the

Malzons aren't only chasing VaRaxians. They see humanity as part of an alliance and a threat. Before we stopped them, they were planning to use the wormhole to jump to Earth."

The room quieted.

"I have decided on our next move, but I want to listen to your thoughts."

Jim spoke up first, his deep voice steady. "We need to get home, Tim. Fast. People must know what's coming."

"Sophie and I agree," Steve said. "Earth's defenses might not be ready for something like this."

Tim nodded. "We'll send *Zara* back through the wormhole immediately. She'll carry a full video report from me and our top officers to President Eisenhower. We'll warn them to prepare a planetary defense and reinforce the Mars and Moon bases."

Murmurs of approval ran around the table.

But Jim wasn't done. He stood up and cleared his throat. "Admiral, I want to go back with *Zara*, and I believe Steve and Sophie want to come with me. We must make ourselves available to the president, Congress, the United Nations, newspapers and television stations, and the people of Earth."

Tim also expected this response, adding quickly. "Unfortunately, *Zara* does not have wormhole protection pods. I can't allow anyone to take this risk. Besides, *Zara* must speed back to Mars and Earth at 10%, possibly 15% light speed. That's an extreme g-force acceleration, far too much for living beings such as ourselves."

Jim pressed. "I don't care. I want to go home and help defend Earth."

This time, Nira spoke up. "No, Jim, I need you here with me."

Surprised, Jim hesitated. "Nira, I didn't know…"

Nira turned her head, embarrassed by her outburst.

Tim noticed Kael's approving reaction and smiled. The moment eased the tension in the room. It also confirmed something Dr. Bo Taber, Con, and John Logan had discussed. Humans and VaRaxians shared many similarities. Now they were exchanging cultures and languages. The next logical step was to share emotional tendencies. Psychologists called this the chameleon effect, but to Nira, it was love.

"Well, you two should discuss this later, but I am sorry, Jim, I've made the decision. We will send *Zara*," Tim said. "As for us, we're going to jump directly to VaRax as soon as we test the wormhole generator."

Jim sat down, visibly disappointed, but he hadn't considered the wormhole protection pods. He glanced at Nira, who smiled self-consciously. He needed to talk with her after the meeting.

Over the next several minutes, discussions arose on several fronts. Should *Horizon* speed back to Earth instead? Should it reinforce its formidable shields? What were the risks of encountering the Malzon fleet? And did the ship have sufficient fuel and supplies to continue the mission?

Despite the rush of conversation, Tim remained silent, his gaze steady, as he listened to the hopes, fears, and strategies of those who trusted him to lead them through what was to come.

As the discussions grew louder, a strange stillness began to creep over him. The voices around him began to blur like distant echoes swallowed by a sudden, illuminating calm.

Suddenly, a sharp flash of light seared across his vision, instantly blotting out the room. He froze, his body rigid, gripped by something vast and unseen—something reaching for him across space and memory, dragging him into a flood of images.

It happened quickly: wave upon wave flooded his mind. The Malzon attack wasn't random. It had been cold, calculated. The Malzon viewed the VaRaxian colony on Celias-3 as a direct threat to their Empire. The single Malzon ship that destroyed *Gammamedus* had escaped with critical data, but there was more to the plan.

Tim's earlier feelings about an ancient threat resurfaced. He saw again that there was another power behind the Malzon Empire, guiding it from outside the Milky Way. Ethan and Lila sensed it. The Malzons now had VaRaxian colony targets, including Earth and even VaRax. Tim envisioned a possible future where the Malzons would attack *Horizon*, VaRax, the VaRaxian colonies, and Earth.

Just as quickly as they appeared, the images faded, leaving Tim breathless and his heart pounding. He hadn't taken Waybegonease in a while. Given the threats, he needed another booster shot, since he sensed he would have more unexpected visions.

Peggy noticed what was going on, and so did Ethan and Lila.

Papa saw them, Ethan said telepathically.

It's about time, Lila agreed.

Tim pushed back in his chair and stood abruptly. Everyone stopped talking. "We're out of time," he thundered, his voice cold as steel. "We must jump to VaRax before the Malzons."

Jim stood up again, facing Tim aggressively. "What about Earth? Are you forgetting about our home? If *Zara* can't take us, we all should leave on *Horizon* to protect Earth. That should be our priority."

"I haven't forgotten about Earth," Tim said calmly,

motioning for Jim to sit down. "There is danger, but there are alien threats out here, and we must make contact with them, face them, before they reach Earth."

"You mean the Malzons?" asked Jim in a lower voice as he sat down. "*Horizon* can't possibly defeat a fleet of Malzon warships. One was dangerous enough, and Arcaayus surprised them. What makes us think they'll make the same mistakes again?"

Everyone grew silent as tension filled the room. Tim didn't want to argue with Jim, but his pause sparked anxious murmurs and debate—some argued to return to Earth immediately, while others believed Tim should make the decision.

After a few moments, Tim stood and said firmly, "We must go, help the VaRaxians, investigate new threats, and meet possible allies."

When Sophie asked if he'd had another vision, he nodded slightly. "A partial one," he said. "But I know this: we will not abandon those in need. The Malzon threat to Earth is delayed, but our mission now leads us to VaRax."

The room hushed at Tim's insistence.

"Thank you. These are my orders. We will send *Zara* and closely monitor the Malzon fleet with our long-range scanners. George, I want you, Peggy, Kael, and Nira to work on boosting those scanners to maximum capacity."

"I want to know if the Malzons follow us to VaRax. I sense they hunger for revenge, and if they attack, we will be ready," Tim said. "Kael said he doesn't believe the Malzons have a wormhole generator, but I want to make sure."

Tim looked at Kael, who shook his head in response. "We just perfected ours and are ahead of any other civilization we know of."

"We will monitor for one, and if we detect the technology, we will change our plans immediately," Tim said.

"I also want Tarel to interrogate the captured Malzon commander," Tim said. "Tarel, bring Joran with you. Find out what the Malzon knows, what they learned from the VaRaxians, and anything about help they may be receiving."

"I will do my best," Tarel said. "It's been my experience battling the Malzons that they simply exist to fight. They have only two thoughts: kill or argue. We never could have rational discussions with them."

"Let me know if he says anything useful," Tim said. "Anything else?"

Father Huey raised his hand.

"Yes, Father?" Tim asked.

"Before everyone goes to their stations, I would like to pray for our success," Huey said.

"Of course," Tim said. "Go ahead."

Huey bowed his head. "Heavenly Father, we ask that you bless and guide us in ways that preserve us and limit the lives we may take and lose. Bless *Endeavor* and *Horizon* and all who sail within her. Let *Zara's* mission be successful and protect our home world from all those who seek to destroy it." He made the sign of the cross and said, "Amen."

"Thank you, Father," Tim said. "After the meeting, Peggy, Maya, and Leonard, I want to meet in the entertainment room. We need to record a warning to Earth that *Zara* can deliver about the Malzons' plans."

Next, Tim turned to Major Andrews. "Prep *Zara* for immediate launch. Once we've recorded the messages to Ike 4, send *Zara* home."

"Yes, Admiral," Andrews replied with crisp precision,

already tapping into his wristcomm. "I'll have engineering and launch bay teams on standby."

"All right, team, let's head to our stations. Meeting adjourned. Dismissed."

The crew quietly exited the staff conference room, everyone aware of the dangers that lay ahead over the next few days.

Within minutes, *Horizon*'s lower launch deck came alive with activity. The lights dimmed to operational red, and warning strobes pulsed along the catwalks as the hangar bay's heavy airlock doors began their slow, grinding separation.

Nira and Nick inspected *Zara* for structural integrity. The mechs fueled her engines.

Steve, Jeff, and Amy uploaded new navigational charts and defensive subroutines, syncing *Zara*'s onboard transmitter with the *Horizon*'s relay. This ensured she could transmit encrypted data to Earth once she crossed the wormhole, even under hostile conditions.

Peggy recalibrated her shielding to handle gravitational turbulence near the wormhole's mouth. George ran diagnostics on all the changes within *Zara*, each indicator blinking green.

Meanwhile, Tim led Maya, Peggy, and Captain Bouchard to the entertainment room to make their recordings.

Tim began by having each officer take turns relaying their part of the message to President Ike 4. They described what happened after exiting the wormhole, the Malzon threat, the intelligence gathered, and their fear that Earth could be next.

Once the recordings were complete, Jeff received the encrypted data packets and loaded them onto *Zara's* secure database.

As the final checks were completed and *Zara*'s engines began their warm-up cycle, Tim arrived at the launch deck and placed a hand on the hull beneath her registry.

"Good luck, girl," he said quietly. "You're carrying the fate of Earth on your wings."

Tim clicked on his wristcomm. "Major, she's ready to launch. Once she's clear, close the wormhole behind her."

"Aye, aye, sir," Andrews said. "*Zara*, prepare to launch. Good luck."

Zara responded, "Affirmative, Major. I'm green to go. I will wait for the launch command."

Tim and the other officers left the launch deck, and the pressurized bulkhead hatch door closed, sealing the ship. Moments later, the bay doors opened to the silent void beyond.

"You are clear, *Zara*, for launch," said Andrews. "Happy trails."

"Affirmative." *Zara* rose gently in the launch bay, her ion thrusters propelling her into space toward the mouth of the wormhole, still shimmering in the distance. In a sudden flash of light, she shot forward into the rift between stars.

Chapter 29

WORMHOLE CLOSES, SHADOW OPENS

4:30 p.m., Wednesday, April 28, 2083

Kael worked with Peggy to remotely connect *Horizon's* wormhole generator control to *Gammamedus*. He nodded to Major Andrews, who started the wormhole closure sequence, noting the ship's reactors were down to 2% power.

"Let's hope this works," said Peggy, looking at the bridge's viewing screen along with the other officers.

A second later, the shimmering wormhole portal snapped shut with a flash of pale blue light. No Malzon would travel through this portal to reach Earth.

A sigh of relief swept through the bridge.

When Tim returned from the launch bay, he found his crew busy at work. An air of cheerfulness filled the room. The wormhole to the Solar System and Earth, which had been open for over a week, was now closed.

"You all have done well," Tim said as he scanned the room. "Has the database and the wormhole generator on the *Gammamedus* been destroyed?"

"Yes, Admiral," said Kael, looking up from his console. "Thank you for leaving our ship intact as a memorial to our fallen people."

"You're welcome. You made a good case. The ship and its technology cannot be used against your people or anyone else," said Tim. "We have closed the wormhole, and I don't want anyone else learning about Earth."

Humanity's home was safe for now. Tim sat in his command chair, relieved in one way, but as he considered the challenges of the next two days, he gripped the console tightly, feeling the weight of the moment settle on his shoulders.

The fate of two worlds now depended on his next move. He felt confident in his actions, but his understanding of the unidentified entity controlling the Malzons remained unclear. He needed more information. After jumping to VaRax, he'd talk with Stephen, Peggy, Ethan, and Lila. It was time for another shared vision. Then, he would personally interview the Malzon commander and use his powers to gather more information.

Ethan stared out the observation window, his small hands curling into fists. *They think they're hunting us. But they're not*

the hunters. Papa knows.

Lila pressed close to him, her face pale, her eyes distant as if looking far beyond the ship.

Something's riding their anger. I don't see it completely, but Papa sees and knows. Something old. It's steering them...and they don't even realize it.

Peggy dropped to her knees beside them, alarmed. "What do you mean?" she asked. "What's steering them?"

Ethan didn't look at her.

A shadow that never died. It found the Malzons. It's using them to break the door open wider.

Lila clutched his hand tightly.

If we don't close it, Earth won't just fall—everything in our galaxy will.

Chapter 30

DESTINATION, VARAX

5 p.m., Wednesday, April 28, 2083

Tim stood at the center of the command bridge, ready to give orders he knew could put his crew and Earth in danger. Still, he trusted his intuition, his visions, and his understanding of the risks of staying or leaving for Earth.

"Kael. Nira. George. Leonard. Peggy," he said evenly. They looked up from their consoles, their eyes steely. "Test the wormhole generator."

The officers moved quickly. They had practiced the procedure and knew it well.

Kael opened the VaRaxian diagnostic panel and softly muttered in his native language. He still had many doubts about whether they would survive the wormhole trip, but the more he thought about what Tim said regarding his daughter being alive, the less apprehensive he felt about trying. Besides, he didn't like the chances of fighting five Malzon warships.

Nira tapped the control panel on the wormhole power generator, warming up the unit as she prepared for Tim's order to initiate the test. George calibrated the power distribution matrix from *Horizon's* hybrid fusion matter-antimatter reactor core.

Peggy watched her monitors closely to detect the distribution of kinetic gamma ray particles in the reactor core. Creating a wormhole required directing power from the engines to the VaRaxian generator, and the energy release would be immediate and substantial.

Leonard patiently awaited orders to establish a course for VaRax, which he would program into the navsystem for Arcaayus to activate when the time came.

The generator hummed. A low-frequency resonance began to vibrate in the *Horizon's* engine room, signaling the activation of the VaRaxian-designed system.

"A few biological tolerance calibrations are necessary," Peggy explained, adjusting the dark matter shielding for the wormhole pods to compensate for human and VaRaxian neurology. "The radiation levels should now remain within the safe envelope."

"We don't have much first-hand knowledge about dark matter, but the data from when *Horizon* went through the first time with Kael and his people will be helpful," George added. "But this should hold."

Kael studied the results in silence. When he finally spoke, his voice was full of remorse.

"We've used this twice—once to reach your Solar System, which led to disaster for my people and Earth's, and the second time to reach Celias-3. One successful jump does not guarantee another."

Tim held up his hand. "Kael, you didn't know the first time what we know now. This will work, and you will see your daughter. Trust me, my friend. You've seen the data; what does it say to you now?"

Kael exhaled. "We've run three simulations, two test pulses. Stability is within 3.7% of expected tolerances. It's acceptable."

Tim nodded. "Leonard needs to know how close we can safely exit near VaRax."

Kael opened his wide mouth and shook his head. "The gravitational influences are stronger than in the Kuiper Belt or in the space past Saturn. For this jump, we'll need to appear on the far side of Tau Cei."

"How many miles past VaRax?" Peggy asked.

"Because VaRax is smaller than Saturn and located in the inner Sol System, I'd say ten million miles, just beyond the outer planetary gravity ring. Captain Bouchard will need to plot it precisely."

"That's about two hours away at half a percent light," Peggy calculated aloud.

"Let's go 15 million miles to be safe," Tim said, glancing at Kael.

After a pause, Kael gave a rare nod of satisfaction. "Yes, but we know wormholes can attract dark matter. We still don't understand why. I've examined our preparations, every subsystem, and the dark matter protection in the pods that Peggy, George, and I designed. It should work properly, but there are still too many variables."

Tim smiled faintly. "It will work." He turned to his crew. "Team, I am satisfied. We will go through our final checks, give instructions to Arcaayus, and settle down in our wormhole pods."

With their plan confirmed, their mission remained clear.

VaRax awaited.

Sitting in his command chair on the bridge, Tim sensed danger ahead but couldn't tell if it was the wormhole or what lay beyond.

Ethan and Lila heard his doubts.

Father, Ethan telepathically said, *you've done everything you can.*

Lila added, *Don't worry; go forward.*

Tim pressed the intercom button on his armrest.

"Crew. We will be engaging the wormhole generator. You may view it on your screens before I give everyone the order to enter your wormhole pods. Good luck to us all."

"Prepare the wormhole generator," Tim ordered.

The lights on the bridge dimmed as immense power rerouted from the core to the wormhole generator. The VaRaxian technology embedded in the *Horizon's* frame responded with a deep, resonant pulse, like a heartbeat amplified through space.

Before them, through the main viewscreen, the blackness began to ripple.

A hush swept over the bridge.

Outside, reality twisted, folding inward until a void tore open, revealing a swirling vortex of violet, indigo, and blue-green cosmic energy. It glowed like a wound, beautiful yet terrifying, a celestial river that folded time and space, leading into what they hoped was the Tau Cei star system.

The crew stood frozen in reverence. Even seasoned officers like Captain Bouchard and Mayor Andrews stared in wonder and amazement.

"Father Huey, you've brought us luck so far," Tim said. "We need a great prayer."

Huey nodded. "We are in your debt, Heavenly Father. Keep us safe as we travel through the universe you created. Guide our minds with wisdom, our hands with courage, and our hearts with compassion, even when darkness surrounds us. As we pass through the veil between worlds, let light follow us," the priest said, giving the sign of the cross. "Amen."

Tim waited a respectful moment, then gave the following command. "Arcaayus, initiate the jump five minutes after we are in our pods and the safety check is performed."

The AI's voice was calm. "Acknowledged. Program accepted."

Tim pressed the intercom once more. "Crew, proceed to the wormhole hibernation room. Children, don't be afraid. It will be a short nap. We will be done in no time."

Officers on the bridge waited for Tim. He stood up from his chair, smiling.

"I don't have to tell you what this means. We have done everything possible for a successful jump. Go now and enter your pods. I will be there shortly," he said.

Everyone filed out except Peggy. "I'm walking with you. Before entering my pod, I want to see that Ethan and Lila are safe."

"They are probably worrying about us as well. Let's check on them and then get settled ourselves," Tim said, stopping and looking deeply into her baby blue eyes. "Peg, have I told you how much I love you?"

"Not enough today," Peggy said.

"We will have time to catch up when we awaken," Tim said as they continued their fast-paced walk down the hall to the wormhole pod room.

"It's been so tense lately, Tim," said Peggy, holding his arm. "We haven't had much time for ourselves and our kids."

"It's true, but don't think too much about that. What we accomplish over the next week will ensure the survival of Earth, our VaRaxian friends, and many other civilizations on this side of the Milky Way," Tim said.

"Oh, Tim, there you go again. Hinting about unseen things. You need to confide in me about what you and the children are sensing. I know you three are talking among yourselves," Peggy said softly.

"We are, but what we sense isn't entirely clear yet. They are so in tune with this danger; it's amazing. I promise, we will have a family meeting once we find out what has happened at VaRax," Tim said as he led Peggy into the wormhole pod room.

"I'm with you. Let's check on our kids," Peggy said.

As before, one by one, the crew and children entered their protective wormhole pods—cylindrical cradles designed to shield them from temporal distortions, radiation, and dark matter bursts. Each pod sealed itself with a smooth hiss and a quiet click, as the internal systems engaged like the closing of a vault.

After checking on Ethan and Lila, Peggy entered her pod. Tim paused next to her, watching as she smiled and peacefully fell asleep.

Then he turned to Kael's pod and briefly placed his hand

on the outer shell. He quietly promised to find Lyara and rescue as many VaRaxians as he could.

"Status?" he asked softly into his wristcomm.

"All pods secure except yours," Arcaayus replied.

Tim took a final look at the over 1,000 secured pods in the huge hibernation room. He inhaled, then slid into his own, and the lid closed.

Just before the sedative vapor put him to sleep, another psychic vision flashed before him. Had they protected Arcaayus enough? What if a dark matter surge damaged him again? They depended so much on this AI computer.

He knew Kael anticipated the danger. He'd collaborated with Peggy and Nira to program *Horizon's* backup AI to activate if Arcaayus failed his post-wormhole safety check. However, something else still felt wrong.

Too late. A second later, Tim fell into a deep, dark sleep. Silence followed.

Arcaayus took control.

Horizon surged forward into the wormhole.

Space peeled apart in cascading ribbons of color: gold, sapphire, and crimson spirals folding into fractal geometry. The laws of physics unraveled into speculation. The stars warped into elongated blurs, galaxies spiraled upside down, and time bent into incomprehensible loops.

To anyone awake, the scene would have been both breathtaking and maddening.

But only one was conscious.

Arcaayus kept the ship steady, navigating through the shimmering throat of space with computational precision. Through gravity storms and dark matter tides, the *Horizon* pressed forward.

Two days earlier, VaRax

The stars above VaRax shimmered as two Ruirulan scout ships entered orbit. They were sent to the planet by the warship Valkis, which was dispatched to VaRax to investigate long-range spectroscopy measurements that indicated the planet was nearing its end.

Upon arriving, they discovered a weakened world abandoned by most of its defenders. The Ruirulans anticipated silence. Instead, the planet's dormant automated defenses activated.

Missiles streaked from hidden silos, targeting the intruders with brutal efficiency. The scout ships were reduced to fragments in seconds.

The Ruirulans retaliated swiftly with a withering barrage of plasma torpedoes and pulse cannons that destroyed several cities. Of the 100,000 VaRaxians who had remained behind, only 10,000 survived the onslaught, including some who had hidden deep in a government VIP bunker.

Once it was over, the Ruirulans sent their last remaining scout ship to VaRax to look for survivors. They found the government bunker and captured nearly three dozen VaRaxians, among them Kael's only daughter, Lyara.

Zara Arrives

Forty million miles beyond Saturn, a wormhole shimmered like a tear in the fabric of space, a vortex of swirling blue and violet cosmic energy.

Then, with a silent burst of light, *Zara* emerged from the wormhole. A few minutes later, it closed upon itself and vanished.

Inside, *Zara's* automated systems rebooted from the protective dark shielding transit mode. Lights flickered green, and the ship's sensors recalibrated to local space.

Within moments, *Zara* locked onto Earth's secure emergency frequency. The first data burst fired toward Earth's lunar comm relay, encrypted and prioritized under presidential authorization, was unambiguous.

To: Earth Command—President Eisenhower IV
From: Horizon—Admiral Timothy Smith

"This is Admiral Smith aboard the *Horizon*." Tim's recorded voice was steady yet grave. "We have just exited the wormhole near Celias-3. The *Gammamedus*, a VaRaxian colony ship that created the wormhole outside Saturn, has been destroyed by a Malzon warship. We believe the Malzons, an aggressive alien race, accessed *Gammamedus's* critical navigation data, including the location of Earth."

The message included footage from *Horizon's* logs of the attack, data on Celias-3, scans revealing the planet's damage from multiple meteor strikes, and why the wormhole was created.

Tim's final words were brief but chilling.

"A ten-ship Malzon fleet has been detected heading to the wormhole entrance, which we have closed. Earth is likely to be their target if they have wormhole technology. We don't believe they do. However, prepare your defenses. *Zara* awaits your instructions. We will return soon."

Approximately 85 minutes later, Marsbase, Moonbase, and Earth received the message.

After sending the transmission, *Zara* accelerated at 10% light speed to Saturn, awaiting confirmation. Back on Earth, deep beneath the new White House in Philadelphia, red lights began to flash.

Standing before a semicircle of top military commanders, planetary defense analysts, and AI advisors, Ike 4 issued orders with precise calm.

"Activate Earth's orbital defense grid. Bring Moonbase and Marsbase to full alert. Tell Earth Defense Chief General Washington I want particle beam howitzers armed and mobile within the hour."

An aide stepped forward, eyes wide. "Sir, should we alert the U.N.?"

Ike nodded. "Yes. Contact Secretary-General Leila Rodriguez. Convene the United Nations Emergency Security Council. Tell them this isn't a drill."

He turned to Dick Button, his congressional advisor. "And call the congressional joint Homeland Security committee into emergency session. I want them briefed. They need to see this data. Top secret. No leaks. They need to know what could be coming."

He stepped away from the war table and addressed the room. "Begin drafting a public announcement to be used only when we are sure there is a threat. We won't start a global panic, but the world deserves a measurable, clear, truthful warning. If this turns out to be real, they need time to prepare."

He turned back to the comm station. "Patch me through to *Zara*."

A moment later, a communications officer with NASA's Space Agency opened a deep-space channel. "Speak when ready, Mr. President."

"*Zara,* this is Ike 4. You are ordered to Marsbase orbit immediately. Your brother *Koren* will brief you on the defense strategy. However, before you return, deploy wormhole detection satellites at the six positions marked on the encrypted star map we're sending. Confirm receipt."

While waiting for the response, *Zara* began placing long-range wormhole trackers in a staggered formation far outside Saturn's icy rings, near the coordinates the VaRaxian cruiser *Gammamedus* had planned to use. Earth would be warned if any threat reached the Solar System.

Ninety minutes later, with Saturn spinning silently in the distance, *Zara* responded: "Message received. Star map uploaded. Wormhole satellites are deploying now. I'm on my way, sir."

Ike closed his eyes for a moment. Then he turned to the room, his voice grim and steady.

"We knew eventually we would face the day when other species on other worlds might find Earth to their liking. The VaRaxians were just the first. We are far from alone in this galaxy—and we may not be ready with *Horizon* so far away."

Chapter 31

SHADOWS OVER VARAX

6 a.m., Thursday, April 29, 2083

The *Horizon* emerged from the wormhole like a magical apparition, its hull transitionally glinting with the negative energy reflected from the portal it left behind.

Fifteen million miles ahead lay VaRax—Kael's home world—illuminated by the golden glow of its expanding orange sun.

Tim felt excitement upon first seeing VaRax. After all, he was the NASA astrophysicist who had discovered the planet through a psychic vision five years earlier and confirmed its existence using spectroscopy.

His excitement was a markedly different emotion from the emptiness and sorrow felt by the 900 VaRaxians on board. They were returning home to a planet on the brink of oblivion, ruthlessly attacked due to a tragic computer error.

Tim understood that Kael, Liora, and the other VaRaxians were hurting. He felt their pain, but he also experienced his own emotions, mainly the many inspiring visions he'd had about VaRax.

In 24 hours, he would face the planet under very different circumstances than he had expected. Peggy, Leonard, Mark, and Maya shared similar thoughts due to their past work with Tim on the SETI program.

7 a.m., Sunday, April 30

As *Horizon* entered the planet's visual range, the fate and truth of VaRax were quickly revealed.

From orbit, they could see the scars left by the destruction that had rained upon the planet's once-vibrant surface. Great cities with majestic towers were now reduced to jagged rubble and black craters. Smoke, visible even from the exosphere, spiraled into the thin upper atmosphere like ghostly fingers reaching out desperately for help.

Kael stood still at the forward viewscreen, his eyes locked on the broken remains of his civilization. He already felt guilty for leaving so many fellow citizens behind, but now, with his daughter possibly harmed, he felt fear.

Maya Patel's voice shattered the silence. "I'm scanning... My God." Her tone, usually scientific and steady, quivered. "Two major urban centers are gone. The energy signatures match high-yield plasma warheads, nearly identical to the patterns we saw during *Arcaayus's* attack on Earth."

"Rhythish and Telos-Varn," Kael whispered harshly, his voice filled with what sounded like hatred. His fists were clenched at his sides, an unusual sight for a VaRaxian.

"Casualties?" Tim asked.

Maya shook her head slowly. "Hard to say. I'm picking up weak biosigns—under nine thousand—in two rural settlements outside the blast zones. The rest..."

She couldn't finish.

"We left nearly 100,000," Liora said, shocked to see her planet in ruins.

Tim turned to Captain Bouchard. "Prep the *Endeavor*. We start evacuating survivors immediately. Maya, Alora, Rykan— gear up. Kael, I want you with us. You know this planet better than any of us."

Kael slowly turned. His eyes burned with anger, grief, and resolve. "I'm coming."

By 8 a.m., *Endeavor* sliced through the dusty air over the desolate plains of VaRax, descending toward a cluster of modest dwellings, one of the two settlements Maya had identified. As they landed, the ramp hissed open, and the team stepped into a profound silence that felt unnatural. Patrick, Tom, Lieutenant McDill, and five Space Marines fanned out in a defensive formation, followed by Tim, Kael, Alora, and Dr. Rykan.

Smoke lingered from nearby fires, and the scent of scorched metal and ozone hung thick in the air. A gaunt, silver-skinned VaRaxian woman emerged behind a crumbling wall as they moved through the settlement. Others followed slowly— dozens at first, then hundreds—starved, frightened, yet still proud.

Kael stepped forward, his resonant voice trembling as he spoke his native language. "Please...I am President Kael. You know me. I have returned to help."

His eyes scanned the multitudes for a sign of understanding. "Fellow citizens, I have brought my new friends, the Earthlings. Tell me, what happened here?"

They all stood dumbfounded, as if they didn't understand.

Kael then made a request that only a parent could comprehend. "We will help everyone. But first, I need to know about my daughter...Lyara. Has anyone seen her?"

An elder VaRaxian, his robes torn and singed, slowly stepped forward.

"The Ruirulans came from orbit," he said in a rasping voice. "We thought they came to help. Then our missiles launched."

Alora frowned. "They were provoked."

"But they didn't stop when our protective shield fell. We had no military to protect us. Rhythish was wiped out in minutes," the elder said.

Another survivor, a younger woman clutching a child, added with disdain, "You have some nerve returning, Kael. I voted for you. I thought you would save us. You left us."

Kael turned away. "I am sorry. I did everything I could to persuade the council. Blame me, but what about my daughter? She stayed."

The young mother, still resolute in her anger, replied unsympathetically. "The government had a bunker in Rhythish for high-level personnel, including scientists, leaders...the 'chosen ones.' You know of this place, Kael. I heard your daughter—the child you abandoned—was among them."

Kael was taken aback by such directness. It was unlike a VaRaxian to be so critical.

"My dear, I am so sorry. I should be blamed for not pushing the council harder, but that is no excuse for what happened. But, please, we are here to rescue everyone. Help us. We had many such bunkers. Where is this place you speak of?" Kael asked urgently.

"Beneath the central obelisk," the elder said. "But we lost contact with everyone after the attack."

Kael looked at Tim for help.

Tim saw the destruction, the desperate people. He knew they had to move quickly to transport hundreds of people off the planet before the Malzons arrived.

Clicking on a universal translator, Tim stepped forward.

"Thank you, everyone. My name is Admiral Tim Smith of the starship *Horizon*. I am a human from the planet Earth. We sympathize with what has happened to your world. We will have time to talk and share common stories."

Tim noticed they were listening with curiosity. He knew he was the first Earthling they had ever encountered, although he suspected they knew Kael took the last VaRaxian ship to Earth.

"We will rescue you all, but please, be patient. We only have one shuttle. We will take 50 of you now and leave supplies. Rest assured, we will return and transport everyone safely."

The VaRaxians solemnly stared as *Endeavor* slowly lifted into the air and moved away.

Thirty minutes later, *Endeavor* found Sanctum Deep, the underground government bunker beneath the shattered ruins of Rhythish.

The city above was gone, nothing but twisted metal and melted stone. The obelisk was toppled and half-buried in rubble. With the help of the Space Marines, Tim's team found the entrance to the bunker. It was sealed but intact.

After Lieutenant McDill set a blast charge that opened the door, Kael quickly led them inside.

They went down a hall and a wide, tall stairway to a large room with doors leading elsewhere. There, they found signs of a struggle—blaster marks on the walls, broken furniture, and abandoned rations.

Dr. Rykan swept the area with his scanner. "They were here. I'm picking up DNA. Thirty life signs. No signs of death. Let me check; yes, Kael, I am getting a reading."

Kael interrupted, gripping the wall, his face pale. "Lyara... she was here."

"Yes, she was," Dr. Rykan softly said.

Alora moved beside him. "She may still be alive, Kael. Someone took them for a reason."

Over the next two days, *Endeavor* continuously traveled between the planet and *Horizon*, ferrying survivors, including elderly individuals, children, families, and the wounded.

The *Horizon* crew worked in shifts, their bodies aching and minds numb from exhaustion. But they didn't stop until the last 9,000 VaRaxians were brought aboard.

The rescued told stories of confusion and fear. "It wasn't a war," said one man in a military outfit. "It was murder. The Ruirulans came down in rage, not diplomacy or compassion."

At the end of the 50th hour, Captain Leonard Bouchard approached Tim on the command deck, data tablet in hand.

"Sir," Leonard said, breath tight. "Deep scan picked up something. A wormhole opened near Celias-3."

Tim's shoulders tensed. "Celias-3? A beginning must have an ending. Did one open in this system?"

Leonard scanned the Tau Cei system. He nodded grimly. "Yes. A second wormhole opened five million miles away." He compared the quantum signatures of the two events. "Same anomalous energy waves."

Tim nodded. "The Malzons have wormhole technology, just as I feared. Do we know what came through?"

"Not yet...but if it's the Malzons, and they travel at the same speed they did coming to Celias-3...they'll be at VaRax in less than six hours."

Tim looked out the viewport, where VaRax's burning horizon met the stars. "Thank you, Leonard. We'll be gone by then, but I have one more thing to do before we leave."

Chapter 32

VARAXIAN MEDICAL CARE

10 a.m., Sunday, May 2, 2083

As *Endeavor* could only shuttle 200 VaRaxians on each run from the surface, *Horizon*'s medical and social transition teams had time to carefully evaluate each male, female, and child.

They represented a cross-section of a culture in crisis: elders with hollow eyes, children too stunned to cry, parents clutching their families tightly. Some were angry, others grateful, but most wore the expressions of those who had witnessed destruction on their dying planet.

From the moment they disembarked from *Endeavor*, Earth and VaRaxian crew members treated them not as strangers but as honored survivors. In the converted landing bay, translators relayed greetings and instructions as Dr. Bo Taber, Con, Corli, Father Huey, and others in the social transition team welcomed the refugees aboard.

The trip to *Horizon* from the surface was short but long enough to offer the VaRaxians one crucial thing: hope. They were promised food, water, shelter, and care, a reprieve from terror and ash.

Colonel Duffy, Major Smith, Lieutenant McDill, and Sheriff Jim ran a tight security operation, ensuring the transition went smoothly. As the VaRaxians exited the shuttle, Earth personnel, including Patrick, Tom, John, Big Nik, and Nick, stood as calming presences. They reassured the nervous arrivals with quiet nods and open hands that they were safe now.

"Greetings, and welcome to you all!" exclaimed Dr. Bo through the translator. "You are safe onboard. We will be happy to answer any questions you may have. We aim to attend to your medical needs, collect your information, and settle you."

One VaRaxian family—a father, mother, and young son—paused, uncertain, as they faced a human, Bo, for the first time. The man held his child protectively, his eyes flicking to the unfamiliar uniforms and alien faces.

"Don't worry," Bo said gently. "We're Earthlings—humans—and we are friends of Kael, Liora, and the VaRaxians already here. Sit with Alora. She's your friend, just like I am."

The intake process was thorough. Basic records were made, and medical histories were documented. The refugees received nutritious synthetic food, including protein-rich vegetables, fruit blends packed with nutrients, and safe hydration drinks, all recommended by Dr. Rykan.

Healthy people were immediately taken to their assigned quarters. *Horizon* had been built to transport 10,000 in protective hibernation pods, but its current mission required improvisation.

"I don't think we have enough quarters for everyone," Dr. Ledbetter said as he reviewed the intake numbers.

"I'd better tell Tim," Paula replied, already halfway out the door.

"He already knows," Dr. Ledbetter said. "Once we max out the available quarters, Tim wants to double up rooms and use the halls until the mechs convert storage compartments into quarters."

"What about Kael? Shouldn't he be coordinating this?" Paula asked.

"He's resting," Dr. Ledbetter said, her voice softening. "The trip to VaRax broke something in him. He only went down to find his daughter...and faced nothing but ruin and criticism. I'll check on him when I can."

Nearly 9,000 VaRaxians had been brought aboard, joining the 900 rescued earlier from Celias-3. Of those 9,000, more than 2,000 needed immediate medical care. The burden was immense.

Kael, who had recovered sufficiently, stood beside Peggy and Dr. Rykan. "We need more space and more of our doctors and nurses to treat the wounded," the VaRaxian said.

"We are creating more space. We will take care of them, don't worry," Peggy told Kael gently. "Your people, they're alive. That's what matters."

Kael nodded solemnly. "Dr. Rykan and Nurse Alora can treat many, but not all," Kael said.

Tim walked up and heard the last part of the discussion.

"Have you been to your medbay? We've got volunteers," said Tim, consoling his VaRaxian friend. "Miracles are happening with your medical equipment. Four of our doctors and two nurses are helping your people."

"I will go visit the medbay soon. It's just...Tim, I can't thank you enough for what you and Peggy have done to bring me to my planet," Kael said, holding his head down. "I failed. I failed everyone."

Peggy thought she saw a tear fall from Kael's eye. She had rarely seen a VaRaxian show emotion. She remembered how happy Veyra was when George announced they were getting married and when Nira expressed her love for Jim.

"What is it, Kael?" Peggy asked softly. "Is it Lyara? Tim said he'd find her."

"She blamed me," Kael said, voice raw, "for leaving so many behind. And now the ones we saved—they blame me, too. I should be blamed. I followed the council's orders, but..."

Peggy placed a comforting hand on his arm. "Kael, we are here for you. We'll find her. We'll make this right. Tim has an idea."

The Prison Planet

It was time again.

Tim, Stephen, Ethan, and Lila were about to attempt another shared vision together—the second involving the twins.

After sharing the initial vision, Peggy felt more comfortable with the twins taking part in another one. She believed they could help gather information that might assist in rescuing

Lyara. Tim's explanation for involving the twins also made sense.

"Peg, before we jump to Earth, I need to know where Lyara's being held, what the Malzons are planning, and who's behind them. There's something else, too…I can feel a presence, an ally out there. Someone who might be able to help us."

Tim tapped his wristcomm as they left their quarters. "Dr. Ledbetter, prepare the medbay. We're ready for the Waybegonease."

When the family arrived, Stephen was already pacing the medbay nervously. Julie stood nearby, arms crossed, trying to appear calm but worried.

Ethan and Lila, on the other hand, were excited and appeared to be already locked into something. "They look like they've started without us," Tim said with a chuckle.

Dr. Ledbetter smiled. "You're not wrong."

Nurse Paula administered the adult doses to Tim and Stephen first, then turned to the twins. Dr. Ledbetter gave them a reassuring wink as Paula gently injected the smaller child-sized doses.

"They're already connected," he said, observing the readings. "Don't be surprised if they lead this one."

"You are right, Grandpa Led." Ethan winked back.

"I feel Lyara," Lila whispered suddenly, her voice calm but sure. "She's scared…but she's nice."

Kael's eyes widened. "You feel her?" The others exchanged glances. Tim smiled. "Let's follow their lead," he said.

The chamber dimmed as the compound took hold. The four sank into a deep, shared state. Colors and shapes swirled through their minds, forming visions that emerged through layers of space and thought.

Suddenly, clarity emerged.

They jointly saw Lyara. She was alive. Her eyes burned with determination. She and nearly three dozen VaRaxian leaders were imprisoned in a secure bunker on Shadow, deep beneath a towering mountain range.

Tim's consciousness shifted. They all followed him.

A second vision surged into view—darker, more disturbing. Stephen groaned aloud, overwhelmed, and dropped out of the connected vision. He collapsed backward and was caught by Paula, who called out for Julie. His vitals stabilized, but he remained unconscious.

Tim, Ethan, and Lila continued.

They saw the force motivating the Malzons: an ethereal, shapeless force, a presence from another distant galaxy. It writhed at the edges of perception, corrupting thoughts and hollowing minds. It wasn't just driving the Malzons; it was using them.

The Xalnyth, Ethan telepathically whispered.

Lila looked at Tim. *If we stop the Malzons, it might not be too late…but we must first stop them.*

Tim opened his eyes. He knew what had to be done. The twins nodded.

Briefing Room, 2 p.m., May 2

The senior officers assembled around the staff conference table, with Tim standing at the head.

"Thank you all," he said, "for helping to rescue the VaRaxians. Let's go around. Status reports. Engineering, George?"

"The power grid and engine are in good shape. Green to go. We've recharged the fusion antimatter pods."

"The wormhole generator has been checked out and is good to go," Peggy said.

"What about our VaRaxian passengers? How are they faring?" Tim asked.

"They are stable enough to enter the wormhole protection pods," Dr. Ledbetter said.

Dr. Rykan smiled. "It could be beneficial for their recovery to go into stasis."

Nick Dragoon looked around and saw that everyone was waiting for his report. "I've checked with all decks, and we are secure. Green to go."

"Anything else?" Tim asked.

"I'm ready to go," said Major Andrews. "I just need to know where."

Everyone assumed the next jump would take them home.

"I've laid in a course for Earth," Captain Bouchard said.

Tim shook his head.

"We're not heading to Earth. Not yet," he said. "We're going to Shadow. Lyara and thirty others are alive and being held there. We're going to rescue them."

Except for Peggy, Stephen, Paula, Kael and Liora, and the doctors, murmurs of surprise spread around the table.

"Tim," Jim said firmly, "we've done our duty. We've rescued those we could. We've seen the danger. We need to get back and warn Earth."

"I understand your concern," Tim replied. "But we have a larger worry, just as I expected when we came here. I saw it...and so did Ethan and Lila."

"There is a larger concern than protecting Earth?" Jim said incredulously.

Sitting on Peggy's lap, the twins climbed on the table and

stood up, displaying their full two-foot, four-inch heights.

"They're being controlled," Lila said in a light but firm voice. "The Malzons...something is guiding them from far away. It's not just about VaRax anymore. This threat is coming for Earth."

The officers and crew were somewhat surprised by Lila. While they knew her unique psychic powers and her extreme maturity for a two-year-old, she hadn't been vocal in public before.

"Lila, you're saying this isn't just a rescue?" George asked. She shook her head. Tim smiled.

"Very good, Lila," Tim said, motioning for her to sit down. "It's a turning point. If we save Lyara and the others with them—if we understand what's happening on Shadow—we may stop what's coming."

The room fell silent.

"What Ethan and Lila saw," Tim said, his voice low and resolute, "is what I saw as well."

Outside the viewports, the stars waited—unblinking, eternal. Somewhere beyond them, something vast and terrible stirred. Yet, there was also hope.

After the meeting, Tim and Peggy walked to the brig with Ethan, Lila, Tarel, and Nira, where the Malzon commander was being held.

"Tarel, ask him again who has given them technology and orders," Tim said, peering through the thick titanium bars.

Tarel nodded. "Thar'kuz ven'taar mek'ta gro'nath or'dul?"

The commander stood up and barked back. "Gra'tel mak

vor'dan...ka'nur vek'tal!"

Tarel shook his head. "He says he knows nothing, and even if he did, he would not tell the enemy."

Tim stared directly at the Malzon commander. He focused his thoughts into the Malzon's consciousness to squeeze out any information on the Xalnyth.

Who are these aliens who are controlling you? What do they want in our galaxy? What do they want from Earth? Why are you helping them?

At Tim's probing thoughts, the Malzon commander's eyes froze. He blankly stared at Tim. Suddenly, the Malzon dropped to the floor. His breathing slowed, then stopped.

Peggy gasped. "What happened?"

Tarel took out his health scanner, pointed it at the prone Malzon, and shook his head. "He's dead. I don't understand it. I'd have to perform an autopsy to give you an answer as to why."

Tim nodded. "Not needed. I have my answers."

Ethan and Lila looked at their father. They also understood the Malzon commander's responses except for what his final thought, "can't block," meant. They looked at each other, their faces filled with sadness.

Chapter 33

PLANET OF SHADOWS

4 p.m., Sunday, May 2, 2083

As the *Horizon* prepared for its next wormhole jump, the crew stood at the observation deck, watching VaRax shrink into the void, a ghost of a once-magnificent world now cloaked in ash and silence.

Its gleaming cities lay in ruin. Its people, rescued but mourning, filled the ship's corridors and sleep quarters with quiet grief. Everyone knew it would be their last time seeing their home world.

But there was no time to linger.

Maya's scans showed five Malzon warships accelerating toward VaRax. They would arrive in under two hours at their current velocity, far too soon and far too many for *Horizon* to engage.

Besides, Tim had a plan. He stood on the command bridge with arms crossed, eyes narrowed, then turned sharply to his senior military officers.

"Colonel Duffy. Major Smith. Lieutenant McDill. I need a strike plan to rescue Lyara and the others."

The rescue mission was triggered by a vision Tim had experienced only hours before. In it, he had seen Lyara and thirty other VaRaxian captives held inside a subterranean prison beneath a jagged mountain range on a remote world cloaked in darkness.

He relayed the name of the planet to Kael.

When Tim finished describing what he had seen, Kael's expression turned solemn. "I know where this planet is. I don't know the mountain range or the prison bunker."

Tim nodded. "Good. That's a start. We're going."

Kael quickly turned to Navigator Bouchard. "You'll want coordinates for the wormhole exit vector. Plot it so we emerge ten million miles from orbit. This should be safe enough to avoid the dark matter forces that could be attracted if we are too close to Shadow's outer planetary gravity ring."

"This will be the farthest planet we have ever plotted a wormhole jump to," Kael added quietly. "It lies fifty light-years from here."

"What's the worst part?" Major Andrews asked, sensing there was more.

Kael's voice dropped. "It's in the heart of the Ruirulan Empire."

The deck fell silent.

"Father Huey, please give us a short but powerful prayer," Tim asked.

"Oh, Heavenly Father, watch over us carefully as we

undertake this dangerous mission of mercy," he said, signing the cross. "Amen."

With the prayer concluded and the course set, Tim issued final instructions. "Everyone to hibernation pods. Arcaayus, begin the five-minute countdown once we're sealed."

Crewmembers knew the drill. This would be their third wormhole jump, the second created by *Horizon's* wormhole generator and the longest distance. Every man, woman, and child moved swiftly to the large wormhole hibernation room.

As each person, VaRaxian and human alike, lay down inside sleek, glass-domed pods, a pale blue mist of oxygen-rich sedative compound filled the chamber, slowing metabolism and brain activity. Within seconds, heart rates dropped, and consciousness began to fade.

Tim watched to make sure everyone was safe in their pods. He walked over to Peggy, nestled in her chamber, mouthed "I love you," and watched her blue eyes slowly close.

He took a quick look at the twins. They were already fast asleep. He thought about what the Malzon commander had told him before the Xalnyth's mind control shut his helpless body down.

Test the humans.

Tim took a deep breath, walked to his pod, climbed in, pressed a button, and closed the lid. Thirty seconds later, his body temperature, blood pressure, and breathing dropped, and he fell fast asleep.

Exactly five minutes after Tim sealed his pod, the ship vanished into the wormhole.

Not long after, the crew slowly stirred from their protective wormhole pods when the *Horizon* emerged on the other side. Maya was first on the bridge, scanning the planet below.

"I have Lyara's DNA signature," she said. "Location confirmed. She's beneath a high-altitude mountain range on the north continent."

"Deploy the strike team," Tim ordered.

Kael listened to the plan to rescue Lyara. "I wish I could go with you."

Tim shook his head. "We will find her and bring her home."

The order was issued, and the *Endeavor* shuttle was prepped and launched within minutes.

Lieutenant McDill led the operation. Tim, Pat, Tom, Jeff, and Nick suited up with reinforced blast armor and disruptor rifles. Jeff carried two satchels of high-impact explosives.

They were joined by VaRaxian volunteers—Joran, Tarel, and Sian, the son of Dr. Rykan and Alora.

"She's my friend," he said, his voice full of emotion. "Lyara and I were close...before the war, before everything. If she's still alive, I must find her."

Dr. Rykan and Alora exchanged glances and nodded. "Go," Alora said. "Find her and bring her home."

Kael stood there, motionless and stoic, with his wife, Liora, who held his arm, trembling. "Save her," he whispered.

Once *Horizon* neared the Shadow planet, *Endeavor* launched and flew directly to where Lyara's DNA signature had been detected. Meanwhile, *Horizon* sped to the other side of the planet and began to bombard a Ruirulan landing base to create a diversion.

The Ruirulans' ground defenses opened fire in response, but the plasma rounds bounced harmlessly off *Horizon's* strengthened deflector shields. After a few minutes of exchanging fire, *Horizon* moved off, looking for other targets to damage—but not destroy.

Meanwhile, *Endeavor* descended through a churning, pale-gray sky to a world half-consumed by darkness. The shadowy planet orbited a distant star, receiving only dim, scattered sunlight, barely half the intensity of Earth's or VaRax's. Yet, it possessed water, an atmosphere, and just enough warmth to support life.

The shuttle touched down on a rocky outcrop at the edge of a narrow valley, where bioluminescent plants illuminated the hillsides. Landing struts hissed as they locked into place on the uneven terrain.

Moments later, the loading ramp dropped with a sharp clank, releasing a faint pulse of warm interior air into the colder, mist-thick atmosphere outside.

The strike team moved quickly, stepping down in full armor, their boots crunching on crystal shards and grit. A strange, almost musical hum drifted on the wind.

"What is that?" asked Nick.

Patrick, who followed Lieutenant McDill and the Space Marines toward the mountain, turned and motioned with his hands up and down for the team to be quiet and stay alert.

They advanced in silence, weapons drawn but lowered, scanning the surroundings. The air was heavy with moisture, carrying the scent of minerals and something vaguely metallic.

Tom paused near a cluster of jagged columns and brushed his fingers against a translucent vine. It shimmered under his touch, pulsing faintly. "This place is creepy," he murmured.

The moment passed. They moved in.

Maya's coordinates guided them along a ridge trail that wrapped around the base of a black crystal spire. Behind it, half-buried beneath moss and stone, they found what they sought: a narrow breach in the mountainside, obscured mainly by tangled vegetation and low-hanging mist.

A metallic structure was faintly visible inside the cave mouth. Tarel stepped forward with a scanning probe, sweeping the opening for energy signatures.

"Artificial," Lieutenant McDill confirmed. "This must be the entrance to the bunker. Why would it be hidden like this?"

"Because this isn't the main entrance," Tim said, touching the dark, metallic door.

Patrick nodded. "All right. Let's breach it. Jeff, blow it open."

Jeff stepped forward with a smile. He attached shaped enhanced C-4 explosive charges to the outer door.

"Step back, everyone," he said after everything was in place.

The controlled explosion ripped the door open.

"Marines, front and center, secure the tunnel," Lieutenant McDill barked.

The 20-foot-long, four-foot-wide tunnel was empty. The rescue party moved forward, entering an open room. The compound inside was quiet.

Suddenly, two Ruirulan guards appeared from an inner checkpoint. They fired at the Marines.

"Return fire, four Marines to the left!" shouted Sergeant Laura Mountbatten. "Stay down and spread out!"

Disruptor fire lit the tunnel. The two guards fell to the ground in a heap.

"Clear this section. We have to keep moving!" McDill shouted.

Tim focused, his purplish-blue eyes glowing faintly. He pressed his hand to the wall and closed his eyes.

"Lyara is…two levels down. Cellblock C." He paused. "There are others: high-level officials, scientists, and more guards."

The team made its way down two levels. Jeff blew another door open. The Space Marines entered quickly, firing disruptors. Three Ruirulan guards fell, as they had no chest blast protectors and were armed only with hand weapons.

"We found them," said Tim, pointing down a hallway.

"Marines, secure the perimeter. They may try a counterattack. Sergeant Mountbatten, with me," said McDill, following Tim, Patrick, and Sian.

They discovered thirty VaRaxians huddled in cells—emaciated, bruised, but alive. Two tall males stepped forward as the team entered.

"I am Councilor Tharan," said one, his voice trembling but proud. "This is High Scientist Kelos. How did you find us?"

"It's a long story," said Tim through his translator. "We will talk about it over dinner once we leave here safely."

Behind them stood another scientist, Mira Levan, who whispered, "We didn't think rescue would ever come."

Tarel stepped forward. "We are so happy to see you, Councilor."

"Tarel, how?" Tharan asked.

"Reunion later. We're getting you all out now!" Tim shouted.

"Sian?" Lyara stepped from the back of the cell. Her voice cracked. "Is that you, Sian?"

Sian's eyes lit up as he rushed forward to her. "It's me, and you're alive. Thank the gods! Your parents want you home... I want you home."

They embraced tightly, clinging to each other like long-separated spouses.

Alarms screamed as the strike team led the rescued prisoners back toward the surface. Twenty Ruirulan guards massed for an attack.

Their commander issued the order to charge. Disrupter fire filled the air. Ten of the guards fell immediately, either killed or badly wounded. Two Space Marines went down, cut off by a crossfire near a corner alcove. Tom and Nick dragged one of them back; the other lay motionless.

Half of the Space Marine strike team covered the retreat of the VaRaxians while Tim and the rest of the group took up positions. Two Marines stayed back and retrieved their motionless comrade.

When Tim reached the exit, he saw a small Ruirulan military transport ship landing in a clearing about 100 feet away, fortunately on the opposite side of where *Endeavor* was scheduled to land.

Ruirulan reinforcements emerged from the transport ship. They began rushing toward the prison entrance.

But the Duffy-Smith rescue plan had anticipated that reinforcements would arrive. Five Space Marines waited for them, their disruptor rifles firing quickly and steadily at the approaching enemy.

Tim quickly called *Endeavor* on his wristcomm. "We are ready anytime you are," he said.

As the second firefight erupted, Nick shielded Mira Levan as she stumbled, dragging her forward. Jeff lobbed a compact explosive grenade that took several enemy soldiers out and threw dust and debris into the air. He then tossed two smoke bombs to cover their escape from the tunnel entrance.

"Now's your chance, Tim! Move toward *Endeavor!*" Jeff shouted.

As the strike team hustled away, Tom and Joran joined the Space Marines in covering the retreat, cutting down the last attackers before the group made its way to the rendezvous.

Endeavor was waiting.

Everyone scrambled aboard, took their seats, and strapped in. "Did we leave anyone behind? *Endeavor?*" McDill frantically asked.

"No, sir," said *Endeavor.* "All life signs accounted for except one."

"All right, then punch it!" McDill shouted. "*Endeavor*, who didn't make it?"

"Sergeant Laura Mountbatten," *Endeavor* said.

The shuttle roared skyward, streaking toward the *Horizon.* McDill bowed his head, trying to hide his tears.

Fifteen minutes later, *Endeavor* docked in *Horizon's* landing bay.

Dr. Rykan, Alora, Dr. Kropt, Nurse Paula, and Dr. Taber were waiting for them with a dozen other medical volunteers. The VaRaxian survivors were assisted off the shuttle with tender care.

Sian held Lyara's arm as he helped her walk into the ship and down to the medbay. In the medbay, Dr. Rykan wrapped her in a thermal blanket, with Sian standing by her side as Kael and Liora arrived.

"Father," she said, her voice fragile. "You came for me."

"Tim found you," said Kael, embracing her. Liora held her daughter's face in her hands, eyes wet with tears.

"Who is Tim?" she asked, glancing at Sian, who smiled.

"He is a great Earthling, now the commander of this ship," Sian said.

"I will introduce you to the admiral later," Liora said. "You can thank him directly. He saved nearly 9,000 of our people on VaRax and another 900 on Celias-3."

Lyara's eyes filled with tears when she heard about the lives saved on VaRax and Celias-3. "Father, mother, I have so much to talk to you about. The dreams I've been having of you, Sian, and a young boy and girl. I sense they are on this ship."

Kael smiled. "You are talking about Ethan and Lila. They are Tim and Peggy's wonderful children. They want to meet you as well."

Suddenly, Maya's voice cracked over the intercom, urgency in every word: "Tim, the Ruirulans just appeared out of nowhere. A four-ship fleet. They're charging weapons."

Tim stared at the screen. In all the excitement, he hadn't seen them coming. "Everyone, to stations!"

Chapter 34
SPACE STANDOFF

Early Morning, Monday, May 3, 2083

A tense stillness settled over the *Horizon's* bridge, like the eye of a giant hurricane passing and the brief wait for the strong back edge.

The VaRaxian rescue had succeeded—but at a terrible cost. Fifty Ruirulan guards and soldiers lay dead, as did one Space Marine, Laura Mountbatten.

Now, streaking out of the gray murk of Shadow's upper atmosphere were the unmistakable signatures of Ruirulan warships. They had evaded Maya's scans, their vessels hidden by the planet's magnetic storms or some unknown cloaking technology.

Tim's eyes narrowed as he stepped toward the command station. "Steve, open a channel. I want to speak with the commander," he said, his voice low but steady.

Before the channel connected, a voice echoed in his mind—

clear, urgent, and familiar. *Father, we can help*, Ethan said telepathically. *There's still a way to avoid war.*

Tim's jaw clenched for a moment, then he answered aloud, "Come to me on the bridge." He turned to Peggy without missing a beat.

"Transfer all power from the weapons to the deflector shields. I want maximum protection. This should send a message to the Ruirulan commander that we don't plan on fighting."

She nodded and moved swiftly to comply, hands gliding over the console as the ship's energy profile shifted. *Horizon* hummed with redirected power around them, a glowing halo forming across its shielding array.

Kael stepped forward to stand beside Tim in his command chair. "Admiral, you should transfer control to Arcaayus. The Ruirulans are our ancient enemy—they will fire. It's only a matter of when."

"Not now, Kael," Tim said sharply, his gaze on the forward display. "I want to talk with them first."

"Admiral." Steve interrupted. "Commander t'Lay of the Ruirulan flagship, *Celara,* is responding."

Tim drew a breath and stepped forward to face the screen, his voice calm but firm as he prepared to make contact. He cleared his throat. "Put her through."

The bridge lights dimmed slightly as the comm link engaged, and a wash of static rippled across the main viewscreen before resolving into the sharp, commanding features of t'Lay.

Kael stood nearby, whispering to Tim that he knew her by reputation as a tough but fair opponent. "Be careful," he whispered.

Tim nodded. "Commander, this is Admiral Tim Smith of

the Earth vessel *Horizon*. We have completed our mission to rescue the VaRaxians. We are preparing to leave your space. There is no need for further conflict."

An aggressive female voice barked through the comm in the Ruirulan language. "Vra'keth nal'suur draya'tekh solanai!"

"Steve, something is wrong. Can you adjust the universal translator?" Tim asked.

"Hold on," Steve said. "Here, try again."

"Commander t'Lay, I didn't understand. Repeat, please," Tim said.

"Admiral Tim Smith, we do not seek war with your kind. But our sensors confirm you are harboring VaRaxians aboard your ship—VaRaxians who have already attacked us and destroyed two defenseless Ruirulan vessels."

A pause crackled through the comm. "Now you arrive unannounced, infiltrate our territory, strike our prison, and leave our guards dead. Who are you to command a VaRaxian warship? And why should I not consider your actions a declaration of war?" t'Lay's voice grew colder. "You leave me no choice. Prepare to be destroyed."

"Commander t'Lay, let's speak openly. The VaRaxian attack on your ships was a tragic mistake—but your retaliation leveled two cities and killed over 90,000 innocent lives," Tim said, his voice steady but firm. "What we did today was not intended as an act of aggression—it was a rescue. We used the least amount of force necessary to recover civilians, nothing more."

He paused, letting the weight of his words settle.

"This doesn't have to escalate further. Let us leave peacefully, and we can both walk away from this. Let this be the end of it."

"You are surrounded. Surrender, and we will hold fire," t'Lay said.

"You're not seeing the full picture," Tim said, his voice steady but urgent. "We're not your enemy. The Malzons are advancing—and they threaten us all. We have a common enemy, Commander t'Lay. We must stand together, not weaken each other, before the true battle."

"The Malzons are nothing," Commander t'Lay snapped. "If you fear them, you must either be weak or foolish. We will give you up to a count of one hundred to surrender. The clock is ticking."

Before Tim could reply, Ethan tugged at his sleeve, his young face earnest and determined. "Let us try," he said, glancing at Lila.

Tim nodded. "Quickly."

He turned to Amy. "Activate Arcaayus. Tell him to wait for my command before taking any defensive actions."

Then, Ethan and Lila did something that no one anticipated. They closed their eyes and reached with their minds, projecting calm thoughts into the telepathic ether.

They sought the young minds aboard the Ruirulan flagship, *Celara*. Within moments, they found two curious and intelligent presences.

Who are you? asked one of the voices, hesitant but intrigued.

I'm Ethan. This is my sister, Lila. We don't want a fight, do you?

I'm Varra, said the voice. *My mother is Commander t'Lay. Why are you contacting me?*

Because we know what war feels like, Lila answered gently. *We've seen our friends hurt; you probably have, too. We don't want more fighting. We want peace. Don't you ever get tired of war?*

Another child joined the connection—Kerin, the son of Dr. Shonta, a Ruirulan medical officer.

We're trained for war, he said. *But that doesn't mean we like it.*

We're learning how to build things, Ethan said. *How to explore space, study stars, and work with others. We could learn together. Don't you think it's time to stop fighting and start learning and playing?*

A long pause. Then Varra's mind voice returned, more thoughtful this time. *I want to meet you,* she said. *I think our parents should talk to each other instead of fighting.*

The children's voices transferred and resonated in t'Lay's mind. Tim and Peggy also heard them as being connected with their children.

t'Lay stepped forward on the bridge and opened a channel.

"Admiral Smith," she said, her tone changing—cool but no longer hostile. "I don't know how, but your children have spoken to mine. They have asked for peace. Call it a mother's intuition, but I will allow you to convince me that the Malzon Empire is truly a threat and that we should stand with you."

Tim stepped forward, steady and composed. "The Malzons attacked my ship at Celias-3 and followed us to VaRax before we left for Shadow. They will be here soon, and this is just the beginning." He paused. "But I don't believe the Malzons act alone. As you have seen, their sudden technological leap points to an outside influence.

"We believe it's the Xalnyth, a species from beyond our galaxy. They're using the Malzon as pawns in a larger invasion plan, one that could devastate not just Earth—my home planet—but this entire section of the Milky Way."

t'Lay's eyes narrowed slightly. "We have heard of the Xalnyth," she said slowly. "We assumed them to be myth... travelers between galaxies, manipulators of lesser species. But if they've reached the Malzon Empire..."

Her voice trailed off. She looked around at her officers,

then returned her gaze to Tim. "We did not realize how quickly the Malzons were evolving. Their species was once barely capable of interplanetary travel. Now they wield weapons that are nearly as deadly as ours."

She stood straighter. "I believe you. And more importantly, I believe my daughter. There will be no attack today. We will talk. The Ruirulan Empire will consider an alliance with Earth and the VaRaxians. For now, you have my word on a ceasefire."

Tim exhaled quietly. "Thank you, Commander. You've taken an important first step. Earth and our friends, the VaRaxians, who now live with us, want peace, friendship, and collaboration in all things."

And so, aboard the *Horizon* and the *Celara*, a fragile but hopeful peace was born, an opening accord between three peoples long divided. Children led the way, their bonds forming the first strands of unity.

Chapter 35

PEACE OR CONSEQUENCES

Later Monday Morning, May 3, 2083

Tim called a meeting in the staff conference room with officers and crew members to discuss the potential alliance with the Ruirulans. He knew Jim and several other crew members would want to know why *Horizon* wasn't immediately jumping through a wormhole to Saturn's outer reaches.

Tim apologized and explained that he had jumped to Shadow to make possible alliances with the Ruirulans.

"My vision told me that Lyara and the others were here, but I also sensed something else would help us protect Earth by coming. This alliance with the Ruirulans is it," Tim said.

Jim nodded. Over the past day, he'd had time to reflect on recent events. His talk with Nira helped. She had convinced him that if Earth was not in immediate danger, then Tim was justified in taking the time to investigate Shadow.

Tim asked Peggy to explain how they decided it was safe enough to risk waiting another day before making another wormhole jump to Earth.

"We calculated that the best the Malzons could do from VaRax, even if they have wormhole technology, would be to jump 40 million miles outside Saturn's gravitational influences," Peggy said. "From there, a trip to Earth would take them 10 days based on their maximum speed of half a percent of light with their engine technology."

"That's right. *Horizon* is capable of near-light speed, although I prefer not to use that within the Solar System," Tim said. "We feel that, right now, it's important to work out our alliance with the Ruirulans. If they agree to help us, we should be able to reach Earth in time."

Tim also explained to the crew that he had received a message from t'Lay accepting their dinner invitation just before the meeting started.

"t'Lay passed on the good news that the Ruirulan High Command agreed with her assessment of the Malzon/Xalnyth threat. They believe it to be credible," Tim said.

With a smile, Tim added, "We will be entertaining Ruirulan guests tonight. Tomorrow, we will jump home. However, I must talk with Commander t'Lay before we set this course. We may need the Ruirulans' assistance at home."

That evening, the dining hall aboard the *Horizon* was transformed into a place of unity. Soft lights cast a warm glow across the long table where Ruirulans, VaRaxians, and Earthlings sat side by side.

Sitting beside Commander t'Lay, Tim rose from his seat, lifting his glass as the room quieted, and offered a brief but heartfelt toast.

"To ancient foes who dared to meet not with weapons but with words," Tim said, his voice steady and warm. "To the VaRaxians, who endured unimaginable loss, and to the Ruirulans, who found the strength to listen. And to all of us—Earthlings, allies, explorers—who believe peace can rise even among stars once shadowed by war."

He turned slightly toward Commander t'Lay and Kael. "May this be the first of many nights where we sit as guardians of the galaxy."

Raising his glass higher, he added with a raised voice and a smile, "To unity and to the battles we'll now fight side by side."

t'Lay responded in kind. "To new friends—Earthlings—and the possibility of peace with our old enemy, the VaRaxians. We will meet all challenges together."

The meal was carefully curated to include dishes tailored for each species: chunky meats, steamed vegetables, and protein blocks for the Ruirulans, bio-nutrient broths, plants, and hearty bread for the VaRaxians, and a rich spread of plant-based foods, lean meats, fruits, whole grains, and legumes for the Earthlings.

After some chatting, Father Huey stood up, as was his custom before large dinners.

"As we gather here and break bread with new friends, oh Heavenly Father, keep us safe and guide our minds with wisdom. May we remember who we are—and why we journey:

not to conquer, but to understand; not to destroy, but to heal; not for glory, but for peace. Watch over all of us as we honor your light in our actions," said Father Huey as he gave the sign of the cross, closing with the customary "Amen."

While the VaRaxians were accustomed to Father Huey's prayers, the Ruirulans regarded the priest curiously, although they couldn't understand who he was talking about.

As the dinner began, the conversation was cautious at first, but as Tim, Peggy, Dr. Taber, t'Lay, and Dr. Shonta became comfortable with each other, laughter began to rise between bites and shared stories, and the tension began to melt.

Even Kael, typically withdrawn, was seen exchanging thoughts with a Ruirulan weapons engineer about the historical battles their worlds had fought against each other.

Kael stood stiffly beside the buffet table, arms folded as he regarded the much shorter, stockier Ruirulan across from him. The weapons engineer's formal dress jacket was filled with medals and ribbons that shimmered under the ship's lights. His name was Vorak, and he seemed equally disinclined to engage in small talk.

"You were at the Battle of T'rassil Prime," Kael said flatly, eyes narrowing. "It was the last time our worlds engaged in combat. I recognize the markings on your jacket."

Vorak's mouth twitched. "That was forty years ago. And I know who you are. You were the president of VaRax, the last in a long line of clever engineers and scientists we nearly defeated in the great Ruirulan-VaRaxian wars."

Kael didn't blink. "I never commanded a warship like you, but I helped to create the technologies that your civilization and others in the galaxy copied."

"We didn't need your innovations," Vorak snapped. "Just

two days ago, we came to investigate your world after you gave it up, and your planetary AI mistook us for an invasion and launched a barrage that destroyed two scout ships and their crews."

Kael, filled with guilt but also with greater anger, lashed back. "And you responded, not with questions, but with plasma fire and missile blasts, killing 90,000 of our people."

Vorak gruffly moved closer to the much taller man. "I don't know why the High Command agreed to peace with the Earthlings with your people involved," said Vorak. "You admitted to killing 50 of our prison guards this morning in a cowardly attack."

Kael began to speak with anger, but then stopped himself, saying in a soft voice, "You don't know; how could you? My daughter was one of those prisoners the Earthlings helped rescue. I am thankful she is with my wife and me again."

A silence settled between them, thick with memory and resentment. Laughter and warm voices filled the dining hall around them, but between these two, the air was as cold as steel.

Kael finally said, "Maybe tonight isn't about forgetting or forgiving. But it could be the beginning of something neither of us could have ever believed—fighting against a mutual enemy instead of against each other."

Vorak, his expression unreadable, considered the possibility. "If the Xalnyth are working with the Malzons against us—and I have my doubts—let's see if this is a new start, as Commander t'Lay hopes."

"And as Admiral Tim Smith believes," Kael said.

They clinked glasses, not in a toast, but in mutual recognition of a past that hadn't been forgiven, only set aside to be proven in peace or against a mutual enemy.

A tranquil silence fell over the gathering as dessert was served—until Ethan and Lila's expressions shifted simultaneously. Their eyes glazed over for a brief moment before they snapped to attention.

Lila leaned toward her father and whispered, "It's *Zara* and *Koren*. They're calling for help. A wormhole opened past Saturn. The Malzons have arrived."

Tim reacted quickly, asking t'Lay if she could step into a private alcove near the observation deck.

"It's happened much more quickly than I imagined. Now, I believe your High Command will soon see with their own eyes that the Xalnyth is behind this," Tim said. "The Malzon alone couldn't have crossed the galaxy so quickly without wormhole technology."

"We just perfected it recently. I am sure they weren't close on their own," t'Lay said with concern. "If they have wormhole tech, the Xalnyth must have given it to them. The High Command is worried they could become dangerous. They are aggressive monsters. Everything has changed, just as you predicted."

He met t'Lay's gaze with unflinching sincerity. "Earth is our home. But if they succeed there, your worlds will follow. I ask you to come with us, not as a soldier but as someone who wants peace. Help defend Earth. Let's face this threat together."

t'Lay studied him for a long moment before nodding slowly. "I will send word to High Command immediately."

Chapter 36

RETURN TO EARTH

4 p.m., Monday, May 3, 2083

The ship's staff conference room was packed as Tim stood in front of the group. He had discussed his plan to beat the Malzons to Marsbase with Peggy, Kael, the officers, and the medical team, and they had agreed. He wanted to explain why this jump would require some unusual but necessary adjustments to the wormhole jump and space-traveling protocols.

The crew was restless. They knew they had completed their mission and wanted to go home to face the Malzon threat.

"Everyone is thinking the same thing: let's go home," Tim began. "I agree."

Many faces were smiling, while others looked too exhausted to react. They had spent ten hectic and stressful days in deep space, encountering numerous aliens and navigating three wormhole passages.

"We're approaching what we hope will be our final jump of this mission," Tim said, his voice steady but charged with anticipation. "But this jump will be unlike the others. Now that we have a strategy to keep everyone safe, I want to walk you through it."

Around the room, the crew shifted in their seats. A few exchanged glances. Murmurs began to ripple through the group as the gravity of Tim's words settled in.

Tim continued, "The Malzons are already in our Solar System. That means we need to reach Earth fast—faster than ever before. *Horizon* must accelerate to 2% of the speed of light and then decelerate just as rapidly to intercept them. But our human and VaRaxian bodies aren't built to endure sustained 2 g forces for very long."

Dr. Bo Taber stood, raising his hand slightly. "Tim, may I?"

"Go ahead, Bo," Tim said, nodding.

"The suspense is killing me," Bo said with a half-smile. "We all want to get home quickly, but we need to do it safely. The human body can handle 2 g of force for a day, but not for six days. How long are you talking about?"

Tim looked out across the crew, reading the concern and curiosity on their faces. "There's only one way to do it. Except for the essential bridge crew, everyone else will enter hibernation pods before the jump. You'll remain in stasis for five of the six days while we accelerate and then begin our deceleration. By the time we reach roughly 1.2 g, the forces should be tolerable for everyone to safely wake up and resume duties for the final 24 hours."

There were a few nods. Some still looked uncertain, but

the logic was hard to argue with.

Bo sat down with a perplexed look on his face. He wasn't sure what that meant.

"And the children?" Alora asked.

"Yes, the children," repeated Bo. "Their developing internal organs and brains should not be exposed to such high g-forces."

"Quite right," Tim said. "The Earth children are used to higher gravity than the VaRaxian children, but to be safe, Dr. Ledbetter and Dr. Ivanova recommended we wake them up when we slow to 1 g, which would be about four hours away from Marsbase."

"How many days would they be in hibernation?" Julie asked. "Our children are just three and five years old."

Tim paused, for he knew his following words would be shocking.

"Five days for the children; four days for the adults, maybe less," Tim said.

At this, a majority of the crew grumbled.

"I knew we should have left immediately from VaRax," said Jim as Nira held his arm and whispered, "Not now."

"I know, I know. It's been a long time," Tim said. "No one has been in stasis this long. Our biosensors will closely monitor us and the children. Dr. Ledbetter, could you explain?"

Dr. Charles Ledbetter stepped forward, his calm voice carrying over the mumbling that continued in the room.

"Dr. Ivanova and I have studied this; it is safe," Charles began. "The hibernation pods aboard *Horizon* were designed with long-duration travel in mind, specifically for scenarios like this. While five days is unprecedented, Earth and VaRaxian physiology have responded remarkably well, based on the three jumps we have already made."

"We trust what you are saying, Dr. Ledbetter, but we are talking about five days for the children," said Kiki Kropt, the mother of a five-year-old boy.

"We conducted simulation tests using our AI computer, and a longer period of stasis showed no problems," he said. "For this extended jump, we'll initiate a gradual neural deceleration sequence to ease the body into a protected metabolic state. Once stabilized, internal systems will regulate oxygen levels, temperature, and nutrient flow.

"As Tim said, our biosensors, linked directly to the ship's AI, will track every vital sign. If anything goes even slightly off-nominal, the pod will wake the individual and notify our medical team instantly."

He turned to the parents among the group and softened his tone. "As for the children, we've taken extra precautions. Pediatric hibernation protocols include neural shielding to protect their developing brains and hormone-balancing microinjections tailored to their growth cycles.

"VaRaxian children possess unique regenerative rhythms that we've mapped carefully. Statistically speaking, they'll adapt better than adults. So, while five days may sound daunting, medically speaking, it's safe. I'll be in the final pod to ensure everyone else is secure first."

Tim thanked Dr. Ledbetter as he took his seat.

"Unless we have more questions, I'd like Peggy and Captain Bouchard to give reports about our jump and trip to Marsbase," Tim said. "Peggy."

She stepped forward, standing by her husband as she began to explain.

"Tim asked me to calculate the safest and quickest wormhole exit point in our Solar System," Peggy began. "It turns out to be closer to Earth than the wormhole we entered that took us to Celias-3—300 million miles from Jupiter and 100 million miles from Saturn.

Kael interrupted. "Isn't Jupiter's gravity much stronger than Saturn's?"

"Yes, about 150%. I know you are worried about dark matter attraction. It's a complex calculation, but we have a near-zero risk at this location. We need every advantage we can get," Peggy said, "and our shield protections are much greater than when you made the first jump from VaRax."

Kael attempted a feeble smile. "Your math is always good. Of course, it would be better if our risk were zero."

"At this exit point, it'll take us five days to reach Mars at 2% light, but due to the 2 g acceleration and deceleration curve, we'll need to use the hibernation pods again," Peggy said.

Tim agreed. "The risk is minimal. We've made the necessary preparations. We'll go under for the push."

"Dad, do you want to speak to our course?" Peggy asked.

Navigator Bouchard stood. He pressed a button on his wristcomm, and the wall viewscreen lit up. A tracking map displayed Jupiter, Saturn, the wormhole exit point, the course to Marsbase, and a timeline.

"Arcaayus has been programmed to adjust to faster light speed and higher or lower g-force acceleration or deceleration depending on where we are relative to the Malzons," Leonard said.

"Thank you, Leonard and Peggy," said Tim. "This means we should arrive at Marsbase four hours *before* the Malzon fleet, giving us time to prepare for its defense."

Patrick Duffy stood up. "Pardon me, Tim, I am neither a science officer nor a navigator, but isn't four hours cutting it close? What if the Malzons go faster than you expect?"

Tim frowned. "As Leonard said, Arcaayus and *Horizon's* AI will be awake—along with most of the bridge officers at different times during this period—to make adjustments.

"Patrick, you, Bo, and the other 90 crew members, children, and VaRaxians in their pods will be asleep. When you wake up after four days, time will not have seemed to pass," Tim said. "Any other questions?"

The crew was silent. Given the Malzon threat and the need to make up time, they knew it was the best course of action.

"Father Huey, give us your words of wisdom," said Tim, motioning for the priest.

"Our Heavenly Father, watch out for us as we pass through your space and time. Give us the strength to overcome whatever obstacles you put in our path. Allow us to arrive safely and do what we must to protect our friends in harm's way," Father Huey said, giving the sign of the cross and closing with, "Amen."

"Amen is right. Now, let's get on with it. Next time I see most of you, we will be ready to defend Mars, the Moon, and Earth," said Tim, adjourning the meeting.

At midnight, the jump from Shadow began as *Horizon's* wormhole generator whirred to life, powered by VaRaxian-designed axion conversion cells humming deep within the vessel's core.

By now, the crew were experienced wormhole jumpers. They went to the hibernation pods, where Liora and Carlyn assisted the children.

Peggy took Ethan and Lila. Before falling asleep, they sent

a telepathic message to Tim: *You were right, Father, we have time, but the Malzon have a surprise.*

Tim, on the bridge with Major Andrews, Captain Bouchard, and Maya, smiled. *We will be ready. Pleasant dreams.*

"Arcaayus will handle the rest. Time for you three to go to the pods," said Tim, who waited alone on the bridge for *Horizon's* rehabilitated AI to complete the pre-wormhole entry protocol.

Arcaayus activated the wormhole generator. A wave of blue-white light arced outward, then collapsed into a shimmering vortex as the wormhole—the once thought impossible Einstein-Rosen bridge—formed in open space.

Captain Bouchard's course had been programmed into the generator: from Shadow to a point 300 million miles from Jupiter.

Tim never got tired of seeing a new wormhole form. Spacetime compressed into a multi-colored point of light, an artificial singularity that expanded into a tunnel through the stars.

"Arcaayus, confirm that all crew and children are in their pods and that life support is functioning."

"Yes, Admiral. May I speak freely?" the AI said in his deep, resonant voice.

"What's on your mind?"

"Thank you for trusting me. And may I say our mission will be a success."

Tim chuckled, thinking Arcaayus seemed to be taking pride in his job.

"You've done well. You are now a critical part of this crew. Let's make this a third successful jump," Tim said.

"Yes, Admiral. All systems are go."

t'Lay's Answer

Commander t'Lay waited until the very last moment to reach out to Tim. Although she lacked his extrasensory skills, she felt a baffling closeness to the human that eased any doubts.

"I haven't heard back from the High Command. I must wait before I commit my fleet," she said, worry tinging her voice and etched across her face.

Tim studied her expression, wondering if her sense of honor would hold. "You have done all you can. We must trust our new friendship will be understood by your friends who make these critical decisions," he said. "This is the burden we share as leaders."

They talked, sharing personal matters about their children. Tim learned that t'Lay's husband had recently been killed in a boating accident while they were on vacation. He expressed his heartfelt condolences to her.

After talking for ten minutes, Tim transmitted the precise wormhole exit coordinates only when he was sure she was sincere and telling the truth. There was no time for mistakes. Earth was in danger.

"Here are the coordinates for the jump to our Solar System and the starmap location of Earth," Tim said. "Hurry, if you can. We shall meet again; I sense it."

"Whatever happens, good luck," she said, her face somber.

Two hours later, after *Horizon* vanished into the wormhole, a message arrived to t'Lay through the secure diplomatic relay: "High Command agrees. The Xalnyth threat cannot be ignored this time."

t'Lay, waiting with her four-ship fleet outside Shadow,

looked toward the stars and whispered aloud: "Admiral Tim Smith, if you can hear me—and I suspect you can with those psychic powers of yours—we will stand with you. My fleet will follow the *Horizon* to Earth."

In deep hibernation aboard *Horizon*, Tim, Ethan, and Lila felt her intent echo across the vastness of space. Though spoken light-years away, her words reached their minds like a vow carried by the stars.

It was a bond formed among Earthlings, Ruirulans, and VaRaxians—not born out of pure strategy but out of sincere trust and hope.

The Malzon Arrive, Saturday, May 1

Darkness parted suddenly. A wormhole—a radiant, twisting rift in space—opened up just outside of Saturn's gravitational pull. Ten Malzon warships emerged from the wormhole's center in eerie unison, their elongated hulls slicing through space to form rows of three ships, with the largest vessel in the front.

Each warship stretched nearly a mile long, armored and bristling with weapon systems designed to intimidate and destroy. However, there was something different about these Malzon ships. Their modified engines pulsed with newly installed, powerful technology.

Inside the vast command chamber of the *Devourer of Suns*, High Commander Rauth Ka'Tar awaited the completion of the tactical ship attack formation. His orders were clear: destroy Earth and its people.

His three oblong eyes narrowed as the wormhole stabilized behind them. He would return victorious or not at all. Before him, holographic projections of the nine warship captains shimmered with resolve. Their scarred, dry, rough, reptilian faces showed only ruthless obedience.

Rauth's voice cut through the silence like a blade drawn in cold vengeance.

"Set course for Earth. Maximum half-percent light. Hold formation until the engines prove themselves worthy of the Malzon Empire. If these new cores fail, let our deaths be lessons etched in the void. If they succeed, let our weapons silence human vanity once and for all."

He stepped forward, claws clacking against the metal floor.

"Transmit no signal. Emit no trace. Show no mercy. We strike hard and fast. Silence until our heat beams and plasma rockets melt their flimsy, soft flesh and bone. The Earthlings will not see us coming."

He raised a clenched fist over his chest.

"This is retribution. This is extermination."

A moment of silence passed. Then, one by one, the captains responded in their native tongue—a guttural, harsh, unified pledge: "For Malzon. For conquest. For final victory!"

Their images flickered and then disappeared. The engines of their warships ignited, filled with potent energy and tainted promises from their new masters, as they raced toward the inner Solar System and Earth.

Horizon Arrives, 1 a.m., Tuesday, May 3

In what seemed like seconds, the nine bridge officers—Tim, Peggy, Mark, Leonard, George, Maya, Kael, Steve, and Medical Officer Dr. Charles Ledbetter—awoke to Arcaayus's booming voice across the ship.

"Attention. We completed the jump. All systems are nominal. Awaiting instructions."

Tim vaguely heard the announcement as he climbed out of his pod. He glanced at Peggy, who was doing the same.

"Morning, how did you sleep?" Tim teased.

"Like I never went to bed," Peggy replied. "How are you?"

"Ready for phase two," Tim said as he saw the other officers waking up.

"Arcaayus, could you repeat what you just said?"

"Attention. We completed the jump. All systems are nominal. Awaiting instructions."

"Thank you. Let's get to the bridge and see where we are," Tim said.

"Is that a question, Admiral?" Arcaayus asked.

"Yes, are we where we are supposed to be?" Tim replied.

"Affirmative. As instructed, I have begun Captain Bouchard's navigation program to Marsbase. We are moving toward half a percent light speed at 1 g acceleration," Arcaayus said.

"What is our medical status in the pods?"

"Everyone is sleeping with zero bio problems," Arcaayus said.

"Thank you. Charles, why don't you make a visual inspection?" Tim asked.

Dr. Ledbetter checked on Paula, then Ethan, Lila, and the rest of the children. "They are fine," he said.

"Good. I want status reports from all departments before we return to the pods and accelerate to 2% light speed," said Tim.

"Engineering is green for go," said George.

"Navigation is go," Leonard said.

"Helm is ready for orders," Mark said.

"Science is go," Peggy said.

"Long-range scanning shows the Malzon fleet is where we expected, just passing Saturn," Maya said.

"At what speed?" Tim asked.

"Half percent light. What we expected based on their approach to VaRax," Maya replied.

Tim paused. "Steve, patch me through to Earth Defense."

"The channel is open, Admiral," Steve said.

"Calling Earth, this is Admiral Smith of the starship *Horizon.* We have returned to the Solar System. What is your status?" Tim asked.

Zara answered first. "Glad to have you back, Admiral. *Koren* and I have been patrolling around Marsbase. The wormhole trackers lit up when the Malzon fleet arrived several hours ago."

"Thank you, *Zara.* We are right on schedule. We should catch up to them soon. What are your orders from Earth?" Tim asked.

"President Eisenhower told us to keep scanning and stay out of trouble until you arrived," *Zara* said.

Just then, another transmission came in. "Admiral, Earth Command is calling," Steve said.

"Hold on, *Zara,*" said Tim. "Patch me through to Ike 4."

"This is President Eisenhower to *Horizon* and Admiral Tim Smith. Dwight to Tim. Do you read me?" Ike 4 said.

"Yes, I do, Mr. President. How are you?" Tim asked.

"I could be better. I wish you were here. We have set up classic defensive positions on Marsbase, Moonbase, and Earth, but we could use some help," Ike 4 said.

"We are coming, and we have assistance from the Ruirulans," Tim said.

"The Ruirulans? *Zara* told me about your meeting. Can

you trust them?" Ike 4 asked.

"Yes, we can," Tim said.

"Welcome home to you and your crew. You've done well in your mission. I hope your friendship with the Ruirulans helps us against this new threat," Ike 4 said.

"It was necessary for our long-term defense. Our little part of the Milky Way is teeming with life," Tim said.

"Get here as fast as you can," Ike 4 said. "I don't have to tell you how tense everyone is."

"I understand. Thank you, Mr. President. Over and out," Tim replied.

The bridge crew listened earnestly. Hearing the president's voice and preparations for another attack seemed surreal.

"Captain, we are ready to lay a course for Marsbase," Tim said.

"Yes, sir," Bouchard said. "Laid and locked into Arcaayus."

"Major Andrews, increase speed gradually to 1% light," said Tim. "How long before it gets uncomfortable?"

"We will feel a slight pressure at about 1.2. Do you feel it yet? As the g-forces increase from Earth's gravity at 1.0 to 1.2 and 1.3, we will feel heavier," Mark said. "We have at least an hour before we should go into our pods."

"This is similar to impulse power acceleration," Tim observed.

Mark chuckled. "We would feel a lot more if we stayed. But what we will feel for the next hour is nothing compared to the three to four g-forces we felt on the Mars mission. Remember, Leonard?"

"Oh, yes, and we were 20 years younger then. I don't want to go through that again at age 55," Leonard said, shaking his head.

Tim smiled, knowing he was working with experienced astronauts who had been through much worse.

"Peggy, prepare the ship for 2% light," said Tim.

"Activating internal gravity stabilizers. This should soften the jolt of acceleration and the kick of deceleration," she said.

"All right, everybody, you know the drill. Back to the pods," said Tim as the bridge crew slowly marched back to the hibernation room.

Four days later, 9 a.m., Friday, May 7

Tim awoke first. He helped Peggy out of her pod and saw the rest of the crew's pods beginning to pop open right on schedule.

He and Peggy walked to the bridge, grabbing bottles of nutrient-electrolyte water. While spending four days in the pods, Tim felt like the time had passed in seconds.

A little groggy, he took his seat and pushed the intercom button.

"Well done, crew. We are home in our Solar System and are beginning to decelerate to 1.5% light. We are less than one day from Marsbase," Tim said. "Report to stations and check your controls."

After a few minutes of recuperation, the officers silently returned to their stations. Shortly afterward, all crew members woke up and began their duties.

"Steve, open a channel to General Washington," Tim said.

"Opening now," Steve said.

"General? This is Admiral Smith. We are 24 hours away. What is your status and condition?"

"We are prepared. The Malzons are approximately 20 hours

away from Marsbase. Will you make it?" Washington asked frantically.

"Twenty hours? I don't see how we miscalculated that much," Tim said. "They must have sped up. I need to check. Our AI was supposed to adjust."

"Whatever you do, get here. We hope we can slow the Malzons. President Eisenhower ordered *Zara, Koren,* and *Indefatigable* to intercept the Malzon warships before they get to Mars, but not to engage," Washington said.

"Good. The twins are good ships. The *Indefatigable* is untested, but it has bigger guns and thicker armor," Tim commented. "What do you mean, not engage?"

"The Earth-VaRaxian ships have been ordered to employ a guerrilla-type tactic to confuse, distract, and lead the enemy warships away without directly engaging them. Their goal will be to delay the Malzons until you arrive with *Horizon* and the Ruirulans," Washington said.

"We will be there as soon as we can. Over and out," Tim said.

Peggy overheard the conversation. "Tim, I calculated the Malzon's speed while you were talking with the president. They are at 1% light and still accelerating."

Tim's heart stopped for a second; then he saw it. "The Xalnyth have modified their engines," he muttered. "They may have made other improvements to the Malzon ships as well. Arcaayus, why didn't you adjust our speed as I instructed?"

No reply. "Arcaayus, did you hear what I said?" Tim asked. "What happened?"

"Yes, Admiral. I don't know what happened. There was one moment during your hibernation when I felt interference... I confirm that the Malzons have increased their speed. I do not have any further data," Arcaayus said.

"I will have Amy and Peggy diagnose your memory. Something blocked your sensors. I didn't foresee it either," Tim said. "Otherwise, you did well while we were asleep."

"Thank you, Admiral," Arcaayus said hesitantly.

Tim turned to Major Andrews. "Stop decelerating. Keep us at 1.5% light. Captain Bouchard, confirm that gets us to Mars two hours ahead of the Malzons."

"Aye, sir," Bouchard replied. "Course calculated. Wait, we may have a problem."

"We won't get there in time," Tim sensed.

"We won't," Bouchard said. "We need to go faster."

"Sir," interrupted Maya. "My long-range sensors indicate the Malzon fleet has matched our speed and accelerated to 1.5% light."

Tim frowned. "They know we are behind them. How could they accelerate so fast?" Then it hit him. "Of course, they are reptilians and can withstand higher g-forces. Leonard, how fast do we need to go to pass them?"

"At least 2% light and at 3 g, and then I am not sure," said Bouchard.

Suddenly, Tim sensed something was interfering with his psychic powers. His inability to sense the Malzon acceleration meant his ESP was being blocked. The feeling was similar to his difficulty probing into *Arcaayus's* databanks as it approached Earth five years earlier. He later found out the Terra Novan ship used a shielding device to block his psychic sight.

He wondered if the Malzons had advanced shielding technology. If the Xalnyth gave them upgraded engine technology, they must have installed a shielding device.

Peggy's voice interrupted his thoughts. "Tim, to pass them, we will need to accelerate to 2% light, but we can't do that in

24 hours. And besides, if they are monitoring us, they could match our speed. I'm sorry, I don't have any suggestions."

Tim turned to Major Andrews, full of frustration. "Mark, we must go faster to pass the Malzon!" Tim exclaimed.

"We can't. We talked about this. We are going at max speed now," Mark replied.

Tim winced. *There must be a way to catch up*, he thought. "For now, I want the Malzons' velocity tracked and reported to me if it changes."

"Yes, sir," Mark said.

"But Tim, even if we accelerate at 3 g, we can't get to Earth before the Malzon," Peggy said.

Tim pounded the armrest of his captain's chair. "I know. The Xalnyth gave the Malzon a shielding device to block me from their attack plan. I can't see through it."

Father, we can help, said Ethan telepathically.

The Malzons are primitive, Lila agreed.

They have a device, but we can use it to fool them, Ethan and Lila said in unison.

Tim's face lit up. *You've both done it*, he said as he rushed over and hugged them.

"The children, Peg," said Tim. "They have given me an idea."

"What are you saying?" Peggy asked, watching Tim embrace their twins.

Tim looked up. "Listen, we have two problems. One, the Malzons are using some psychic blocking technology that prevents me from penetrating their ship. Two, we cannot accelerate faster than 2 g without experiencing physiological damage."

"Yes," said Peggy, curious about what her husband was thinking.

"Tanya mentioned before that she believes Waybegonease might be used to minimize the extreme g-force effects we feel when accelerating."

Peggy looked puzzled. "This is the first I've heard about it."

Tim said, "She discovered this during separate experiments she conducted about using Waybegonease on the human and Terra Novan children.

"I need to check with the other doctors, but if we can use it that way, we can all take doses and accelerate to catch up with the Malzon."

"Yes, father, yes!" exclaimed Ethan and Lila together.

"What do you three mean?" Peggy asked.

"Tell Mother everything!" they shouted excitedly.

Tim took a deep breath. "I also need to have another shared vision with Stephen, Ethan, and Lila—a type we have never attempted—to plant an idea in the Malzons' collective brain."

Chapter 37

THE DIVERSION

10 a.m., Saturday, May 8, 2083

Tim now saw the problem clearly. The Malzon fleet was estimated to be four hours ahead of *Horizon*. *If* he could convince the Malzons to slow their ships *and* if he could push his ship beyond safe limits for humans and VaRaxians, the *Horizon* could close the gap between them.

Could he achieve both? He thought so.

"Dr. Ivanova, Dr. Ledbetter, and Dr. Kropt, meet me in the medbay. We're going to test Waybegonease for a secondary use," Tim said, pressing the intercom. "We need volunteers. Make the calls."

He turned to his wife. "Peggy, come with me. Major, you have the bridge. Keep an eye on the Malzons," Tim said.

Peggy followed him into the hallway. "What are you thinking? We all take Waybegonease? Isn't there another way? It hasn't been tested on anyone without visioning powers," she said, her voice filled with concern.

"Do you feel that pressure? G-forces are increasing," Tim said. "Charles and Tanya will tell you what effects that will have on us, not to mention the children, over the next 24 hours."

"The children? No, Tim. We must keep them in their pods until the last minute," Peggy said.

"Yes, you are right, but Ethan and Lila must be awakened. They have used Waybegonease before. Besides, we need them for what I have in mind," Tim said.

"Oh, Tim, I want Dr. Ledbetter's thoughts on this," she said as they reached the medbay.

Upon entering, Tim saw Dr. Rykan, Dr. Kropt, Alora, Paula, Kael, and Dr. Ledbetter standing by Dr. Tanya Ivanova as she explained how Waybegonease could minimize the effects of g-forces on the brain.

"Waybegonease is a derivative of newvidium, the daughter isotope of an unknown space element that gave Tim and Stephen their psychic abilities," Tanya explained as she pointed to her drug development flowchart on the large, high-resolution display. "When they take it, the drug stabilizes the brain's electrical impulses and widens their blood vessels, thus reducing epileptic-like symptoms."

"Therefore," said Dr. Ledbetter, "you believe Waybegonease can increase blood oxygenation in the brain and reduce other neurological impacts of the high g-forces we all could experience?"

"Yes, with three more modifications. We added a small amount of nootropics, benazepril, and levodopa, plus Dramamine for the children," Tanya said.

Dr. Kropt stood beside the screen as Dr. Ivanova concluded her presentation of the findings. He nodded thoughtfully before speaking.

"I've reviewed the latest data from Dr. Ledbetter and Dr. Ivanova on using Waybegonease for this application," Kropt began. "With the vasodilator additive, I believe it could be very effective. The main issue under high g-forces is reduced blood flow to the brain—gravity pulls it downward, away from the cerebral area. This enhanced version should stimulate the heart just enough to keep that flow steady and restore what the acceleration takes away."

Dr. Rykan stepped up beside him, arms crossed, eyes on the chart. "But let's be honest, most of these additives are stimulants, except for levodopa. Isn't that risky? Especially in a sustained dose?"

"It would be," Dr. Ledbetter acknowledged, "but Tanya and I ran simulations. A single dose designed to last 24 hours for an adult should be safe. It's not something we'd repeat daily, but for a fast transit situation, it's viable."

Dr. Kropt raised a brow and smiled slightly. "This version of Waybegonease could be an anti-g-force fuel—a powerful additive that keeps the brain properly supplied with blood during high acceleration. If we're making a hard burn to Earth, this is what we'll need."

Tim, who had been listening intently from his seat near the console, chimed in, "So we're calling this version 'The Additive' now?"

The doctors exchanged amused glances.

"I like it," Tim said with a grin. "But like with original Waybegonease, we're going to test it first...right?"

"Absolutely," Dr. Ivanova replied. "Clinical validation is next. We'll start with a small control group. No one's taking 'The Additive' until we're certain it's stable under high acceleration conditions."

Tim nodded. "Sounds like a plan. We need to do this fast. Remember, we're doing this to catch up with the Malzons, not seek FDA approval."

No one smiled. Everyone's gaze shifted to Dr. Tanya Ivanova as she turned to Dr. Ledbetter.

"We need four adults and two children to test," he said.

Tim interrupted. "Peggy and I talked about the children. We won't test them. We decided that keeping them in stasis until we approach Mars is still the best option," Tim said.

"Fine," said Dr. Ledbetter. "We still need four adults, two human and two VaRaxian. We take their vitals, EEG, and EKG before and after. The results should be nearly immediate."

Kael stepped forward. "I volunteer. It should be me."

"I also volunteer," said Sian, standing next to his parents with Lyara.

"Could you use us? Mary and I?" Tom Terry asked.

Tim nodded. "We sure can. Thanks for coming. Now, let's start."

"We should also monitor two undosed individuals for comparison purposes," Tanya suggested.

"What about Peggy and Thomas? Could you two be our control group?" Tim asked.

"Of course," said Dr. Kropt, glancing at Kiki for support.

Peggy smiled. "Tim read my mind. He does that a lot."

"Not all the time, but this time, I did," said Tim with a chuckle. "Now, if we're ready, let's proceed. We're running out of time."

Paula dimmed the medbay lights slightly as the testing protocol commenced. The doctors and nurses moved with focused coordination, prepping the volunteers for a dose of "The Additive" with cautious optimism.

As Tom rolled up his sleeve, he said, "I've seen what this does for Tim. If it works on him, I am confident it will work on me. Mary feels the same."

Sian lay on one of the treatment tables as Paula began to prep him for a shot. Lyara watched him with admiration. "This has to work. We must stop the Malzon Empire," Sian said.

Kael took the last dose as he lay on a treatment table next to Sian. "We should know the results very soon," he said.

Paula and Tanya began by recording baseline vitals for Tom and Mary, Kael, Sian, Dr. Kropt, and Peggy—taking temperature, blood pressure, pulse, EEG, and EKG readings. They also collected a small blood sample from each subject for later analysis.

As soon as the drug entered the test subjects' systems, the medbay monitors sprang to life. Real-time EEG and EKG readouts streamed across the digital displays, showing brainwave patterns and heart activity. The automated systems accurately tracked oxygen saturation, pulse, and cranial blood flow.

"Vitals baseline and live data captured," Paula reported, eyes fixed on her tablet. "We're already seeing early effects."

Tanya scanned the evolving readouts. "With g-forces steadily increasing during our burn to Mars, I'd expect a rise in key indicators—reduced blood flow to the prefrontal cortex, elevated heart rate and pulse, and possibly some motor tremors."

"That's exactly what's happening with Peggy and Dr. Kropt," Dr. Ledbetter noted. "Look at how their vitals are climbing."

Dr. Rykan leaned forward, eyes wide. "But look at Sian and Kael's EEGs. They're holding strong. No jitter. No drop."

"Same with Tom and Mary," Tanya confirmed, scrolling through the scans. "Neurological and vascular activity are stable. No signs of stress."

Tom and Sian exchanged a glance, smiling as their brainwave patterns displayed healthy signs.

"Look at that symmetry," Tanya whispered. "They have different brain structures, but their minds are adapting together."

"I feel...light," Tom said softly. "Like I'm grounded but still floating. That pressure in my head is gone."

"Me too," Sian added. "I feel energized."

Mary turned toward Kael, curious about the VaRaxian's reaction.

"I do feel better," Kael said, nodding slowly. "The internal strain is gone. My organs feel...at ease."

After three minutes, each test subject was rechecked. The after-readings were astonishing: oxygen saturation remained high, EEG alpha and beta wave distribution remained stable, and, most remarkably, the usual strain symptoms common during ever-increasing g-force acceleration were completely absent.

Dr. Ledbetter looked at Tanya and Dr. Rykan, nodding slowly. "It works. It absolutely works."

Tanya smiled, catching her breath. "We just proved it. A derivative of Waybegonease—The Additive—doesn't just stabilize psychic fields. It protects the brain and body from g-force stress, at least less than 3 g."

Dr. Rykan folded his arms, clearly impressed. "The Additive, indeed."

As the medbay erupted in celebration, Kael turned to Tanya with a rare VaRaxian smile. "I feel good. You may have just saved more lives than you know."

Tim patted Tom Terry on the back, then glanced at Sian. "You okay?"

"Yes. It doesn't hurt now," Sian said. "I feel better. Can everyone take this?"

"You bet," said Tim with a smile. He walked over to the doctors and shook each of their hands. "Tanya, Dr. Ledbetter, Dr. Kropt, and Dr. Rykan. You did it."

Listening to the discussion, Dr. Kropt stood up, unhooked his electrodes, and cleared his throat. "Excuse me, but aren't you forgetting something?"

"What Thomas means is, we'd like a full dose of Waybegonease, please," Peggy said with a smile.

"Paula, give our control group their shots," Tanya said, pausing. "We do have one more problem."

Dr. Rykan stared at Tanya. "What is it?" she asked.

"We have enough Waybegonease Additive for the 30 humans and the 10 VaRaxians already awake," Tanya said.

"But not the 9,000 in stasis," Dr. Rykan concluded.

Tanya shook her head. "It would take some time to synthesize that much."

Tim stepped forward. "If we don't have enough, it's best they stay in stasis. At least until we wake the rest of the children when we slow to 1 g an hour or two before we arrive at Marsbase."

"Well, then," Dr. Ledbetter said. "I'd like to wait one more hour before we start giving everyone their shots, just to be sure there are no unusual side effects."

"Give the bridge officers their doses as soon as possible, then take care of the rest of the crew this afternoon," Tim said. "Charles, you and Tanya need to give yourselves doses now. I want the medical team assembled in the medbay in 30 minutes."

Psychic Misdirection, 11 a.m., May 8

In the *Horizon's* medbay, the lights dimmed to a soft blue. Everyone necessary had gathered—Tim, Stephen, Ethan, and Lila seated in a semicircle at the center, surrounded by Doctors Ledbetter, Ivanova, Kropt, and Rykan.

Nurses Paula and Alora moved quietly around the room, checking monitors and preparing each participant with neural caps and vitals sensors.

Tim held a small vial of Waybegonease, swirling it gently. "We'll do this as we did before," he said. "One dose each, with a quarter dose for the twins."

Ethan and Lila were calm, eyes glowing faintly with anticipation.

"The Malzons must believe we're lagging far behind at 1% light," Tim explained to the group. "In truth, we'll be gaining on them fast at 2% light speed. If this works, we'll have the element of surprise."

Everyone nodded. Paula administered the Waybegonease, one dose injected into their arms. The effect came quickly. Tim felt the familiar lifting sensation, the blurring of spatial boundaries. As the others closed their eyes and exhaled in synchrony, the room pulsed with quiet energy.

"Follow my mind," Tim said. "We'll reach across the void together."

Within moments, their consciousnesses slipped into the ether. Stars blurred past them in luminous streaks. The cold expanse of space was replaced with patterns of concentrated thought directed toward Earth.

Then the darkness changed.

Before them loomed the Malzon fleet, cocooned in a

swirling shell of Xalnyth shield distortion. Black and iridescent, the field repelled their thoughts like water against glass.

"We've hit the barrier," Stephen said in the shared mindspace. "Xalnyth shielding is stronger than the VaRaxians'."

Tim focused, reaching out with every ounce of mental precision he could muster. His thoughts bounced off the shielding. "We need more power."

"We've got this," Ethan said firmly.

Lila reached for his hand in the vision. "Let's draw from the VaRaxian children. They are ready to help."

In the distance of their minds, fifty young VaRaxian psyches flickered like stars waking from slumber. With a rush of clarity, Ethan and Lila pulled their latent psychic energy from them—untapped, raw, and pure. Shimmering tendrils of light wove through the twins, flowing into Tim and Stephen and jointly pushing through space toward the fleet.

The barrier trembled.

"Push together!" cried Lila.

The shield cracked.

In the next heartbeat, they were through.

Inside the Malzon fleet's mindspace, they found cold, calculating logic, a hive intelligence coordinating velocities, trajectories, and sensor sweeps.

Tim focused and planted the thought: *The Horizon is falling behind. Its engines are damaged. It travels at only 1% the speed of light and is slowing further. No threat.*

Stephen, Ethan, and Lila joined him, amplifying the message with images: flickering lights, limping thrusters, the *Horizon* drifting slowly across space.

The falsehood took root. The scene dissolved. The four returned to the medbay, breathing heavily, sweat on their brows.

"We did it," Ethan said softly, awe in his voice.

"Papa, we helped!" exclaimed Lila, smiling broadly.

"I didn't have a doubt," Tim said, opening his eyes and winking at his twins.

"Vitals stable," Dr. Ledbetter said, checking the readouts. "They're back."

Peggy hurried over to Ethan and Lila, hugged them, and whispered, "I'm so proud of you both," then turned to face the others. Julie ran to Stephen, who looked tired but had a big smile, and hugged him. The doctors and observers shook hands and exchanged congratulations.

Tim smiled. "Let's hope the Malzon bought it."

Before anyone else could respond, an alert chimed from the comm system. Paula crossed the room and pressed the intercom button.

"What is it?" she asked.

"We have an urgent signal on a secure channel for the admiral," Steve said. "I will pipe it through."

A burst of static, then a voice: "This is Commander t'Lay." Everyone turned.

"We've entered your Solar System safely. My fleet is on its way. We will fight beside you."

The room exhaled with relief. Tim stood slowly, a spark of fire in his eyes.

"The Ruirulans are here, and the diversion worked. We have a fighting chance," he said. "Now, let's dose everyone and finish this."

Tim pressed his wristcomm. "Major, let's not waste any time. Begin acceleration to 2% light at 2 g. Wait for my command for 3 g."

Within the darkened command chamber of the *Devourer of Suns*, High Commander Rauth Ka'Tar stood before a shifting space map of the Solar System. His red eyes narrowed as data streams scrolled down a vertical column beside the display.

"Report," he barked.

A subordinate officer bowed low. "We have received a signal from *Horizon*. Its speed remains at 1% light. They are far behind."

Ka'Tar's spined brow rose.

"Is their engine damaged?" he asked.

"They either are damaged or conserving power," the Malzon officer replied.

Ka'Tar exhaled sharply through clenched teeth. "Pathetic. Earth's champions falter again. They have weak bodies and minds."

He turned to the tactical map. "Let the fleet maintain its current speed. We keep to our strike plan. Earth will be ours soon. Then we will destroy *Horizon* and her satellites."

The bridge crew nodded in silence.

Rauth Ka'Tar clasped his hands behind his back, unaware of the psychic lie now worming its way through his entire fleet's decision-making algorithms.

Chapter 38
'THEY'RE EGGS!'

5 a.m., Sunday, May 9, 2083

The next day, ten hours from Mars, Ethan and Lila awoke with no effects of the Waybegonease dose and the shared vision other than a good night's sleep. The drug had stimulated them for a few hours until their metabolism adjusted.

After breakfast, Ethan said calmly to his sister, "We need to try one last time."

"I know. We talked about this. Are you ready?" Lila asked.

Ethan nodded. Sitting cross-legged on the floor of the space school, the twins closed their eyes. They reached out telepathically to the lead Malzon command vessel, skillfully bypassing the Xalynth shielding technology.

They sent peaceful thoughts—images of harmony, unity, children of all species playing on Earth's lush fields. Their minds reached out to any spark of empathy, any flicker of reason, and to the Malzon children, whom they sensed were aboard the invading warships.

What returned was a wave of hostility. Ethan flinched and shook his head. Lila's face twisted in pain. The minds they connected with were aggressive in every way: dense, mechanical, lacking nurture or compassion. There were no emotions, no questions, no wonder. The only feeling they experienced was obedience to something darker and more profound.

Papa, these Malzons are monsters, Lila cried, tears forming in her small eyes. *They are angry, awful, and cold. I never knew there could be so much hate.*

Tim, on the bridge, heard his twins. He projected calm. He had never sensed or seen them so worked up. *I'm coming.* He rushed out of the bridge, calling for Peggy as he ran down the hallway to the space school. She followed.

"Ethan! Lila!" said Tim as he entered the room. "Did you reach the Malzon children?"

Ethan halted his pacing long enough to answer his father. "Papa, there are no children. There are only eggs. When they hatch, they're nearly full-grown. They don't learn. They act."

Lila was even more upset. "There are no parents, no school, not even any singing."

Ahead, the Malzon fleet pressed forward toward Marsbase, Moonbase, and Earth—relentless, mindless, and marching to a rhythm that the children of Earth, led by Ethan and Lila, could not reach.

A grim silence settled across the ship as *Horizon* surged forward on its approach to Marsbase, with the Ruirulan fleet somewhere in the Solar System.

Everyone knew what was coming. Diplomacy had failed. Earth's survival would depend on strength, tactics, unity, and the will to fight.

Chapter 39

THE SECOND MALZON ATTACK

3 p.m., Sunday, May 9, 2083

At Marsbase, Commander Rhea Myles stared at the flashing red lights across her tactical display. Her voice, calm but edged with dread, echoed in the command center.

"They're nearly here. Ten ships. And... Stars help us... They're already scanning us."

All across Mars and Moonbase, defense personnel snapped into action. Laser and particle-beam cannons, drone fleets, and planetary shields came online, humming with charged plasma. Earth Command activated every available defense satellite and began emergency population relocations into deep bunkers.

Onboard the *Horizon*, Tim stood on the central ops deck, watching as the Malzon fleet neared Marsbase. Despite the speed increase, *Horizon* was still two hours away.

Horizon's AI confirmed Maya's scans: the Malzons activated their targeting systems. They were not communicating or hesitating.

"They are not here for a neighborly visit," Tim said quietly. "They're here to burn us to ash."

To his left, Peggy studied the telemetry, her fingers dancing across the console. "They're stronger than we thought, Tim. Faster. Their power output is off the charts. Xalnyth tech is all over them."

"And the Ruirulans?" Tim asked.

Captain Bouchard looked up from his station. "Commander t'Lay's fleet still cannot be located."

Tim shook his head. "Steve, try to raise her again. She said she was coming."

Steve pressed the space comm button, all frequencies. "I've been trying the original signal she messaged us on, and alternatives that seemed reasonable. She's not there."

Tim could not understand. He sensed she was within several million miles but couldn't pinpoint her exact location.

"Admiral, is it possible the Malzons destroyed their fleet?" Amy asked.

"No, she's here...somewhere," Tim replied, perplexed.

"Perhaps you are sensing her final thoughts," Amy suggested.

Behind him, Ethan and Lila hovered near the observation window. The children were uncharacteristically silent, their eyes locked on the distant shimmer where the enemy had emerged.

"Papa," said Ethan in his light but firm voice, "t-Lay will come."

Lila added confidently, "What she is doing is all to surprise the Malzons."

Tim smiled. He knew they would have an answer. Their psychic senses told them what the sensors could not: this would be a battle unlike any other.

Chapter 40

THE BATTLE FOR EARTH

4 p.m., Sunday, May 9, 2083

Commander Rhea Myles stood nervously in the command center of Marsbase. She had done everything the book advised her to do to prepare for the Malzons. The civilians were already in underground shelters, and the recently installed defensive weapon arrays were primed and ready.

"We have eyes on them. Four warships are scanning us with something we can't identify. It's a strange feeling in my head."

Athena, Marsbase's AI, responded in a calm, synthetic voice, "They're attempting mind-penetration using some form of a neural breach. Defensive mental shielding countermeasures holding...for now."

Myles shuddered as she squeezed out an order: "Shields full. Launch countermeasures. *Indefatigable*, flank and intercept."

One of the Malzon ships broke formation and launched dozens of hypersonic nanotech missiles that moved swiftly, spinning toward the Marsbase.

"Divert all power to the shields!" Myles shouted. "Everyone not in the bunkers or operating weapon systems, go to the underground shelter."

"They're getting into our heads," Athena warned. "Xalnyth energy signature confirmed."

Myles grabbed a neural stabilizer and pressed it to her temple, causing the haze to clear.

"Athena, flood the base with VaRaxian psychic shielding. Now."

The lights flickered. Strange golden patterns pulsed across the hull—ancient alien runes. The mental invasion halted abruptly.

"Focus, everyone. Target their flanks."

Two of the ten Malzon ships broke off their attack and headed for Moonbase, and four others headed for Earth.

Back on Earth and at Moonbase, giant railguns rose from their bunkers, pointing skyward. The planetary defense system, complete with nuclear missiles, went on high alert.

On Marsbase, a laser cannon and particle beam railgun batteries opened fire, striking a Malzon ship in its engines and causing it to spin out of control. A wave of attack drones launched from a bunker buzzed like angry hornets and circled a second ship.

But the Malzons adapted. One ship directed a beam weapon that scrambled the drones' anti-targeting systems. A moment later, they retaliated with plasma warheads, destroying a battery of Marsbase cannons.

Koren spotted a third attacker, pulled away from the observation distance, and fired its lasers at the missiles targeting the Marsbase dome. Several missiles were intercepted, but two managed to get through, destroying half of the dome.

The fourth Malzon warship identified *Koren*, recognizing its VaRaxian design, and pursued him. *Zara* fired her laser gun, momentarily distracting the Malzon ship and allowing *Koren* to escape the firing range. However, the Malzon ship launched two hypersonic nanotech missiles; one struck *Zara* midships and exploded. Wounded but still operational and able to navigate, *Zara* crept away.

After taking heavy damage, Commander Myles ordered the final weapon to be used.

A massive antimatter cannon codenamed the Judgment Arc emerged from a hidden underground cave and took aim at the nearest Malzon warship.

"Give them a message from Earth. Fire the Arc," Commander Myles ordered.

The cannon fired a beam of pure antimatter, slicing cleanly through the Malzon ship. As the target imploded, a nearby vessel was nearly drawn into its collapsing core.

At 5 p.m., Tim stood at the center of the bridge as *Horizon* neared Mars, where two remaining Malzon warships continued their attack.

He pressed the intercom button. "All hands, this is Admiral Smith. Battle stations. Strap in. We'll be taking evasive maneuvers and engaging shortly. Nick, have your maintenance and damage control teams ready."

Turning to the bridge crew, he continued, "Engineering, monitor all systems closely."

Around him, seatbelts clicked as crew members locked in, eyes forward, ready for the fight ahead.

"Commander Myles, we have arrived. Stand down. You've done well," Tim called out.

The admiral shifted his focus to the tactical map. "Arcaayus, take out the Malzon ships," Tim said. "*Endeavor* and *Koren,* employ hit-and-run Viking tactics."

"Affirmative," Arcaayus bellowed.

"Admiral, we have help. The *UNS Indefatigable* is approaching our flank," said Steve. "*Zara* is wounded and needs assistance."

"*Indefatigable*, this is Admiral Smith. Escort *Zara* to Earth for repairs at the fastest possible speed. Return to Moonbase at flank speed and await instructions. Do not engage the Malzons on your own. Arcaayus, target the Malzons."

"Yes, Admiral," Arcaayus confirmed in his deep, almost oddly gleeful voice.

One of the Malzon ships broke off from its attack on Marsbase and headed straight for *Horizon*, its plasma cannons blazing. However, *Horizon's* shields held, absorbing the high-energy bursts.

Arcaayus increased speed and slightly altered course as the Malzon ship fired more deadly plasma torpedoes. The missiles missed *Horizon* by yards.

While once inferior to the *Horizon*, the Malzon warships surprised Arcaayus with new tactics, heavier shielding, and more accurate shooting. But after a brief recalculation, Arcaayus countered the Malzons' new strategy like a chess master.

"Admiral, I sense the Xalnyth have improved these warships, but they underestimated our upgrades. I can destroy these two in a few minutes," Arcaayus proudly stated.

"Once you have finished them, engage at maximum impulse speed to Moonbase, then Earth," Tim said. "The Malzons are nearly in firing range."

"Yes, Admiral," Arcaayus replied, firing *Horizon's* powerful laser beam and cutting a Malzon in half.

Two Malzon ships were out of action, one destroyed by Judgment Arc and the other by *Horizon*. The third attacker, damaged by Marsbase, turned toward *Horizon* and charged at flank speed in what appeared to be a suicide attack.

"Admiral, watch me as I neutralize this attacking Malzon," *Arcaayus* bellowed as he targeted the enemy ship with six photon torpedoes, firing three in two groups, five seconds apart. The impact of the first three torpedoes neutralized the Malzon shield, while the last three blew holes in the ship.

"Good work, Arcaayus," said Tim.

"Admiral, the last Malzon ship is turning around for an attack," Maya said.

The Malzon flagship, the *Vrex'Zal*, which had been directing the attack, bore down on *Horizon* in what appeared to be a frontal assault.

Steve interrupted. "We have an SOS from Moonbase. They are under attack by two Malzons."

"Take out this ship, Arcaayus. We've got to get to Moonbase and Earth. It doesn't appear our Ruirulan friends will make it," Tim said.

Suddenly, *Horizon's* engines shut off. The AI computer screen went dead.

"Admiral, we have a problem," Amy called out. "I'll check

for a program malfunction. Jeff, run a diagnostic on the connection."

"Admiral, the ship's not responding to Arcaayus," Major Andrews said.

"Or Arcaayus isn't responding to the ship," said Tim, immediately understanding what happened. "What about the backup AI?"

"Not responding either," said Amy. "Something happened. I'm checking."

"Mark, until Amy and Jeff get Arcaayus working, you must fly *Horizon* manually. Leonard, you'll have to take charge of the weapon systems. Start firing," Tim ordered.

"I can only fire the forward weapons. We need help," said Leonard.

Kael saw what happened. "Nira and Tarel, come to the bridge immediately. You need to operate the starboard, aft, and rear cannons."

Nira and Tarel dropped their repairs in the engine room and rushed toward the bridge.

The Malzon flagship fired its plasma beam in pulses, also launching multiple hypersonic nanotech missiles at *Horizon* as it drifted without engine power toward Marsbase.

"You are at my mercy now, and I don't give mercy," said High Commander Rauth Ka'Tar to *Horizon*. "Prepare to die."

Just in time, Major Andrews regained control of the thrusters, turned the ship around, and headed toward the Moon at flank speed.

"Admiral, we need to buy some time until we get all the guns operational," Mark said.

"We are here," said Nira. "Where do you need us?"

"Over here, next to Leonard," said Mark. "He will show

you how to operate the cannons."

"We know," said Tarel. "I was a young lieutenant once on a battlecruiser."

"That was twenty years ago," Nira said.

"Just watch me," Tarel said.

"George, I need a damage report," Tim said.

"We took a hit to our lower decks. No injuries. We vented air before the hatches shut," George reported. "The thicker shielding Kael and Peggy created held up well enough."

"*Koren* and *Endeavor,* come alongside. We will turn and fight in ten minutes, halfway to the Moon," Tim said.

He turned to the pilot. "Mark, I want you to fly erratically. Let's let this Malzon catch up and think we are damaged."

"Yes, sir."

Tim shifted channels. "Nick, can you hear me?"

"Yes, Tim, how are we doing?" Nick asked.

"I have an assignment for you, Jim, Big Nik, and whoever else can help. I want you to gather spare parts, trash containers, and damaged equipment. Move everything to the lower deck C, next to the damaged bulkhead where the hole is. Once everything is there, get out, close the hatch, and vent everything from that section," Tim said.

"Yes, Admiral. I know what you have in mind. The old trash ejection deception," Nick said with a chuckle. "I read about that in novels from the 20th Century."

"Same thing, but I don't think the Malzons read those books," Tim said without humor. "Let me know when it's done. Hurry."

"Yes, sir," Nick said.

"Mark, I want you to be ready to turn when Nick calls out," Tim said. "Start slowing and weaving now."

Nira and Tarel switched on the starboard and aft laser beams, the rear phaser, and the particle cannons, then readied the photon torpedoes.

"Admiral, we are ready for action," said Tarel, studying the scanners and viewscreen. "The enemy is coming."

"All we need is a few seconds of indecision to finish this Malzon, then we can join the *Indefatigable* on the way to Earth at the Moon," Tim said. "Steve, contact Earth Defense."

"Yes, sir," Steve said. "I've got General Washington on the line."

"General, what is your status?" Tim asked.

"Four Malzon dreadnoughts are about 15 minutes away. Earth Planetary Defense is activated. Earth-based and orbit-based missile systems are armed. We will get a first shot at them," said General Washington, a distant cousin to the famous Revolutionary War general and America's first president.

"Very good," Tim replied.

"When will you arrive? We need help," said Washington.

"General, I have to level with you. We won't be there in time. We have three Malzon ships out here to neutralize, unless Ike 4 wants us to abandon Moonbase and disengage from the approaching enemy. Over," Tim said.

"Admiral, I am here," Ike 4 said. "Save as many lives as you can. I leave it to your discretion, but we must deal with those three anyway."

"Yes, sir. We will be there soon," Tim said. "Steve, open a channel for *Koren, Endeavor, Indefatigable,* and *Zara*."

"Yes, sir. You got it," Steve said.

"Change of plans. *Koren, Zara,* and *Indefatigable*, I want you three to speed directly to Earth. Hit those Malzon ships from the rear and get away if you can. Maybe you can distract them. We are counting on you to do everything you can to slow them down," Tim said. "*Endeavor*, go to Moonbase and support its defense the best you can. I will meet you there."

"Yes, Admiral," *Endeavor* replied.

"Admiral, what about my order to return to base for repairs?" *Zara* asked.

"Earth needs help. Are your weapons still working?" Tim asked.

"Yes, sir," *Zara* confirmed. "Let me understand. My brother and I are expendable?"

"Yes, I'm sorry to issue that order," Tim said. "*Horizon* can't get there in time before the Malzons attack. Your job is to save as many lives on Earth as possible."

"We understand. It will be an honor," said *Koren*, charging up his weapon systems.

Commander Archie Sullivan of Moonbase activated his defensive systems when the Malzons passed Mars. He ordered all civilians and non-combatants to take shelter in underground bunkers.

"I want those ion group batteries charged and ready to fire as soon as the enemy is within range," Sullivan barked.

Six Malzon ships approached the Moon, with four breaking off toward Earth.

"Fire cannons," Sullivan ordered. Firing concentrated particle beams, the leading Malzon ship's engine was speared, causing it to spin out of formation and lose power.

"Launch drones to their flanks," Sullivan ordered. Swarms of anti-ship drones, designed to confuse enemy weapon targeting systems, sped off in a sweeping arc maneuver.

As the drones approached, the second Malzon ship countered using anti-targeting beams.

"It's not working. We are being targeted. Keep firing those cannons as long as possible!" Sullivan screamed.

Moonbase sustained 50% damage in seconds, with its central dome shattered and several adjacent smaller domes venting atmosphere.

"Admiral Smith, we can't hold on much longer," Commander Sullivan said. "We got off a lucky shot and damaged one ship, but the other is attacking."

Nick Dragoon's voice crackled over *Horizon's* comms. "Trash ejection's vented, Admiral. Bulkhead hatches sealed tight." He glanced at the overhead panel as indicator lights turned green one by one. "Everyone pulled their weight: Jim, Big Nik, Con, Logan, Terry, Father Huey, Sophie, Veyra, Colonel Duffy, and Major Smith. Even the Space Marines led by Lieutenant McDill helped shove waste canisters into the ejection bay. It's done."

Tim nodded in gratitude, his eyes fixed on the tactical display as the fake debris cloud drifted away from the *Horizon*. Soon, he hoped, the Malzons would see the illusion of a crippled vessel, venting garbage and floating helplessly in space.

"Mark," Tim said, voice low, "shut down thrust. Let her drift."

Mark Andrews complied without hesitation, halting forward acceleration. The *Horizon* glided silently, pretending to be wounded prey.

"It's working," whispered Nira, eyes wide. "They've taken the bait. They're catching up."

As the *Vrex'Zal* drew closer, sensors detected a massive power buildup along its underbelly. Torpedo bays opened. The enemy prepared to fire weapons.

Tim stood from his command chair. "Let them get closer. Ready. Fire," he said, his voice sharp with authority. "Give that Malzon everything you've got."

Without delay, *Horizon's* entire weapons array sprang to life. The forward particle cannons, VaRaxian plasma rails, and six photon torpedoes fired in a coordinated sequence, one after another.

Leonard Bouchard's targeting matrix calculated the weak points in the Malzon armor while Nira and Tarel fired the beam cannons and hypervelocity rounds with brutal precision.

"Four incoming torpedoes!" Maya shouted.

"Mark, evasive—now," Tim ordered.

Pilot Mark Andrews didn't flinch. He had anticipated the moment and slammed the helm controls hard left and down, executing a corkscrew spin that jolted the *Horizon* out of the torpedoes' lock. The enemy projectiles flew past, detonating harmlessly in open space.

The Malzon battleship never stood a chance.

As it tried to adjust course, *Horizon's* barrage tore through its shields and into its central hull. A final railgun blast from Leonard struck the enemy's core reactor. The Malzon ship erupted in a blinding explosion, its burning hull spiraling into the void.

"Direct hit!" Leonard called. "I got him."

"Enemy neutralized," Nira confirmed.

A cheer rose on the bridge.

"Mark," Tim said, adrenaline still surging, "get us to Earth at maximum speed. I hope the Waybegonease Additive is still working."

"Aye, Admiral," Mark replied, hands flying across the controls. The *Horizon* surged forward.

Tim turned to the crew, eyes blazing. "Let's defend the Moon and Earth," he declared.

With that, the *Horizon* sped toward the final battle, leaving behind the wreckage of a deadly foe and racing toward its home planet.

Still, the *Horizon* was three hours from Earth. Tim knew the Malzons would arrive before the *Horizon*, and they would unleash everything they had in their arsenal on Earth. He stretched his mind but still couldn't sense where the Ruirulans were.

"Steve, let's hear the Earth Planetary Defense broadcast through the bridge speakers," Tim said.

The *Horizon's* bridge went quiet except for General Washington's strained yet resolute voice crackling to life across space.

"This is General Washington to all defense units. Hold the line. Repeat, hold the line. The Malzon fleet is an hour away. They are firing long-range missiles and torpedoes. Planetary shields are holding...but barely. We've lost *Zara*. *Koren's* down. Repeat—*Koren* and *Zara* are both hit and unable to help."

As Tim listened, he could almost hear the rumble of distant explosions echoing faintly through the comm feed. He sensed *Zara* and *Koren* were seriously damaged.

Putting aside his concern, Tim stood at the edge of his command platform, watching the viewscreen display the last four Malzon warships navigating into low Earth orbit, just outside the atmosphere.

Their formation was tight, and their shields radiated with reinforced energy. Earth's orbital satellite batteries unleashed volleys of kinetic warheads and laser fire, but they fizzled against the enemy's newly enhanced defenses. The satellites were destroyed in retaliation.

"They've adapted again," Nira said grimly. "Nothing's getting through."

Horizon continued to race toward the Moon and Earth at flank speed. For the most part, the Waybegonease Additive somewhat mitigated the effects of traveling up to 3 g; the crew reported instances of muscle cramps, increased heart rates, and headaches from the constant pressure on blood flow to the brain.

Tim ordered that anyone feeling ill should report to the medbay. Several Space Marines required IV fluids and rest to endure the long day.

Still, the *Horizon* held course, hurtling at 2% light speed toward the Moon and Earth. The crew settled into a rhythm, forcing their bodies to adapt: shallow breaths, controlled movements, and scheduled micro-rests in their acceleration couches.

As they neared the Moon, the feed from the Moonbase command center cut in. The voices were frantic.

"This is Commander Sullivan—targeting systems ineffective.

Repeating fire patterns has a negative impact. They're closing in."

Tim clenched his fists. "We're still five minutes away. Hold on," he said.

The bridge was chaotic. Scanners flashed, voices became layered with tension, and the Earth and Moon trembled on the brink.

Then Steve's voice cut through the chatter. "Admiral, I think you'll want to take this call."

The bridge fell silent again as a new voice emerged, calm, assertive, unexpected.

"Admiral Smith, I apologize for being late to the party, as you Earthlings say," said Commander t'Lay. "We are launching an attack."

Tim blinked, stunned. "Where are you? I felt you, but...we don't have you on our scans."

"Neither do the Malzons. We engaged our cloaking device and approached from the far side of your Sun and the dark side of your Earth."

Tim almost laughed with relief. "Wonderful. Are you in a position to engage the Malzons before they start firing at our cities?"

"Not yet," t'Lay replied. "But we will be there soon. Will you inform your defenses not to fire upon us?"

"I can do that. Peggy, let General Washington know that our Ruirulan allies are converging around Earth for a head-on attack."

"Yes, Tim," she answered, tapping into secure lines.

"We will be engaging the Malzons in five minutes," t'Lay said.

Two surviving satellites caught the battle on video and transmitted the signal to Earth and the *Horizon*.

The first Ruirulan drone, the *Dravik,* a sleek, torpedo-like craft the size of a naval yacht, screamed in from the blackness and rammed a Malzon cruiser from below. The collision ruptured the Malzon's hull, and the drone self-detonated in a brilliant burst of white light, atomizing the vessel instantly.

Tim and the crew erupted with a unified cry. "Direct hit!"

The rest of the Ruirulan fleet poured in behind *Dravik*, firing plasma bursts and phase-pulse warheads. Their agile ships sliced between the remaining Malzons with deadly grace.

After a series of dogfights over the next 30 minutes between the Ruirulans and the Malzons, *Horizon* arrived to support t'Lay's four ships, flanking one of the cruisers with a precise salvo from Leonard and Nira.

Under the combined assault, the Malzon ships began to falter. They hadn't expected the Ruirulans and found themselves surrounded.

Another Malzon ship exploded under the combined fire from the Ruirulans, Earth cannons, the *Horizon*, and the *Indefatigable*. The allied fleet directed its attack on the remaining two Malzons, closing in with deadly precision. *Horizon* and *Indefatigable* approached from one side while the Ruirulan flagship, *Celara,* swept in from the other.

Coordinated blasts of plasma and ion fire rained down on the third Malzon warship, hammering its shields until they collapsed in a burst of blue-white static. The ship shuddered, sparks erupting along its spine. Its engines failed, and it began to drift—dark and silent—caught in a slow spin over Earth's upper orbit.

Then, without warning, its core detonated in a blinding flash, scattering fragments like a collapsing star.

The last Malzon destroyer veered away, trailing smoke and

molten debris. Fires burned across its hull as it fled toward Jupiter, its engines faltering, its weapons silent. The fleet held position, watching the wounded ship disappear into the darkness.

"Admiral Smith, do you want me to give chase?" Commander t'Lay asked calmly.

Tim took a breath, his voice firm. "No. I'll have *Indefatigable* follow and report on its condition." Suddenly, a bright flash erupted in the space the Malzon ship had occupied.

Admiral, the Malzon has self-destructed," Maya confirmed.

Tim nodded. "I have to say, we've achieved a great victory. The battle for Earth is over."

Cheers erupted across the *Horizon* and echoed from every remaining defense station on Marsbase, Moonbase, and Earth. For the first time in days, the sound wasn't fear or warning— it was triumph.

"Steve, contact *Zara* and *Koren*. Ask how they are and if they need assistance," Tim requested.

Steve's console lit up with a reply. "Admiral, *Zara* and her brother report heavy damage. Their engines are gone. They'll need a pickup."

Tim's voice warmed. "Major Andrews, let's give our friends a hand. Set a course."

As *Horizon* angled toward Earth—where Ruirulan patrols still swept the void in case the Malzons had left hidden weapons behind—the tension began to ease. Plans for a small celebration quietly spread among the crew, a much-needed chance to breathe after the long, brutal mission.

Tim opened a channel to the *Celara*. "Commander t'Lay," he said through the translator, his tone steady with gratitude, "your courage and skill in dispatching the Malzon warships made all the difference. We would be honored if you and your senior officers would join us aboard *Horizon* later tonight for a joint celebration."

t'Lay inclined her head, her voice calm yet touched with warmth. "We are honored and accept your invitation. May we bring our children? Varra and Kerrin would very much enjoy meeting Ethan and Lila in person."

"Of course," Tim replied with a faint smile. "And I hope Dr. Shonta can attend as well. My communications officer will send over our coordinates and the details."

But as the echoes of celebration faded into the steady hum of the *Horizon's* engines, the silence of space returned. Beyond the glow of victory, the stars burned cold and indifferent, and a darker reality began to take shape.

At Marsbase, Commander Rhea Myles stood alone amid the wreckage of the command deck, her face lit only by emergency lighting and the flickering stars beyond the shattered viewscreen.

"We won this battle," she whispered to herself, her voice hollow in the ruin, "but was this only the first invasion from the stars?"

Ethan and Lila, watching on the viewscreen silently from the observation balcony on the bridge, heard Rhea's question.

She is right. That was the first wave, Ethan telepathically projected to Lila, Tim, and Peggy. *The Xalnyth used the Malzons to test us. Next time, they will come themselves.*

And far beyond the Milky Way, in the depths of the void, Tim felt anger. An ancient presence stirred.

Chapter 41
THE AFTERMATH

11 p.m., Sunday, May 9, 2083

Above the blue-green Earth, *Horizon* sailed quietly in high orbit. Its once-tense corridors hummed with strange yet welcome energy mixed with relief, exhaustion, and the unmistakable joy of returning home to Earth safely.

Carlyn, Julie, Mary, and Kiki organized the staff conference room into a spontaneous celebration space. Decorations were made from medical gauze, data printouts, and children's artwork, creating an atmosphere of hope, joy, and calmness—exactly what everyone needed.

Just before the celebration began, Amy finished reactivating Arcaayus, who had been shut down earlier in the day by a hidden Xalnyth remote command originating from the Malzon flagship. The intrusion revealed a buried backdoor in the AI's original programming—an old vulnerability the Xalnyth had twisted to their advantage.

When Tim was briefed, Major Andrews tried to lighten the mood with a quip: "Guess Arcaayus choked under pressure."

Tim fixed him with a steady look. "Major, I want you to assemble an engineering-security team with Amy, Jeff, and Peggy. Lock down every line of code. No backdoors, no gaps, not one overlooked pathway. If the Xalnyth exploited it once, they'll try again one day."

At that moment, Arcaayus's voice resonated across the deck. "For the record, Major, I do not choke. An external corruption vector incapacitated me. A rather embarrassing one, I admit. I would prefer not to repeat the experience."

Andrews smirked. "Sounds like you're calling it a software hiccup."

"Call it what you will," Arcaayus replied, almost dryly, "but I assure you—next time, the Xalnyth will find themselves on the receiving end of *my* pressure."

As crew members filled the conference room from every corner of the ship, the service mechs wheeled in champagne, crystal glasses, and trays of hors d'oeuvres. Laughter rippled through the air, mingling with the hum of voices as old friends reunited and new bonds were sealed in the glow of victory.

Even the VaRaxians, usually stoic and precise, appeared slightly more relaxed in their posture. They smiled softly, their heads occasionally tilting in curiosity at the laughter, the music, and the human way of allowing joy to emerge after hardship.

Kael and Liora stood near the edge of the room, the soft glow of the stars spilling through the viewport behind them.

Kael smiled as Liora handed him a glass. "You carried more than your share of the burden, Kael," she said gently. "Tonight, you're allowed to simply... breathe."

He looked at her for a long moment, the unspoken weight of VaRax heavy between them, then raised his glass. "To those we lost," he said quietly, "and to those who remain to carry the light." Liora touched her glass to his, her eyes shimmering with hope.

As Kael lowered his glass, a soft voice caught his attention. Lyara stood a step away, her hands nervously clasped in front of her. Sian urged her forward. For a moment, her usual boldness was absent, replaced by the hesitance of a daughter unsure of how her words would be received.

"Father..." she began, her eyes searching his face. "Back on VaRax...when you and Liora left aboard *Arcaayus*, I was so angry. I thought you had abandoned us. Abandoned me." Her voice faltered, then steadied. "I should have trusted you. I see now you were fighting for us in a way I didn't understand."

Kael's face softened. He set his glass aside and placed a steady hand on her shoulder. "Your anger was born of pain, Lyara. And I deserve much of it. But know this—every choice I made, even the ones that cost me your trust, was for you... for our people. I could never abandon you."

Tears welled in her eyes, but she blinked them back quickly, unwilling to let them fall in front of the others. She leaned forward, resting her forehead briefly against his chest. "Then tonight, I forgive you. And I'll never doubt you again."

Kael held her close, a rare but unbreakable bond rekindled in that simple embrace.

Tim and Peggy stood next to the VaRaxians as Ethan and Lila brimmed with excitement, their words tumbling on top of one another.

"Mama, Varra and Kerrin are coming!" Ethan exclaimed, his eyes shining. "And they already told us they want to play hide-and-seek!"

Lila chimed in, giggling as she hugged her mother. Peggy brushed a strand of hair from Lila's face, her heart swelling. "You'll have plenty of time for games tonight," she said softly, "but remember—this is a chance to make friends who may be part of your lives for a very long time." The twins exchanged a secret, knowing glance.

Suddenly, the conference room doors slid open with a gentle hiss, drawing everyone's attention. Commander t'Lay stepped through first, dignified in her deep violet ceremonial tunic, followed closely by Dr. Shonta, whose calm presence softened the room, and several other Ruirulan officers. Just behind them came Varra and Kerrin, their youthful energy barely contained as their eyes darted curiously over the bustling celebration.

Ethan and Lila spotted them instantly. Their faces lit up, and before Peggy could even caution them to slow down, the twins darted across the room, weaving between crewmembers and trays of food.

"Varra! Kerrin!" they cried in unison.

Varra's pale face broke into a broad smile while Kerrin laughed aloud, his arms open wide. The four children collided in a joyous hug, their laughter ringing louder than the music that had just begun to play.

Peggy followed a few steps behind, shaking her head but smiling as she watched the reunion. The sight of the children embracing—Earthling and Ruirulan, as if no gulf had ever existed between their worlds—drew a ripple of warmth through the crew, many pausing in their conversations to quietly admire the moment.

t'Lay glanced at Dr. Shonta, her eyes reflecting something rare: hope. "Were we like this?" she said softly.

He replied with a smile, "Once, a long time ago." Even Vorak chuckled.

Ethan pulled back from their embrace first, grinning. "You made it! We have so much to talk about."

Kerrin gave Ethan a playful tap. "I thought you wanted to play hide-and-seek? You're it!" He turned and ran behind the refreshment table.

Tim watched the lively energy with some concern. He could see trouble ahead. "Peggy, could you take our children to the space school where they have room to play? I'm afraid someone might get run over."

Ethan laughed. "C'mon, Kerrin and Varra! We can have more fun at our school. I'll introduce you to the rest of the kids."

Lila crossed her arms with mock seriousness. "Yes, but who is going to keep an eye on these adults?"

Everyone laughed. It was a sound that carried through the room and lifted the hearts of everyone watching.

Stephen and Julie sat in the back of the room, a little removed from the laughter and chatter. It had been a tough trip for Stephen. Even though the Waybegonase helped him manage the shared visions, his mind still carried the weight of all he saw and heard. He would need a long rest on Earth to recover.

He leaned back in his chair, exhaling slowly, and glanced at Julie with a tired smile.

"You know," he murmured, voice low enough for only her to hear, "I think I've had my fill of wormholes, alien warships, and psychic storms for a lifetime. When we get home, I want quiet mornings, long walks, and maybe a chance to remember what normal feels like. That's the life I'm looking forward to now."

Julie squeezed his hand and whispered back, "Then we'll make that our life, Stephen—and I'll be right there with you."

Across the room, Veyra and George sat close to each other, next to Nira and Jim, who planned to get married in the fall at the bioshelter by Father Huey. Sian and Lyara, wondering where they would live, sat next to Dr. Rykan, Alora, and Tarel. John Logan and Jennifer sat beside their new friend, Joran.

For the first time in months, the room hummed not with orders or alarms, but with simple dreams—where to live, who to love, what to do. The fighting was over, and everyone had survived—except for Sergeant Laura Mountbatten—giving way to lighter concerns of choice and hope.

Lieutenant McDill and his Space Marine squad gathered near the refreshment table, talking quietly. Each wore an honor bracelet to remember Laura.

Father Huey stood near the viewport, bathed in starlight, and gently tapped his glass. The room quieted. "Let us give thanks," he said. Heads bowed. "To the hands that protected us and the hearts that stayed strong in the storm. We don't understand all that's out there. But we are still here. And for that, we are thankful."

A hush followed, and then a soft chorus of "Amen!" rippled across the room.

Tim stepped forward. He hadn't slept in two days, and his face still bore the weight of command. But he looked like a proud leader. As he started to speak, Ethan, Lila, Varra, and Kerrin entered the room to join their parents.

"This wasn't easy," Tim said softly. "You all know that. We were far from home, among hostile forces, with little time to think. But none of you gave up. You did your job. You kept each other alive. You believed."

His voice caught for a moment. "We fought not just for Earth but for the kind of future worth fighting for. And because of that, we won. I couldn't be prouder to serve alongside each of you."

Tim sat down next to Peggy, Ethan, and Lila as applause erupted, some of it emotional, some raucous, and all well-earned.

Afterward, the mood softened into something more personal. Dr. Ledbetter stood up. He spoke about resilience and healing—about how the human body wasn't the only thing that needed care after war.

"We need time now; time to relax, play with our children, be with friends, and soak in the warmth of our home planet—Earth," he said.

"Here, here," said Dr. Bo Taber as he recounted a moment on the med deck when two injured Marines shared a joke about their injuries.

"Guess I'll be limping back to 'Bama with a scar that'll make my grandma faint," the Marine from Mobile drawled, grinning through the pain.

The Marine from Kennebunkport snorted, adjusting the bandage on his arm. "At least you'll still be walking. Up in Maine, we call that kind of limp *character*—helps us charm the summer tourists."

The Alabamian chuckled, wincing as his ribs protested. "Character, huh? Well, maybe I'll borrow a little of that Yankee spin if it means I get free drinks when I'm home."

"Deal," the Mainer replied, reaching out his good hand. "But only if you teach me how to make grits that don't taste like paste."

Dr. Bo, recounting the story, said he couldn't help but smile at the levity. "That's when I knew we'd make it. Laughter means hope is present."

Con raised a glass to the fallen on Mars and the Moon.

"I didn't know those who died to protect others, but I can tell you who they are. They are you and me," he said. "All of us would fight hard to protect our way of life and our fellow brothers and sisters. Here's to them. May they be forever remembered."

Kael, flanked by Liora, Nira, and Tarel, spoke: "We once feared that trusting humans would be our undoing. But instead, it has given us hope. We started this mission with nine VaRaxians. We finished with nearly 10,000 of our people."

Everyone clapped and cheered. t'Lay stepped forward, her head bowed toward Tim and Kael.

"Together, Earthling resolve and VaRaxian strength created a harmony neither could have achieved alone," she said through a translator. "It was not only our weapons that defeated the Malzons, but the bond of trust that grew between our peoples."

"Thank you, Kael, t'Lay, and everyone," said Tim. "Now, we have a special musical treat. Corli, you have the floor."

Corli, who often entertained the children and crew with her musical abilities, walked to the front of the room with her guitar.

"I'd like to introduce my new band. The Sky Pilots. Gentlemen?"

Steve and Jeff picked up their guitars, and Bo lugged an upright acoustic bass hastily made by the ship's 3D printers. After a quick tune-up, they nodded to Corli.

"A one, two, a one, two, three, four," counted Corli as they began playing a new Earth folk song, "Safe in the Sky." Her voice rang out, clear, sweet, and soulful.

We sailed through the void, where the silence cast wide,
With starlight as a compass, and love as our guide.
The battles are fading, the memories drifting by,
But we held one another, and are now safe in the sky.

The Earth may be small from the black velvet sea,
But the hearts of the brave beat in you and me.
With children now dreaming where once they would cry,
We rise with the dawn, now safe in the sky.

Even the bridge crew joined in on the chorus.

We're safe in the sky, where the stars still burn.
Through fire and fear, we found our return.
With hearts made of light and wings that won't die,
We carry each other—safe in the sky.

The VaRaxians and Ruirulans listened intently, visibly moved by the unfamiliar yet catchy harmony. They smiled as new friends Patrick and Carlyn, Tom and Mary, Dr. Thomas Kropt and Kiki, Nick and Nancy took to the dance floor.

Patrick, twirling Carlyn a bit too fast, laughed. "Guess I'm safer in the sky than on the dance floor."

Tom, holding Mary close, grinned. "If I step on your toes, just remember—it's still better than zero gravity."

Dr. Kropt, adjusting his glasses as Kiki pulled him along, muttered with a smile: "Safe in the Sky? I'll settle for surviving this dance."

Colonel Duffy and Major Smith, standing near the Space Marines, watched the Sky Pilots' music fill the room and the dancers spin across the floor. Both men wore easy smiles, the kind that came from knowing they'd made it through the fire together.

"Never thought I'd see a party like this after what we went through," Duffy said, folding his arms but grinning as the band picked up the tempo.

Smith chuckled, shaking his head. "You've got that right. I'll enjoy it tonight, but what I'm smiling about and most looking forward to is heading home. My wife's been waiting a long time, and I've promised her this is my last tour."

Duffy raised his glass in quiet agreement. "Same here. I'm ready to hang up the uniform, sit on my porch, and let someone else save the galaxy for a change. But tonight—" He nodded toward the dance floor where the crew laughed and celebrated. "—tonight we let them know it was worth it."

Down on Earth, celebrations echoed around the world. Despite the scars of war—flaming craters on Marsbase, charred structures on Moonbase—humanity was able to breathe together once more. President Dwight Eisenhower IV and U.N. Secretary-General Leila Rodriguez addressed the planet in a global broadcast that was relayed to *Horizon*. The celebration paused momentarily while the president spoke.

"The Malzon threat has been neutralized," Ike 4 said, standing before a large window showing Earth's curvature. "And we have *Horizon* and her brave crew to thank for that."

Brief applause and cheers broke out on the *Horizon*. The president kept speaking.

"Today, the nations of Earth have pledged ten billion dollars to rebuild our orbital outposts. We mourn the three hundred souls lost at Marsbase and Moonbase, including Mr. Tusck, who gave his life to ensure that evacuation protocols were executed. But we also celebrate the millions saved."

He added to a wave of cheers, "The *Indefatigable*, the only undamaged shuttle, will depart tomorrow for *Horizon*, bringing a new crew to replace our heroes. Admiral Smith and his crew—including our VaRaxian friends—will return home to a grateful Earth. We hope someday to be able to pay back our new Ruirulan friends."

Left unspoken was where exactly the 10,000 VaRaxians, saved from their dying planet and Celias-3, would live: Alaska, where they were initially promised, or Mars, or somewhere else.

However, Tim and Kael spoke privately and pledged to find homes on Earth and Marsbase for VaRaxians. They knew that healing from war meant more than treaties and pledges. It meant offering roots, belonging, and dignity.

Always the diplomat, Kael emphasized that scattered

settlements could weaken their sense of unity, while Tim believed integration with Earth communities would foster the roots of mutual understanding.

Together, they revived an old plan: a coastal settlement in northern Alaska rich in geothermal energy and new greenhouses near Olympus Mons for those who chose Mars. The new location was a joint Earth–VaRaxian research hub on Tetepare Island, a peaceful paradise where families could rebuild and children could thrive in warmth under blue skies.

Although none of the Ruirulans wanted to stay on Earth at this time, Commander t'Lay held a video conference with President Eisenhower and Secretary-General Rodriguez to discuss an exchange program for scholars aimed at fostering lasting peace between the civilizations.

Back on *Horizon*, no one cheered louder than Peggy. She embraced Tim tightly, whispering, "We did it. We're going home."

The party stretched into the ship's night, full of stories, songs, and plans for rest.

A hush settled over the staff conference room as the viewport slowly rotated to reveal the sunrise over the Pacific. Even laughter paused as every soul there watched the first golden light hit the curve of the Earth.

They had won. They had survived, and now they were going home.

A week later

On the following Sunday night, Ethan and Lila sat with Tim and Peggy around a table on the roof of their bioshelter. They were home, and it felt good.

"The Malzons weren't evil," Lila said softly, looking up at the stars. "They were alone—so alone. And they had been alone for so long that they didn't know what family meant, what a friend meant, or what community meant."

Tim put an arm around her. "You always try to see the hopeful side of everyone, even though they were monsters, as you described them."

Lila shuddered. She remembered entering their minds, feeling the hate, the alienation, the loneliness.

"You tried to save them," Tim said, "and I am proud of you for trying."

Ethan climbed up on his father's lap. "Papa, we need to find a way to help them. They aren't hopeless."

Tim hugged them both. "If we can find a way to do it, we will." He looked above into the dark sky, and the stars shone brighter.

EPILOGUE

Ten years later, Sarasota, 2093

In the following years, Ethan, Lila, and the other Earthling, VaRaxian, and Ruirulan children continued to meet, learn, exchange ideas, and share feelings and sensations.

Tim, Peggy, and all the parents encouraged the children's interactions. Friendships blossomed, and a new generation of leaders began to take shape from those seeds. As Ethan and Lila grew older, the stage was set to reach out to youngsters from other species and civilizations.

A few months after the victory over the Malzons, the Ruirulans formalized their alliance with Earth and the 10,000-plus VaRaxians, creating the Orion Galactic Alliance.

After a year of debates and negotiations, the United States and the U.N. agreed to allow the VaRaxians the option to live in northern Alaska, Marsbase, or Tetepare Island, an uninhabited 46-square-mile island in the Solomon Islands in the South Pacific.

Meanwhile, the Orion Galactic Alliance expanded with new species, including the Thalureans, the Xenara, and the

Q'Maari, distant civilizations more than 50 light-years from Earth.

Each year, messages promoting peaceful coexistence were sent to the Malzon Empire. Ethan and Lila added invitations to the younger Malzons. But nothing was returned—no signals or acknowledgments, not even static.

Horizon's crew returned to Earth, settling in various cities and states. Tim, Peggy, Ethan, and Lila returned to their bioshelter home. So did Stephen and Julie, Dr. Charles Ledbetter and Paula, and Captain Leonard Bouchard and Dr. Tayna Ivanova Bouchard.

George and Veyra Clarke, now married, became ambassadors to the VaRaxian and Ruirulan people. They traveled often but came home for special occasions.

Lyara and Sian also married and lived near their parents, Kael and Liora, on Marsbase, with plans to eventually settle in northern Alaska.

Years passed, and Ethan and Lila, now teenagers, were no longer the wide-eyed kids who had once shared each other's thoughts in whispered silence. Their powers had matured into something profound. Together with their closest friends— Earthlings, VaRaxians, and Ruirulans—they had created a shared consciousness, a bond not just of thought but of purpose.

They could read truth in the hearts of others, weave ideas across languages, and project calming waves of emotion across great distances. Where the Orion Galactic Alliance began with treaties, it grew strong through the unity of its youth.

Varra, the daughter of Ruirulan Commander t-Lay, and Kerin, the son of Dr. Shonta, the Ruirulan medical officer, along with dozens of other young VaRaxians and Ruirulans, lived and learned side by side with their human peers on Earth, Mars, and the newly built United Alliance Space Ring.

But through it all, Tim and Peggy, now in their late 30s, remained the heart of the Alliance's founding. Their steady and unshakeable love was the glue that held their family and the growing galactic community together. It was a profound bond forged in respect, science, and struggle.

They found time for stargazing, long dinners, and laughter with their friends and children. Even as Ethan and Lila grew and their responsibilities increased, their love remained simple: founded on trust, illuminated by wonder, and strengthened by every battle they endured.

Yet, even in moments of peace, Tim could still feel that familiar tug at the edge of his consciousness, a quiet but persistent pull, unlike the benign invitations they occasionally received from new alien civilizations. Those encounters had become routine for NASA and the United Nations Space Agency, which investigated and engaged with new species as part of the growing Galactic Alliance.

But this was something else. It wasn't only the Malzon. Tim sensed a darker intelligence, ancient and patient. He knew what it was: the Xalnyth were still out there. And this time, they were searching for an even more powerful ally.

One night, as Ethan and Lila stood on the observatory roof beneath a violet dusk sky, their hands brushed, and their eyes widened in unison.

A message arrived through the psychic thread they shared with dozens of others: *They are coming, and we must be ready.*

Tim watched them, knowing what that meant. A new chapter was beginning—not his, but theirs.

COMING SOON:

CHILDREN OF THE STARS

A new generation rises to meet the future... and the ancient power that stirs beyond the Milky Way.

How to Contact
Jay B. Greene

Visit my website, review my books, and sign up
for my newsletters at www.jaybgreene.com

By subscribing, you'll get:

- Early sneak peeks at upcoming books
- Bonus chapters, deleted scenes and exclusive short stories
- Insider updates on Jack Kendall and Tim and Peggy Smith's worlds
- Special offers and giveaways
- Author insights and personal notes

Sign up now at: **www.jaybgreene.com**

Love My Books? Help Others Discover It!

If you enjoyed one of my Jack Kendall Mystery books or Tim and Peggy Smith Space Adventure books, please consider leaving a review on **Amazon, Barnes & Nobl**e, **or wherever you bought your book**. Your reviews help other readers discover the series—and they mean the world to me as an author.

Thanks again for reading, and I hope you'll join Jack Kendall or Tim and Peggy on their next thrilling adventures!

Pursue the Truth, **Jay B. Greene**

More Tim and Peggy Smith
Space Adventures

Tim Smith gains psychic powers after discovering a mysterious space rock during a summer camp hike. This event propels him into a career as a NASA astrophysicist, where he uncovers an exoplanet called Terra Nova and foresees an alien threat approaching Earth.

A massive alien mothership, its AI corrupted by dark matter, emerges from the Kuiper Belt and begins attacking a world devastated by pollution and climate change.

Tim, his wife Peggy, and a small group of survivors retreat to a bioshelter, using Tim's visions to strategize against the invaders. Discovering that the Mothership holds technology capable of restoring the planet, Tim and his team race to reset the ship's AI to its peaceful prime directive of "no harm to humans" and "assist in cleansing Earth of pollution."

In *Danger From Space*, join Tim and his team as they confront an alien menace and the pressing realities of our world's environmental crisis. Discover a story of survival, unity, and hope for transformation in the face of overwhelming odds. Help inspire change and embrace our responsibility to protect the planet.

About the Author

Jay B. Greene was born, grew up and lives in Sarasota. He studied environmental science and journalism in college and graduated from the University of Florida. His love for stories propelled him into a 40-year career covering health care, government, crime, and the environment for several newspapers across different states. He is also the author of the *Jack Kendall Mystery series*: *Mountain Crossing*, *Becky* and *Bone Valley*. *Nokomis Hospital* will be out next.